Bury me in Valletta

Bury me in Valletta

Book Two of
The Siranoush Trilogy

Stuart Campbell

Third paperback edition [i], 2023
Published by Stuart Campbell
www.stuartcampbellauthor.com

ISBN: 978-0-6457198-0-2

Contents

About The Siranoush Trilogy

The Siranoush Trilogy comprises the novels *Cairo Mon Amour*, *Bury me in Valletta*, and *The Sunset Assassin*. The three stories are stand-alone episodes in the tribulations of reluctant British spies Pierre Farag and his wife Zouzou Faris. The couple are exiled from Cairo to London in 1973, and then to Malta in 1975, ending their quest for freedom and anonymity in the northern Australian tropics in 1978.

Siranoush, meaning 'sweet love', is the stage name of a legendary Armenian actress who began her career in Constantinople, but left Turkey after the banning of Armenian plays. Her acting and operatic career continued in Yerevan, Tiflis and Baku. She died in 1932 and is buried in Cairo. Pierre is Armenian on his mother's side; like Siranoush, he is forced to make a life in exile.

I used Siranoush as the codename of the espionage operation that Pierre and Zouzou are enmeshed in during the 1973 Yom Kippur War. By literary chance, Pierre's great-aunt saw Siranoush perform at the Cairo Opera House in 1928.

The novella *Ash on the Tongue*, is a prequel to the trilogy, introducing the main characters in the run-up to the Yom Kippur War between Israel and Egypt. *Cairo Rations* is a collection of essays that I wrote to jog my memory before embarking on the trilogy.

Chapter One

Pierre Farag dug in his pocket for change. He lit a match and fed two twenty-pence pieces into the electricity meter. The beige standard lamp clicked back on to feebly illuminate the unglamorous flat: Camden Town, their seat of exile. The television news resumed. Unemployment had hit one million; the Labour Party had voted against joining the Common Market; Saigon had fallen to the Viet Cong.

He considered Zouzou's declaration that she had given up her job. Resigned, just like that, from the perfume counter at the department store. Where was it? – Woodford, Watford, Walham? These soft English town names with their *-fords* and *-hams*. How was a man to tell one from another? In Egypt the towns and suburbs had names you could get your teeth into - Zamalak, Zagazig, Az-Zarqa.

"I'm not sure that I approve of that, my dear." He had sounded priggish, he knew, but he wished she had asked him first. Where were they to find thirty pounds a week?

"Not approve, *habibi*?" she had asked. "You speak of approving or disapproving? I'm thirty-five years old and I have endured six lifetimes of disapproval."

1

She was right, of course: Zouzou Paris, Egypt's most notorious actress, the 'national bitch' some called her, now living secretly with him in London. What did he know of disapproval, a man of thirty-eight who had spent his life in the shadows, in no need of the approval or disapproval of others? They hadn't spoken of the matter again.

Zouzou settled into the sofa to watch *The Two Ronnies*. How did she find their juvenile jokes funny? He'd tried hard to see the point of it.

"We're out of cigarettes, Zouzou. Do you need anything else from the shop?"

"A box of sunshine, bring me that."

Outside, a bluster of April wind chased away the sooty bus fumes and the smell of damp pavements. He waited in the Pakistani shop behind an orderly line of lumpy British in their anoraks and bobble hats. The shelves bore the packaged goods that spoke of stuffy flats just like Pierre's: Kit-E-Kat, Spam, PK chewing gum, HP Sauce.

He glimpsed himself in a narrow strip of mirror tiles above the shelves. They'd maintained their disguises for the first few months after arriving in England. But Pierre's chestnut hair dye had grown out and the horn-rimmed glasses were discarded. Now he was just another anonymous immigrant: Medium build, indistinct age, short dark hair with a Brylcreemed quiff. The raincoat and grey trousers marked him out as unremarkable. He could be a librarian, a water board clerk, a science lab assistant at some suburban Secondary Modern. And just as he had in Cairo, he moved unnoticed through the city. If anybody gave him a second look, they might have said, 'an Italian or a Turk, perhaps', or 'one of those bloody Cypriots'.

Later that night Zouzou sat him down in an armchair with a bottle of Blue Nun, dimmed the lights, and retired to the bedroom before ordering him not to move. He winced at the expense of the wine, but swigged off two glasses, poured a third and watched the door. Five or six minutes passed. What could she be doing? Experience had taught him there was no point in guessing Zouzou's next move.

The door hinge creaked.

"Pierre, close your eyes!"

He heard a rustle and then the click of a cassette player, followed by some languorous music.

"Now open!"

She stood there in a luminous black cocktail dress, thin straps at her white shoulders. She waited for a cue in the recorded music, and began to sing. Her voice started huskily, and then built to a serpentine flow. It was a song by Jacques Brel that she used to hum around the flat - but not like this, not with this depth of ardour and regret. He was stunned at her skill, smitten by the pure erotic charge of the voice, her body, the wine, the French lyrics.

The song ended and the click of the cassette recorder broke the thrall.

"What do you think, Pierre?" Hands on hips, head cocked to one side.

What did he think? Could a man drowning in wonder think in the normal sense?

"You never told me you could sing," he whispered.

"You should have watched my films, Pierre."

Her films. He must have been the only man in Cairo never to have seen her films. Pierre Farag, the man on the shaded side of the street, too preoccupied with keeping tabs on his clients and his network - and keeping out of some police interrogation cell. When had there been time for films and music?

She slid onto his lap and he ran his hand over her thigh.

"How did you pay for the dress, Zouzou?"

"I stole it. In Watford. I'm going to sing for my living. In Soho. Do you disapprove of that?"

Pierre shook his head. He slid the straps from her shoulders and unzipped the stolen dress.

***

A brief June downpour hadn't quenched the alcoholic fervour of the Tuesday night crowd at The Orient club in Soho. The tiny cube was crammed with drinkers at 11pm when Pierre and Zouzou arrived. A girl in a caftan belted out a song in front of a guitarist with a hairy chest, and another girl played a jewelled electric violin. A boy with an extraordinarily thick mop of orange hair walloped a drum set in the smoky shadows behind the guitarist.

The music seemed pointless to Pierre's Egyptian sensibility. Music was meant to be convoluted, poetic, enigmatic. It was supposed to lead the listener to unexpected places. This stuff was repetitive, the same pattern played over and over, the drums bashing alongside to keep it from straying.

Zouzou pulled his ear to her mouth and yelled something about 'West coast sound', whatever that was. She stood rocking her shoulders to the music, then joined a knot of dancers in the midst of the half dozen tiny tables.

Pierre watched Zouzou gyrate and laugh with the dancers: A British late-night *mélange* - girls in gauze and feathers and almost nothing else, businessmen in unbuttoned white shirts, youths of interchangeable gender in leather waistcoats and huge hair, Iranian students on the loose, a red-faced Welshman capering in a tweed jacket.

Even Pierre began to be enthralled by the hypnotic pounding. Zouzou stepped out from the tight circle and pulled him onto the dance floor, where he jerked and shuffled, now with Zouzou, now with an African man in a kaftan, now with a saucer-eyed blond girl, now with a slinky Persian boy in black, all bathed in a miasma of patchouli, beer, hashish and perspiration.

How he had changed, he thought: Eighteen months ago, he was a man 'turned in on himself', a man who'd never had a youth. Zouzou had given him back his years and fixed him to a spot in the universe - next to her.

When the music stopped, Zouzou went to the backstage lavatory to change and fix her make-up, while Pierre stepped outside and strolled up to Greek Street, where the air smelt of taxi fumes, urine, and frying spring rolls. A fat man laughed with a bouncer at the doorway of a strip club. A crowd of cackling men – a stag night party? – stumbled out of the sex shop next door under the flashing yellow and mauve *DUREX* sign.

Pierre hooked a squashed lager can from the gutter with his toe, and dribbled it down the alley towards the Orient; a policeman coming in the other direction tackled him and booted the can under a car. "You'll be playin' fer West 'Am soon, son!" he said, and Pierre laughed without mirth. He hadn't the measure of these London coppers yet.

Inside the Orient, the lights were up and the crowd had thinned to twenty or so, mostly at tables – couples, single men, small groups. The Iranian students had stayed. Zouzou seemed to have developed a following among them. Pierre nodded to the manager, Cash-in-Hand John, who hit the light switch.

Zouzou had had a huge following in Egypt – magazine articles hinted at her lascivious liaisons, and on the hand-painted movie billboards it was a contest between her bust and her panda eyes. She'd worried that she'd be recognized by Egyptians who might stray into the club. But, he told her, why should London be so different from Cairo? The intelligence services of the United Kingdom and the USSR probably knew the colour of his socks each morning before he'd got them on. And why not throw in Mossad and the Egyptian General Intelligence Directorate for good measure? Their lives were only loosely connected to their free will: Trouble would come when a faceless member of some country's *mukhabarat* decided it was time.

The speakers crackled. "Ladies and gentlemen. Time to wind down the tempo as we approach midnight. The Orient club is delighted to present our Tuesday night taste of the mysterious East, the exotic, the beautiful, the inimitable ... Z i z i !"

A single spotlight flicked on. She stood, a voluptuous contour of shimmering black, her hair pinned up high, large black glasses covering half her face, the white arms and shoulders almost blinding in contrast.

Zouzou waited. Someone shushed a couple giggling at the bar. There was silence. She tipped up her chin to sing.

The drinkers leaned forward spellbound as she began. It was a lilting, sinuous song by the great Fairouz, and she sang in the airy dialect of Lebanon, so unlike the earthy Egyptian Arabic she and Pierre spoke at home. If the audience understood not a word, they didn't seem to care.

At the end, there was a warm sprinkle of applause, and Zouzou thanked the audience in breathy French. She upped the tempo with the song by Jacques Brel. The drinkers glowed in the passion she radiated from the tiny stage.

But something was wrong. After ten years as a private investigator in Cairo, Pierre had an instinct for trouble, a feel for a room or a street where the balance of things was out of kilter. From the corner of his eye, he saw the barman make a brief hand signal. The bouncer was on tiptoe, scanning the crowd. The smell of fresh air above the fug meant that the external door had been propped open. The trouble was here. Their time had come.

Now there were strangers flitting in the gloom: Pierre made out two wraiths in tight suits. He tensed himself in readiness for the diversionary move he'd planned for this moment. His hand gripped the heavy spanner in his pocket. The mirrored bar with its bottles of gin and *crème de menthe* would shatter. He'd grab Zouzou and rush for the stairs.

But the dark shapes headed for the table where the Iranian students sat. The men snatched one of the students from his chair and walked him swiftly out of the club, unnoticed by the drinkers at the surrounding tables. The remaining Iranian students had noticed, and were discreetly slipping on their jackets and heading for the exit while Zouzou sang.

SAVAK – it had to be. Pierre had heard whispers about how the Shah's secret police had infiltrated the Iranian students at London University. But there had to be more to it; there always was.

Zouzou finished her set just after midnight and went backstage to change. One of the Iranians was still hanging around, and Pierre watched him palm a roll of banknotes to Cash-in-Hand. When would their time come, he wondered?

***

They took a taxi home. There had been another burst of rain, and the black streets threw up silver stripes from the street lights. The police squeezed them past a traffic accident outside Euston Station. Zouzou turned away from the injured motor cyclist, but Pierre stared at the supersaturated colours of the scene: The rider's black helmet, his tartan scarf, the brown boot wrenched and twisted sideways, the mangled knee through torn blue jeans.

After a year and a half in London, Pierre's sense of dislocation could be suddenly sickening and disorienting, and he had adopted the remedy of an existential stare, forcing his eyes and his mind deep into the present moment to convince himself that now was real, that he wouldn't wake to find himself in his old room in Cairo.

The taxi driver was saying something.

"Pardon me, Sir?"

"Motorcyclists. They'll never bleedin' learn."

"I suppose not," Pierre said.

But now was real, this blandly cruel city where the mundane bumped up against the horrific and the bizarre: A city where Irishmen blew up trains and litter bins, where firemen rescued old ladies' cats from trees, where drugged-up teenagers wore safety pins in their noses, where a family man on a bus could ogle a Page Three girl.

They whispered as they undressed in the flat. Despite the rain, it was warm; a blistering summer lay ahead, the papers said. Garden hoses had been banned.

A neighbor coughed and broke wind in his sleep beyond the jerry-built wall.

It was time, Pierre thought, to tell her. The near-miss in the club was a sign, surely? He had held back the truth from her for too long. She must know.

"Pierre, I can't sleep."

"Nor me, *habibi*."

"What is on your mind?"

Yes, now.

"Zouzou, the day we left Cairo, when we drove to Alexandria to take the ship to France, how do you think we were allowed to leave?"

She pulled him close and said nothing for a few seconds, as if rehearsing her answer.

"Your brilliance, *habibi*, I suppose. Or your *shabkah*." He knew she was making light of it. His *shabkah* – his network of spivs and informers - were hardly up to the job of extracting him from a country at war.

"Not the network. I made a *safqah*."

"A bargain, Pierre *habibi*? My whole life was a story of bargains before you took me away. What was special about your *safqah*?"

"There was a man in Cairo, an Englishman. His name doesn't matter."

"Names. What are names? Go on, *habibi*."

"He gave me the passports. Mr Rogers and Miss Patchett."

Zouzou laughed bitterly. "I got sick of being Miss Patchett with her ridiculous blonde hair. I looked like a chicken."

"You're still her, and I'm still him. That's what our papers say."

"And the bargain? What was the price, Pierre?"

"I fear I paid too much."

"The price, Pierre? Tell me."

"I gave him ten years of my life."

She stared at him, this woman who could not be surprised, this feline beauty who had faced down the powerful old men of Cairo and Beirut and survived with her honour intact.

"Go on, *habibi.*"

"I agreed to work for them, for the British *mukhabarat*, whenever they need my services, for ten years. After my term of servitude, they will give us papers for America."

"Tell me the name of the man in Cairo, Pierre. Tell me the name of this devil."

"Donald Waters, damn his soul."

Chapter Two

Emma Stonehouse pulled the front door shut and followed her mother down the flag-stoned path. Despite the June shower, the neighbour was in the next-door garden fiddling with a flower pot among the beds of chrysanthemums; you could rely on the old cow to be snooping around when there'd been shouting. She looked up with that sour-milk stare.

"Having a good eyeful?" Emma said, just quietly enough for her mother not to hear.

"I beg your pardon?" Mrs Littleproud said, but turned to jab murderously at a clump of roots, evidently not game to tackle the Stonehouse family at war.

It was the kind of weather that put you on edge: Windy with sudden drifts of rain, too warm for a scarf, too blowy for an umbrella. The forecast said they were in for a heatwave in July.

Looking back to the house, Emma saw her father staring through the bay window with his neat haircut and a pipe jammed between his jaws. He turned away without expression, and disappeared behind the deep curtains of the living room. Let him bloody stew.

"Close the gate, darling," her mother said from the front seat of the Range Rover. Emma glanced across: Blonde hair pinned up, hounds-tooth skirt, pastel blouse and green wellies. The pencil-thin ex-air hostess stuck in 1960, never changing, that was Mrs Susan Stonehouse.

The wrought iron gates clanged shut, and Emma wiped the raindrops from the glass-covered name plate. It was a habit she'd had since she was a little girl. 'GHAWDEX', the house was called, the Maltese name for the island of Gozo where Grandad's holiday house was. "Not 'gor-decks', her father told visitors. "It's pronounced 'ow-desh'." Always had to be the expert on everything. She glanced up to see if he'd come back to the window. Of course not. He'd have his nose in a book on medieval military strategy by now.

"Daddy just wants the best for you," Emma's mother said, holding down the accelerator to warm up the engine. She checked her make-up in the mirror, dabbed at an invisible flaw. The dogs settled into the back seat. The windscreen was fogged from the sodden air, and Emma wiped it with her hand.

"It'll smear, darling. Here, use a tissue." Emma ignored her mother. She needed a bloody cigarette.

They drove the two miles to the railway station past the big detached houses surrounded with damp fields and copses of beech and oak. Her mother tut-tutted when they passed the gypsy camp by the disused chocolate factory a half mile out of the town. A small girl in a plastic mac and bobble hat stopped to watch them, and then went back to bashing an oil drum with a stick.

When they stopped in the station yard, her mother said, "Emma, please write to him while you're away. But in a way he can understand."

"He'll never understand. People like him just don't get it."

"Your father isn't 'people', Emma."

She knew how childish she sounded. Of course, her father couldn't be dismissed as 'people'. But why the sodding hell wouldn't he make the slightest effort to understand her? Where had it all gone wrong? She knew he had some sort of inner life: There used to be communion on Sunday mornings, and he still spent the afternoons in the conservatory reading about Mediterranean history and listening to symphonies on the BBC. OK, Brahms and the Knights of St. John weren't her thing, but Ralph Stonehouse wasn't a pillar of marble. Of this she was sure. So how could he not feel her anguish at the world, at the lousy injustices, the hypocrisy everywhere you looked? How could he walk out of the room when they'd watched the fall of Saigon on television yesterday?

This time it had been Ireland. She'd said a stupid thing at dinner, something about serving the English right if they got blown up in Marks and Spencer. He'd refused to talk about Ireland and she'd come out with it to shock him. He didn't immediately say anything, just continued to eat his consommé, but in very slow motion while his face reddened. Then he looked up at her and said, in the quietest of voices, "You know nothing of these matters," got up, brushed a breadcrumb from his shirtfront, and left the room. No 'stupid girl' or 'for God's sake grow up'. At least she could have retaliated, forced him to react, asked him why the fuck he couldn't even make a pretence of taking her seriously.

The carriage clock on the mantelpiece sounded a funeral chime.

"See?" her mother said. "You've provoked him again. And there's the turbot still to come." The unfinished consommé sat in mute reproach while they ate the fish.

The windscreen of the Range Rover cleared as warm air blew from the vents. The car had the sweet, meaty aroma of damp Labradors. Funny, she never noticed it when she used to live at home, but a year at college in London had flushed the doggy smell from her nostrils. Now she was slightly repulsed by the whiff that clung to the sofas and the bedspreads in her parents' house.

Her mother leaned over the back seat and handed her a Boots carrier bag.

"Some things to tide you over at university."

"It's Poly, not university."

"You've only yourself to blame for that."

The bag contained toiletries, moisturiser, and at the bottom, a brochure for the Family Planning Association. Emma mumbled her thanks and felt herself blush: Communication with her mother on the subject of S-E-X was always carried out in code, but she appreciated the gesture behind the brochure more than she could say. At least someone regarded her as an adult. Susan Stonehouse extended her cheek to receive a goodbye kiss.

"Bye, Mum."

When the Range Rover was out of sight, Emma slung her rucksack on her back, and walked to the bus stop. Bugger wasting her allowance on a train ticket to London when she could hitch. The bus dropped her by a petrol station near the motorway ramp. She'd expected a string of hopefuls with their thumbs out, but today there was just one student there, a boy she'd been at school with. His parents were communists, she remembered, and there'd been a big fuss about him getting exempt from Religious Instruction. He was wearing a college scarf, but she didn't recognise the colours. The cardboard sign in his hand said 'London'.

"Sorry, have I nicked your spot?" he asked. He had a scrappy bit of beard and was wearing an anorak with a CND badge sewn on. It must be his dad's – CND had gone out with the beatniks. Eric, that was his name.

"It's OK. You were here first. Have you got a fag?"

The boy offered a packet. There were only two of the tiny cigarettes left. Players No.6. Two puffs and they were gone.

"Are you sure?"

He nodded and put his hands around hers to shelter the lighter from the wind.

"Might as well stick together," Eric said.

"Might as well. Proletarians of the world unite, and all that."

"Blimey Emma, you've got a good memory."

"Are you still communists?"

"Nah. My mum left my dad, and after that he joined the Tories. He's on the council now."

"Bloody hell, Eric. Anyway, what are you studying?"

"Engineering. Imperial College. What about you?"

"Political science and history," she said. "North London Poly."

"I would've got the train but I'm waiting for my grant," the boy said.

"It's a sod, isn't it?" Emma said. Her father earned too much for her to get a government grant, but that was a fact she preferred to keep to herself. The Barclays Bank cheque was buttoned up in her Levi jacket. He never gave it to her directly. That was Susan Stonehouse's department. "He's added a little extra, darling," she'd say, and Emma would stuff the cheque in her pocket with calculated indifference.

She and the boy stood with their thumbs out for half an hour.

"This is useless," he said, as another clot of cars fed onto the ramp. The drizzle was back.

"Eric, that bush, stoop down behind it. Give me your sign."

Emma took off her cap, shook out her long blonde hair and unbuttoned the Levi jacket. The low-cut T-shirt would do the trick. A lorry skidded to a stop and she grabbed the handle as the door swung open.

"Hang on," she said, and Eric scrambled into the cab after her.

"Fuckin' 'ell," the driver said.

***

The rain stopped as the lorry hit the outskirts of London. The driver dropped Emma and Eric at Brent Cross. She took the Tube to Archway, he set out on foot. The afternoon was warming when she swung her bag onto her shoulder and walked down the street of terraced houses lined with parked cars and scooters. A burst of Bob Marley from an upstairs window lifted her mood. She looked up to see a West Indian couple snogging. The girl glanced down and smiled at her. My London life, she thought: Music, sex, books, drugs, ideas, politics, people who give a fuck.

She worked the key in the outer door of the two-storey terraced house. The hallway was empty and the door to the bottom flat was closed. Upstairs, there was a note from Linda on the bookshelf: 'Whoever gets in first, we need 20p pieces and milk'. The kitchenette smelt of bacon and cigarettes. The sink was filled with dirty glasses. Linda - dirty cow. When she tried the gas, there was none. She wasn't prepared to wash up in cold water but she tidied the little sitting area, which littered with LPs, old Sunday papers, magazines, and ashtrays. On the sofa was a book she'd never seen before: *The Green Book* by Muammar Al Gathafi. She flicked pages at random: Stuff about people being pushed around by conquerors, and democracy not representing the will of the people.

Linda's bedroom door was open. The bed was unmade and the dressing table – a stack of wooden Mateus Rosé boxes - was strewn with make-up and cassette tapes. The sash window wouldn't open under the fifty coats of paint. It was Linda's problem if the room smelt like a sheep pen. Emma went into the bedroom she shared with Jules, lay down and fell to sleep.

In the evening, she was awoken by voices and a savoury smell from the kitchenette. Jules was frying something and Linda was rolling a joint. A night in, just like in a dozen shared flats where her student friends lived across North London. Fry-ups, hash, Mars Bars, cheap wine, talk of exam questions, politics and sex.

"How was polite society, Emma?" Jules asked in his funny half-French, half-Cockney accent. She slid her arms around him. He smelled scrumptiously of man sweat and patchouli. She glanced at their reflection in the window. God, they looked good together.

"Too polite for my taste, Jules. Christ, if I ever end up living in Berkshire, can someone arrange to have me put down?"

"C'mon Emma," Linda said, "You're missing the doylies and bone china already. What the fuck are you cooking, Jules? It smells vile". She had the joint alight now, and her voice was raspy.

Jules took a drag from the joint, held the smoke down, and puttered it out slowly. He looked down at the pan. "Looks like *beignets à pain de viande*."

17

"Fucking spam fritters again," Linda said, passing the joint to Emma.

Emma took a deep pull, turned Jules' face towards her and blew the smoke into his mouth. God, she needed to get his clothes off.

After they'd eaten, she went down the corridor to check if the shared bathroom was empty. She shoved someone else's damp Y-fronts to the far end of the washing line, scrubbed away the grey ring around the tub, and turned on the taps. Jules came in and locked the door, and they stripped. He sat on the edge of the tub and she rolled a condom onto him the way he'd taught her. In her English head, she said the words 'French cock' because – well, because she could do what the fuck she wanted. Then, in a rush, they folded their bodies into a wet tangle of hot breath and searching hands.

Afterwards they lay at opposite ends of the bath with their legs entwined. She raised her pale hips and opened herself to the gaze of her swarthy lover. When he made a dirty chuckle, she vowed that her life would never resemble that of her mother in the dead heart of Berkshire.

***

A week of lectures and tutorials ground to an end, and the real point of being in London came into view: Friday night at Stash's place and the weekend ahead.

But drugs and alcohol were on hold for the night: Stash said that revolutionary action demanded clear thought, unclouded by the enemies of the oppressed; the CIA controlled the drug trade, and the alcohol industry was an international capitalist conspiracy designed to keep the working classes in drunken servitude. Well, that might be the case on Friday night, but there was the rest of the weekend to catch up. Her father would have a bloody stroke if he knew about Stash.

They'd done their weekly reading. Linda made copies on a Roneo machine in the student union: Stash had prescribed *The Art of Insurrection*, a chapter from Trotsky's *History of the Russian Revolution*. It hadn't been exactly gripping, Emma had to admit, but you don't expect Trotsky to read like Barbara Cartland.

Stash's group didn't have a name: "When you name a thing, you reify it as a component in the systems of production and exchange," he'd said. "But the unnamed is unaccounted for and unidentifiable." Emma wasn't sure of the logic of this.

When she asked Linda what Stash meant, her flat mate said, "It's fucking obvious. Maybe you're just not ready for this level of analysis."

So that was that: Emma was feeble-minded doylies and bone china material. Well, bugger Linda and her phony intellectualism. In fact, Emma suspected that Stash declined to name the group because he wanted to avoid it appearing on a Special Branch list. They were just friends meeting at the caravan for a chat.

There were actually two caravans, perched side by side on bricks in the front garden of a house in Willesden that backed onto the Bakerloo Line. One caravan was the living quarters of Stash's family – a wife and some toddlers who Emma occasionally saw peeping from behind the curtains. Stash's group met in the other caravan, which contained six or seven wine boxes for seats and a poster of Mao Tse-Tung. Emma had once asked to use the lavatory, and was sent into the house, which seemed to be a dormitory for immigrant shift workers. There was an overwhelming smell of curry and garlic in the corridor, and a sour stench in the shared bathroom. A man knocked on the door and shouted in some harsh language as she squatted above the cracked toilet seat.

The usual six members were there tonight – Emma, Jules, Linda, two older Irish men and a girl from New Zealand.

"Evening everybody," the New Zealand girl said. Nobody answered. You waited for Stash to speak. He made his preparations in silence, checking his papers, looking up thoughtfully and then making a note or two. When he was done, he moved his box below the Mao poster and sat in a meditative pose. His ginger hair was tied in a pony-tail that hung half-way down his back. The porcelain eyes were unblinking, almost blank above the thick beard. He was older than Emma; she thought about her father's age - forty-five perhaps. He had the look of a man who'd led a rough life: Spidery tattoos on his hands and a livid scar along the neckline above a khaki tunic.

When he began to speak, she was immediately beguiled. Despite his appearance, his accent was refined and his quiet voice metronomic. He forensically analysed Trotsky's chapter, laying out its faults like pieces of spoiled fruit. Emma only half-understood his argument about the lack of a psychological dimension in Trotsky's work, but it didn't matter. She had struggled to read the chapter, as she had the passage from Jung the week before. Was she thick? Was the posh girl from Berkshire enrolled in Political Science a dimwit? She didn't think so, but a feeling of inadequacy nagged at her. Stash forged on. His narrative was utterly compelling, even if she barely grasped its essence.

At the end, Stash looked around the circle, waiting for questions. One of the Irish men made a rambling statement – not really a question – about the manifesto of some splinter group of the IRA, and Stash nodded sagely.

He looked around the group again, untied his pony-tail and released the cascade of red hair over his shoulders. Emma heard a gasp; Linda's mouth was open and her eyes were wet behind her glasses.

"There is a final item this evening," Stash said. "An item that you have been leading up to even if you did not consciously know it."

What's this, Emma wondered, some kind of sex ritual? Linda was practically begging Stash to shag her. Jules frowned at her and made a 'let's go' face. Emma ignored him. This could be interesting.

Stash raised a forefinger, guru-style. "Friends, we have been meeting for six months. We have satisfactorily reconciled the political and the psychological. We hold firm the conviction that the act of insurrection arises spontaneously from the collective unconscious." He swept his disciples with a piercing eye.

"But the time has now come for each of us to enact our individual acts of insurrection. How will we accomplish this?"

Emma felt a quiver in the pit of her stomach – the terror of a nightmare mingled with the thrill of the forbidden. Individual acts of insurrection? What the bloody hell?

Stash moved his wine crate into the middle of the circle and took a tobacco tin from his tunic. Emma saw a pipe and a screw of foil. She looked at Jules, who shrugged.

"The collective unconscious," Stash said, "is, by its nature, not accessible to conscious thought."

He held the pipe before him like a priest offering the host.

"Yer mean, we've got to get bolloxed to find this feckin' collective thingo?" one of the Irish men asked.

"I mean that it requires a sacrament. A sacrament that will bridge the gap between what we know and what we are not permitted to know." Stash let the thought sink in.

The New Zealand girl said, "So we smoke the sacramental shit and then our acts of insurrection will sort of bubble up on their own?"

Stash nodded. She continued: "So we might find out we want to blow something up?" but he ignored her. Instead, he reached for a cassette player and pressed PLAY. There was the hiss of the tape loading, and then Emma recognized the hypnotic opening notes of Erik Satie's *Gymnopédies*; she had bought the record for her father's birthday when she was fifteen, before he turned against her. She chased the thought away. Ralph Stonehouse had no place in this caravan.

Linda was the first to draw on the pipe. Stash went around the circle, kneeling in front of each of the members, using a lighter to keep the substance glowing. He repacked the bowl after the two Irish men. Jules was next, and then Emma.

As the smoke hit the back of her throat, she tasted the harsh vegetable bite of cannabis, but with an edge of something else sweet, something incensey. She opened her eyes for a moment to see Stash, a bronze sun-king, surveying his nodding acolytes.

And then she gave herself up to the furriness, to the mellow sexiness, to the inside-out void, to the sure knowledge that Erik Satie was playing a tiny piano in a room deep inside her brain.

***

Stash was in no hurry for the group to carry out their acts of insurrection. But at the beginning of the next meeting, he invited them – if they wished - to tell what their unconscious had proposed during the 'sacrament'. The two Irish men fidgeted and winked at each other, but weren't prepared to tell. The New Zealand girl said she was going to paint-bomb a police car, and the Irish men sniggered. Emma thought she heard one of them say, "pathetic". Jules mumbled something about graffiti, although Emma knew he was wary about getting caught doing anything that might get him sent home to France. Linda kept quiet.

"And Emma? What will you do?" Stash asked.

"I'm going to steal something." No hesitation. Wow! Where did that come from?

The others looked at her, waiting for more.

"That's it. I'm going to steal something, something important."

The Irish men were looking at her keenly. "Would that be a gun, then?" one of them said.

"Not a gun. No violence." That was all she was prepared to say.

On the way home, Linda pestered her with,"Come on, tell us what you're going to steal," until Jules told her to shut up.

"And anyway, you didn't say what you were going to do, Linda," he said.

Linda took off her glasses and wiped them.

"Yeah, so you're so curious about me. Tell us," Emma said.

"Stash wants me to do something for him."

"What?"

"Suck him off?" Jules asked, and Linda ran on ahead.

"You're such a bastard, Jules."

"I'm French, remember? I can't help it."

She didn't care whether Linda sucked him off or made him a birthday cake. What really occupied her was that she'd vocalised her thoughts about stealing something. The inchoate idea had suddenly acquired form: Sounds, words, grammar, out in the world, potent. She was going to steal something, and the shit was going to fly.

Chapter Three

Jules had arranged to go back to France for a month, but Emma decided not to head to Berkshire for the summer break. She'd stay at the flat and get a temp job. Her parents weren't due to take their annual month in Gozo until August, so there wasn't the option of using the Berkshire house as a quiet hideaway. And at any rate, her old school friends grew duller the longer she was away; the prospect of halves of bitter at the Greene Manne with Alex and Jennifer and Peter and ... well, no thank you, Berkshire.

But on the morning that Jules left, she lay in bed with a hollow spirit. The low rays of the glaring sun filled the room. There should have been some kind of afterglow from her farewell lovemaking with Jules, but she felt sticky and unfresh. The sheets needed washing and the ashtray by the side of the bed had a cold, dead stink from his *Gauloises* dog ends. It wasn't meant to be like this, with the prospect of a summer in London before her, a summer of music, protests, pubs by the Thames, new friends.

The void wasn't the absence of Jules. She was wise enough to know that her feelings for him were superficial and mostly sexual. It wasn't that she didn't feel affection towards him; he was quirky, he mangled

English jokes hilariously, and he was always the magnetic centre of any social gathering, with Emma basking in his alluring Frenchness.

But he could also be vain and secretive, and there was a streak of crudity in him that she tried not to dislike. She put up with sex on park benches, pretending to match his enjoyment and satisfaction, but often feeling afterwards that she was a clumsy apprentice who hadn't quite come up to the mark. Once she said to him, "I haven't finished," when he was already pulling on his jeans, and he'd shrugged and made a silly face. But then, there were the times when it was bloody amazing.

Emma wasn't intellectually naive about women and men. She'd read patchily in the feminist texts since tackling *The Female Eunuch* at sixteen, to her mother's dismay. When she tried to interest Jules in Julia Russ's *The Female Man*, he'd turned his French nose up: "Feminist science fiction? Dykes in space rockets?" It wasn't his bloody business anyway. She had some lesbian friends at college and had fantasised about them when she'd been in bed with Jules. But the fire wouldn't light when she was alone. Still, it would be a blast to turn up at Berkshire smooching with a woman. Almost worth it, really, to see her father's face.

No, the void wasn't about Jules. It was the fear that her life - with its ideas and ideologies and anger and altered states - was ephemeral. What if she woke up one day and never again gave a fuck about Vietnam or the exploitation of the miners or the military-industrial complex? Who'd care if a pretty girl with a quarterly cheque from her father just went home to Berkshire and married a solicitor? On days like this, she didn't give a shit about anything, and she didn't know if she'd give a shit tomorrow.

The pay phone in the downstairs hallway rang and kept on ringing. It stopped and started again.

"Soddin' thing!" This was the downstairs tenant, a Jamaican nurse who had the bad luck to have the phone bolted to the wall next to her door.

"Someone for Emma!"

The receiver was swinging on its flex when Emma hopped down the stairs in one of Jules's shirts.

"Emma, it's Mummy."

"Hello, Mum. Is something wrong?"

"You sound tired, darling. Are you quite well?"

"I'm fine. How's Dad?" Her question was no more than a matter of form.

"Daddy's fine but, well, that's the thing. There's a big flap on in the Cabinet Office, so I've decided to go to Gozo to keep out of his way. Auntie Kay's there with the girls for a week."

"Good idea. It'll be lovely there right now. Hot."

There was a pause.

"Well, thanks for letting me know, Mum. When are you going, by the way?"

"Tomorrow. The travel chap found me a spare seat on Air Malta. He's a marvel."

"Love to Auntie Kay, then. And the girls."

"And, Emma?"

"Yes, Mum?"

"You'll be all right in London while I'm away, won't you? You know - it's not Berkshire, is it?"

***

The farmhouse in Gozo had been a constant in her life as far back as she could remember. Her grandfather had bought the place when he retired from the diplomatic service, but he rarely used it. Emma's parents spent every July there, and often Auntie Kay joined them with

Emma's cousins. It was a traditional flat-roofed farmhouse, two hundred years old, with walls two feet thick, and a well in the internal courtyard. The rooms were cool and high-ceilinged with rough plastered walls, tiled floors, and cane blinds. The house nestled on the edge of a meadow of dry grass, prickly pear, and wild thyme just outside a rustic village. Another old farmhouse sat alongside; the local story was that two brothers married to two sisters had built the properties. There was a hide on the opposite hill, from which the local men shot tiny birds.

Their month in Gozo followed a well-worn routine: Mornings in Victoria, Gozo's dinky capital, where the flea market and the fish market tumbled into the main street, and the cafés served clumsy versions of the delicate pastries sold across the water in Sicily; afternoons swimming at Ramla Beach where a white statue of the Virgin Mary watched over the bathers. In the evenings, Dad would spit-roast a chicken in the courtyard, and British expat friends would drop by to drink bottles of Double Diamond and smoke duty free cigarettes.

Emma's last visit had been a year ago, her last summer before college. She'd been bored to hell for the first week, picking quarrels with her father, and making sour faces at her mother when she suggested she go to the disco in the village.

"Nobody forced you to come," her mother said. "It's not our fault Amy didn't turn up this year." Emma's summer friend was Amy Russell, a girl of her own age whose parents had a holiday house in the next village. They'd team up to escape their parents, buzzing around the island on a scooter by day and getting stoned at the disco by night.

After ten days without Amy, Emma told her parents she'd decided to go home early.

"I'm going to take the ferry to Sicily and hitch back with Joseph and Charles." The two boys were their Maltese neighbour's sons, travelling back to London to finish medical school. Her parents thought they were models of Catholic propriety. Emma knew better. The boys were planning to stop in Rome for a few days, and they'd all have a blast.

Her father said, "Absurd. You'll fly home."

Emma snapped: "Dad, why don't I get a say in this? I'm nineteen. I can vote. I'm going to college next month." She bit her lip. God, why did she always fly at him like a kid having a tantrum? Stupid, stupid idiot.

He looked at her. Was there a softening in his eyes? Was he on the verge of hugging her? The look hardened. "You'll get a say when you behave like an adult." He stood up to go.

"Ralph," her mother said, "Why don't we sit down and just talk it over?" He was already putting on his sandals.

"I'm going for a walk, Susan." He pulled his white canvas hat firmly down to his ears, jammed the pipe between his teeth.

"It's over a hundred out there. Let me get you a cool drink, Ralph, and we'll have a chat."

"There's nothing to chat about. I've made up my mind. Emma's to fly home."

Susan crossed the room to block his exit. Emma froze.

"Please sit down, Ralph."

"Mummy, let him go. It's pointless. He never listens to me."

"Emma, stay out of this, please," her mother said. Her shoulders were rigid, her arms stiff by her side, knuckles screwed into her palms. There was a decisiveness in her voice, something Emma wasn't used to hearing.

Her mother raised her voice: "Sit down, Ralph."

Her father grasped the stiff shoulders and firmly moved his wife aside. As he opened the door to leave, her face turned a furious red.

"Ralph, I'm warning you."

He stopped, a mulish look on his face.

Emma looked from one parent to another during a long moment of mutual defiance.

"Fuck off, then!" her mother said.

He stood there astonished, his jaw hanging open, the pipe rattling on the flagstones. He composed himself and went out. Emma heard him bang the front door shut and walk out into the gravelled path. A cicada struck up its song, and then another until the dry meadow rang with a discordant electric buzz.

Susan Stonehouse sank into a chair, alternately laughing and sobbing. "I was so angry. I've never said that word in my life, Emma. Forgive me, dear."

Emma was mortified. Her mother's outburst was so raw that she could barely begin to imagine what pressures were pent up behind the wall of respectability.

"But I would have flown back. It wasn't worth all the shouting."

And then for the first time, it occurred to her that her father's sour hostility might not be her fault. She'd assumed in recent years that it was his disappointment in her - her mediocre O-levels, her politics, her drug case - that caused the pall of unhappiness that shrouded their relationship. Could the source, she wondered, be something between Ralph and Susan?

"Mummy, tell me, what's wrong with Dad? Why does he behave like this?"

"Emma, my darling girl. I'm so sorry. I don't know. He's lost to us. I barely know him anymore. And it wasn't just the hitchhiking that got me worked up. It was ... everything."

"Everything what?"

"I don't think I want to talk about it anymore, Emma, if you don't mind."

"Why do you put up with it? Go after him, tell him - I don't know ..."

"That's enough, Emma." Her mother dabbed her nose and stood up, Berkshire composure re-established. She opened her handbag and counted out eighty pounds.

"Here, darling. Hitch hike home tomorrow with the boys. I wish I'd had the chance. Don't worry about Daddy. I'll talk to him."

***

After she hung up the phone in the downstairs hallway, Emma went up to the flat and began to clean up. She packed her dirty washing in a plastic bag and walked to the launderette. All the machines were busy, so she sat down for another go at *The Female Man*. A good-looking guy in a yellow vest sat down next to her and took a book from a Moroccan shoulder bag. He had long black hair to the shoulders and a Che Guevara moustache, and there were silver rings on all his fingers. Emma peeped sideways: *The Politics of Ecstasy* by Timothy Leary - the textbook on acid; she'd heard about it but never read it. When he peeped sideways at Emma's book, she was struck by his expression of sincerity - a guy you might trust.

"My machine's nearly finished. You can have it next," he said.

They sat in chummy silence for a few minutes. He knelt down, fished out his clothes, and tossed them in a drier.

She loaded the machine, dribbled in some powder from a Tupperware, and put some coins in the slot. He seemed amused by something.

"What is it?"

"Your Tupperware," he said.

They both laughed. "My mother gave me it. She's got loads of them," Emma said.

"Mine's the same but I'm trying to give them up. Do you live around here?"

"Just in the next street. How about you?"

"No," the man said, "South of the river. I'm just visiting a friend up here."

"Do you usually take your washing when you visit friends?" Emma asked. He was nice, easy to talk to. "I'm Emma, by the way."

"I'm Kit. Nah, it's my friend's washing. I'm doing her a favour." He was right: A red bra floated across the glass window of the drier. "Hey Emma, do you like Ravi Shankar?"

"Yeah. I've got *Shankar Family and Friends*, the one George Harrison did. It's amazing. Why do you ask?"

"He's on at Southwark Cathedral this evening. I'm going with some friends. I've got a spare ticket. Do you want to come?"

Why not, Emma thought.

"Great. Where do we meet?"

"The Southwark Tavern. Six OK?"

"Six is perfect." The void was filled, at least for tonight.

***

She spotted him in a corner among five or six girls and guys a bit older than her. She bought a half of shandy at the bar and joined them. Two of them were in outer space, wide-eyed and stifling giggles. Kit introduced her to the others. One guy said he was a cook, and one of the girls - she was from the North - mentioned a bar job. Emma hadn't been in London long enough to get to know people outside the student tribe, except for Stash's group. She'd hardly ever met anyone from the North, never been north of the Watford Gap motorway services.

Kit said they all lived in a squat, but she thought they looked like ordinary people, not down-and-outs. There were squats everywhere in London. But from what he said, it wasn't easy: Strangers breaking in, dodgy electricity, no hot water.

She soon realised that all of them but Kit were stoned; he said his job was to look after them at the Ravi Shankar concert. "We do it this way in case someone has a bad trip; there's someone to help."

"Does that happen very often?" Emma asked.

"You mean you haven't tripped before?"

"Not really."

"Not really?" Kit said.

"No, not actually. I haven't."

"Do you want to? I've got a tab if you want it. I'll be around to help. It's good gear."

Emma took a sip of her shandy. She looked around the group. Two more had moved into their own worlds, one gazing at her hand as she moved it side to side, the other eyes closed and smiling as if he had entered some variety of paradise. She'd always been too scared to drop acid, but she felt secure in the gentle rapture radiating from Kit's friends. He looked at her and raised an eyebrow in query.

"I think you want to," he said.

"OK." It came out almost without her realising. It was now or never, among a group of people who seemed to know what they were doing. She was leaving the Berkshire twerps behind for good.

She moved to sit next to him, and he opened his wallet under the table. There was a photo of a middle-aged couple in the little plastic window.

"Is that your parents?"

Kit nodded and smiled. He slid a little square of blotting paper from behind Mum and Dad. It had a cartoon face printed on it. Emma put it on her tongue and washed it down with shandy.

***

She sat on the cathedral floor among a crowd of young and old people, lots with flowing clothing and bits of coloured scarves. She began to find herself floating on the strands of fluid melody overlaid on the drone strings of the sitar, and then chasing the melody to its endless end. The musicians melted into swirls of waxy colours that she had never seen before. Her body was at the center of a vast cylinder of rhythmic drumming. She moved her hands, and her fingers made trails of colour that resonated with the sitar, which was making solid ropes of harmonies that wove and unwove and smiled and unsmiled inside her face with intense clarity. She felt precarious, unbalanced, controlled and uncontrolled. When she closed her eyes, the music became a blanket of rhythmic colour; she knew truths that she'd never known before, that she was connected to a truth so much bigger than herself, that there was no limit to her journey. She had a sense that hours had passed and now she was in control of a beautiful mystery.

But after a minute - or was it ten minutes or ten hours? - the music grew jangly and she felt her smile going upside down, and she saw that the girl next to her had a flopping mask for a face. Emma's watch grew very small so that she couldn't read the time. She looked up at the grey vaults of the ceiling and saw them sinking towards her like clouds of soft rock, and then she was crying and trying to disappear into the cold stone slab she was sitting on. She wanted it all to stop but it went on and on and on. Arms lifted her gently. She floated on a wave of terror into the dark street. Hours, minutes, days she walked and walked with Kit through a nightmare town of glowering buildings and diabolical strangers.

Much later, she woke up to find somebody pawing at her. It was dark. It was indoors. She had her clothes on, but she was under a blanket. It smelt. A man was trying to undo her jeans. She sat up and punched him, and he yelped.

"That was my fuckin' nose."

A cigarette lighter flicked on somewhere in the room and a candle was lit. The candle approached, with faint smears of turquoise trailing from it, and Kit's face above it.

"What are you doing, Pete? She's coming down. She had a bad trip. Piss off out of here."

The man rolled over and disappeared.

"Are you OK?" Kit asked. "You freaked out a bit. I brought you back here."

"Here?"

"The squat."

"I want to go home," Emma said. She felt around the blankets. She was on a mattress on the floor.

"I've got your stuff. Hang on." He went away and came back with the denim shoulder bag she'd had at the pub.

"Do you want something to eat?" he asked.

"What is there?"

"Cornflakes."

"No thanks." Where the bloody hell was she?

Kit prised open a corrugated iron sheet and let her out. Her watch said 5am. Although it was still dark, the smokestacks of Battersea Power Station were visible against the glow of Central London. She was still south of the river, then.

"See you again?" he said.

Emma snorted and headed for the smokestacks and the glow. She'd walk off the jangling in her head - an hour and a half to home, she estimated. She cursed herself for her stupidity; anything could have happened.

She stopped for a moment and visualised herself as a tiny figure at the centre of the street, at the centre of London, at the centre of the universe. The tiny figure got tinier and tinier until it wasn't there at all. She groped for an insight that kept slipping away. What had happened to her last night? There was something different, something to do with God, the universe, and then it slipped away again. She shivered.

And as Emma crossed Chelsea Bridge, with the breaking dawn and the rising metallic smell of the river at low tide, the night's events evaporated and all that was left was the void.

An old car passed her and slewed to a stop. A skinhead leaned out of the window and said, "Wanna lift?" He opened the door and the interior light went on.

There were three more men in the car, with raw shaved heads and red eyes.

"Leave me alone."

"Come on, dontcha fancy a bit of this?" The man was groping in his trousers and she caught a glimpse of dirty white.

She ran across the road and was caught full in the face by headlights. Brakes screeched. The tarmac came up to meet her shoulder as she lost her footing, and she was flat on her back looking up at the front of a taxi. It reversed into the kerb behind the skinheads' car. The door opened and a wrinkled face under a checked cap loomed over her.

"Blimey, you gave me a start. 'Ere, darlin', let's get you on your feet." The taxi driver hoisted her up. Nothing broken. She hadn't been hit.

He sat her in the back seat and turned towards the other car. Emma saw that he had a wicked-looking wheel brace in his hand.

The skinheads' old banger jerked away. She heard one of them shout, "Fuckin' lezzie," and they were gone but for the whiff of engine smoke.

The taxi driver said, "Where to, my love?"

"Holloway," Emma said. "But I can't afford a taxi."

"My treat. I've just clocked off. I live at Crouch End. You look a bit peaky. You haven't been to one of those cannabis resin parties, have you?"

"Just a bit too much to drink. I'll be fine, thanks."

"I've got a daughter your age. Does your dad know where you are?"

The wrinkled man in the checked cap was a dad. She had a dad. A dad she loved and didn't love. The tears came under a shroud of desolation. She wept until she was devoid of any feeling whatsoever. As they turned into Seven Sisters Road, the low beams of dawn sunlight crinkled the drops on her eyelashes into a silvery aura. It was suddenly all so clear: It was time to act.

***

Early on the following Sunday, Emma dressed in old Levis and tucked her long blonde hair under a denim cap. She'd get to Berkshire with hours to spare, but she wanted to avoid bumping into anybody she knew, and she couldn't be bothered with Linda's questions. She scribbled a note for her flat mate, who was still asleep 'Gone to St Albans for the day. Back tonight'. Her bike was chained up in the side alley. She cycled the quiet streets to Paddington, not quite believing what she had decided to do, but knowing that it was right.

The arguments tumbled over in her mind: Her father's coldness, her mother's oppression, the futility of their Berkshire lives, their inability to understand her, the injustices all around, the hideous hypocrisy of the old men who conducted the tone-deaf orchestra that passed for international politics. Yes, what she was doing was surely right. Her father would suffer some inconvenience, perhaps even embarrassment. Let him. They'd close ranks as usual, anyway; bloody government people always did.

There was a spray of rain as she approached the station. Shit! She'd forgotten to pack a waterproof. But the sun was out when the train reached Reading. Emma put on her sunglasses before getting out of the carriage; there were people around here who might recognise her. The conductor helped unload her bike from the luggage car, and she muttered thanks, keeping her head down. He'd been too interested in getting back to the tits in the News of the World to even look at her.

It was a twelve-mile ride to the house. Emma avoided the main roads, getting lost several times and having to backtrack through wooded lanes to find junctions with uncertain signposts. When she spotted the disused chocolate factory through a gap in a hedgerow, it was well after midday. She pulled the bike into a clump of bushes and took an apple from the panier.

Her father's Sunday afternoon routine was family legend: Ralph Stonehouse never worked on Sundays, however serious the 'flap'. A year or two ago, she and her mother had sat at the lunch table in awe as her father spoke into the phone: "You may inform the Cabinet Secretary that I will provide a written briefing for the PM on Monday morning, and no sooner."

The big flaps usually coincided with some international crisis. She knew nothing about his job except that he had a stratospheric security clearance: One more thing for them not to talk about, which left just about sod all. She mourned - yes that was the word - mourned the bond they'd had. The family used to walk to the Anglican church in the village every Sunday. Her father always took the sacrament, but her mother, being from Presbyterian stock, would not: "It's rather showy and a little unnecessary, darling". Emma was never confirmed, but loved to kneel next to her father when he filed back into the pew after taking the blood and flesh of Christ. She was never sure about the strength of her faith, but those words! *Grant that all who share this bread and this cup may become one body and one spirit, a living sacrifice in Christ, to the praise of thy Name.* Whether she believed any of it or not, they were moments of perfect unity, her father deep in prayer, the organ playing the ceremony to its end.

One day, he made an excuse - too much work to do - and left Emma and her mother to go to church without him. There were more excuses and more absences until Emma herself began to skip church. She'd edged towards asking her mother about Dad's indifference, but the response was uniform: "He's so busy with his work these days". There was an increasing grimness about him from that time. Sunday lunches were eaten in silence. He bought a pair of big headphones that he plugged into the stereo. Listened with his eyes closed. Clear off, little girl, I'm busy with Mendelssohn.

She guessed that if the current 'flap' were serious enough to send her mother off to Gozo, her father would be working late into the weeknights and even staying over in London for a night or two if necessary. But Sunday would be sacrosanct, and she could be sure that he would be out of the house with the dogs from five o-clock. His walk would take him over the wooded hill behind the house, across the brook, down Fidget Lane to The Lamb for a solitary half of bitter, and back through the Public Footpath that threaded along the boundary of the horse stud. It took an hour and a half.

But there were still a few hours to kill. The midday heat was retreating as a bank of ragged clouds obscured the sun, and Emma shivered in her thin denims. She jumped at the sound of voices in the lane and ducked into the undergrowth: It was a troop of boy scouts loaded down with khaki rucksacks, and dangling tin mugs. The boys - six or seven of them - stopped not ten yards from her and dumped their packs by the side of the road. One of them - a big lad with a pink face and acne - lit a tiny spirit stove and started to boil water. A smaller boy lit a cigarette. The others passed around a magazine and made 'whoa' noises: "Look at the tits on that," she heard a boy say in a squeaky voice.

The pain of cramp speared her calf like a sudden knife wound. She cried out. The boys froze. After a few seconds, the acne kid apparently remembered his leadership obligations.

"All right, lads," he said. "First aiders, stand by."

The undergrowth parted and the pink face loomed.

"Is somebody hurt, Missis?"

"No. Leave me alone." Emma's mind raced: How old was the bloody boy? Fourteen, perhaps fifteen? Got to get rid of them. An idea hit her.

"I know your mum."

The acne reddened on the pink flesh.

"My mum?"

"Yes. You're from around here. I've seen you."

The boy's Adam's apple sank and rose in terror.

"So what would she say if she knew that you lot were smoking and looking at dirty magazines? And you in charge, too? Didn't your mum tell me you're a sergeant scout or something?"

"Patrol Leader, Miss."

"That's right, that's what she said."

"You wouldn't tell her?"

"Depends. I'm on an undercover job with the police. Now clear off. You never saw me, OK?"

The troop decamped and clanked off down the lane.

The clouds drifted away and the afternoon warmed. Emma dozed in the hollow her body had made in the undergrowth, occasionally waking to massage her calf; the cramp must have been from the long bike ride. At four-thirty, she pushed the bike deeper into the bushes and broke off some big ferns to cover it. It was a half-hour walk to Ghawdex through the fields.

There was an old shed a hundred yards from the house from which she could see the front garden. Stooping behind the splintered door, Emma suddenly went cold: What if the dogs smelt her scent and barked at her hiding place? But the wind was blowing gently away from the house, and she was pretty sure she was safe for now.

At just after five, her father appeared in the porch with the excited Labradors pulling on their leashes. He turned left and made for the side of the garden, where there was a gate into the field. He was out of sight in five minutes.

The line between the shed and the front door ran almost completely out of sight of Mrs Littleproud's house. Emma let herself in with her key. Inside, the smell of dog and lavender polish brought back the life she'd abandoned, the parents she'd loved but given up on.

His security pass was in its usual hiding place; she'd seen him drop it into the Art Deco vase hundreds of times. It was an unimpressive thing: An oblong plastic-covered card bearing his photo and a long serial number, threaded onto a neck cord. No name on the card, but 'Property of Her Majesty's Government' on the back. Ralph Stonehouse peered out from his clandestine world, stern-faced, clean-shaven with neatly parted hair. Emma saw herself in his confident demeanour. She touched the side of his face with her forefinger.

The door chime rang. It was fifteen minutes since her father had left. It couldn't be him. He had a key, anyway. Emma dropped to her knees and crawled to the front door, pressing her ear to the thick timber. The chime rang again.

"Mr Stonehouse?" It was the muffled voice of the wretched neighbour, Mrs Littleproud. Emma had underestimated the STASI surveillance unit next door.

"Mr Stonehouse. I have those hydrangeas for you." The chime rang again. The neighbour wasn't interested in giving anybody flowers; she must have been spying at the window and wondered who her father's visitor was. Emma stayed on the floor until she heard steps on the gravel. The cow had given up. Time to sneak out through the back door before she launched another foray. Shit, it was deadlocked, different key, she remembered. The front door, then.

With the security pass inside her shirt, she took a last look around the room. Had she forgotten anything? An irregular shape caught her eye: The corner of something black sticking out from under a settee. She knelt and pulled it out: Her father's briefcase, an ancient creased thing with the faded gilt initials RJS. Her heart smashed against her ribs. There was a buff folder inside. The words TOP SECRET jumped out.

The door chimed again.

It was now or never. Emma buckled up the briefcase and held it fast. She pulled the cap low over her brow, put on the dark glasses, and opened the door a crack. The old bat was standing in the middle of the path looking up at the bedroom windows. Emma flung the door open and bolted for the front gate in a crouching stance. It was raining. She swerved to avoid the neighbour, slipped on the wet ground and collided with the woman's hip, pitching her sideways. There was a hideous crack, but Emma didn't look back. She ran across the road into the field, crying over and over, "Christ, what have I done, what have I done?"

Chapter Four

Ralph Stonehouse raised his gritty eyes to the portrait of
the Queen on the far wall of his office. He fiddled with
the temporary identity pass around his neck. The fingers
of his right hand drummed the desk of their own accord.
He wondered if his heart would hold out; and
wondering about his heart sent his pulse soaring.
Another cigarette. Another cup of tea. His teeth were
furry and his stomach felt like a drain. Her Majesty
looked down brightly.

There were days when he dreamed about killing
Donald Waters - most days, in fact. But none so much
as today: Ralph Stonehouse, an Assistant Secretary in
the Joint Intelligence Organisation, dreaming about
smashing Donald Waters' face in with a shovel. And
then piercing his heart with a stake.

The telephone rang for the umpteenth time. He
snatched it and said, "Stonehouse," removing the top of
his fountain pen with his free hand. The desk blotter
was covered in a crazy doodle of mountain tops and
satanic faces. While he listened, he began to sketch a
pendulous drop of blood.

"Morris here, Ralph. The PM's got to be told sooner
than later. I can't cover for much longer. Either find it

or bloody well own up. It won't be dainty, but it's not exactly Burgess and Maclean stuff."

"It's not anything like Burgess and Maclean, and I don't like your insinuation, if you don't mind me saying so. I simply mislaid it." He hung up. Insolent bastard.

Ralph tore the blotter from the pad and ripped it into pieces: Doodling, childish. He'd started doing it at school and had never broken the habit.

The air in the old-fashioned office was soupy. A blade of hot afternoon sunlight cut through the long sash windows onto the parquet floor. The heavy wooden furniture and velvet curtains exuded a smell of antique dust. Ralph looked up at the sovereign, her faithful servant who had lost the file that would have put Donald Waters in Dartmoor for a very long time.

A sonnet. It all started with a sonnet, a lumpen declaration of puerile love by a cockstruck schoolboy. He still blushed to think of it: Waters' crony Hodge creeping into the bed in the school sick bay to 'fix him up'; the desperate loneliness of a boarding school adolescent that made him an acquiescent partner in one brief episode of sticky intimacy; his infatuation with Hodge's luminous good looks. And his pathetic travesty of Shakespeare's fifteenth sonnet, given confidentially to Hodge, who passed it straight on to Waters. The next day, smirking boys were reading handwritten copies in every corner. By the end of the week, the whole school were covering their bottoms when they passed him in the corridors.

In their lower sixth year, Hodge returned from the Easter holidays bursting with news. It was around the school in a flash: He had shagged the *au pair*. Boys sat slack-jawed as he led them through the unimaginable details: Enormous tits, juicy cunt, rubber johnnies.

Hodge basked in the sun of adulation. Whatever the facts of the matter, his holiday adventure had cleared him of any taint of being a queer.

That left Ralph Stonehouse as the brown-hat who'd written a love poem to another chap.

***

Ralph had been promoted to Assistant Secretary five years ago, charged with the task of establishing a channel of communication between Whitehall and Ealing. The Government needed Ealing to run covert operations in the Middle East without any come-back. Plausible deniability, that was the handy term they'd borrowed from the CIA to cover Ralph's task.

He took Susan out for a celebration dinner. They giggled at the silly cover story he'd invented: Assistant Secretary in the Department of Deckchair Maintenance.

"I can't say a word about it."

"But really Ralph, you'll tell me one day?"

"You know I can't, Susan." They finished the second bottle of champagne.

"You know what I'd love to do right now, Ralph?"

"I think so, but I still won't tell."

He woke in the early morning and untangled himself from Susan's naked body. Assistant Secretary. Assistant bloody Secretary. And well-deserved, too.

Ealing fell under the eye of Marjorie Byers, a Permanent Under-Secretary who had trained as an Arabist and anthropologist.

"She's tough as a camel, that one," the Cabinet Secretary had told him. "School of Oriental and African Studies of course, like most of the ruddy Arab Mafia. But she knows her stuff. I can't give you too much detail, but she did two years in *mufti* in Jordan and Syria, and we're a damned sight safer in our beds as the result."

Marjorie Byers was also well-connected, as Ralph soon discovered. There was a strict prohibition on Ealing staff visiting Whitehall and on Cabinet Office staff visiting Ealing. The solution was to meet at country houses - opulent places with long private driveways in rural corners of the Home Counties. Some were said to be highly exclusive bordellos. Ralph would be picked up by a minicab which he assumed was arranged through a cut-out that eliminated a connection with either party.

The first meeting took place at a Tudor mansion somewhere in North Hertfordshire; the last road sign Ralph had seen was for Ware, after which they tunnelled through lanes of black hedgerows. It was after ten at night when a manservant admitted him to the house. He was led through thick-carpeted reception rooms hung with tapestries and oil paintings of moustachioed grandees on horses. The servant knocked at a door, and a voice called. "Come".

Marjorie Byers was Britannia epitomised, with the implacable expression of a woman who might lance dragons from atop a war horse. She sat with imperial aplomb behind a vast antique desk. Her perm appeared to be made of fibreglass. He could not fail to notice a handbag large enough to contain a disassembled Bren gun.

"Sit."

He sat.

"Well?"

"I've drawn up an agenda, some key points on how the two departments relate to each other," he said.

"Mr Stonehouse. I have no intention of discussing your agenda. I have asked you here so that I can assess your character."

"My character?"

"Don't repeat what I've said. If you have a proper question, then ask it."

Ralph considered her remark. Being talked down to by a woman was quite outside his experience. Not normal procedure.

"If I may say so, I do not need to be assessed. I was selected for this position through the normal Civil Service procedures."

She ignored him. "What does your father do?"

"What's that got to do with the price of eggs?"

"Please answer the question."

She was obviously mad. Best to humour her. "He was an Ambassador."

"Graham Stonehouse? East Africa specialist?"

Ralph nodded.

"School?"

"Hepworth Castle."

"Never heard of it. Oxford or Cambridge?"

"Edinburgh. I read English and Philosophy. First class honours ..."

Marjorie Byers swatted his answer away and focussed her glare at a point in the middle of his brow. He wondered if she was attempting to penetrate bone, the better to learn his character.

At last she said, "You'll do, I suppose."

This was intolerable. Ralph must object to such treatment. He rehearsed his response as she continued to stare: 'If you don't mind me saying so, if I might just interpose here, if I could ask you to clarify'. But before his lips parted, his rejoinder wilted, made a final twitch, and expired.

The woman opened the enormous hinged handbag, looked inside, and then snapped it shut.

"Mr Stonehouse, you and I will likely not meet again. Your point of contact will be my Assistant Secretary Mr Waters." She beckoned to a figure in the corner of the room who Ralph had not noticed.

Donald Waters. Ralph's stomach lurched. His career was down the sewer.

Waters stepped forward and offered his hand.

"Jolly good to meet you again, Ralph. What's it been? Twenty, twenty-five years?"

Ralph stood paralysed, perspiration breaking out under his armpits.

"Hwot's the matter with you, Stonehouse? Struck dumb?" Marjorie Byers asked.

Ralph mumbled something like, "Last person I expected," and extended a hand which he knew was slick with sweat.

Waters chuckled.

"Stonehouse and I are old school pals, Ma'am. I think we can look forward to a first-class partnership."

He raised an index finger as if a fond memory had just occurred to him: "Now you were a bit of a poet at school, as I remember, Ralph. Are you still writing sonnets by any chance? Do have one of these sandwiches. *Gentleman's Relish*, by the look of it."

There had been no explicit blackmail since the reunion with Waters five years ago; his foe was too subtle for that. But Ealing had got away with murder - several times, literally - because of Waters' hold on Ralph. At their infrequent country house meetings, it would be, 'No point in upsetting the PM at this point,' or 'There were casualties, unfortunately. But if you're asked you might say that on balance, it was in the national interest'.

The Bellamy and Vickers affair was the nadir of Ralph's so-called liaison job. From what Waters had deigned to tell him, it was a royal cock-up. How else to describe two British operatives abducted to Moscow, and an Egyptian double agent occupying a desk at Ealing? Something stank, and it came from Waters' direction. How many times had he been on the point of warning the Old Man that Waters was a national security risk? But where was the solid evidence? And who'd believe him if Waters revealed his pathetic schoolboy secret?

But three years into Ralph's misery, a gift of inestimable value fell into his hands. On his Sunday walk, the dogs went into a frenzy when a man stepped out from behind a tree. The individual was gangling and middle-aged, dressed in hiking gear that looked too large in some places and too small in others.

"Are you lost?"

"I wish to give something to you, Mr Stonehouse."

"And who might you be?"

"My name is Zlotnik. I am a Soviet diplomat."

"So why do you sound like an American?"

"Please do not waste my time, Mr Stonehouse. I am who I say." The man handed him a Soviet diplomatic passport and waited while Ralph examined it. He'd seen a few of these before. It looked authentic.

"Why me? How did you find me?"

Zlotnik sighed and rolled his eyes. "Ralph John Stonehouse, born 4 October 1930 in Godalming, Surry, school Hepworth Castle, cross-country gold medal 1946, father Graham Stonehouse ...

"All right. I've got the idea, Mr Zlotnik." Bloody hell, this was highly irregular. Under-Secretaries weren't supposed to bump into spies. The man gave Ralph an envelope and strode down the hill.

For once, he didn't postpone the job until Monday. By Sunday dinner time the outline of a plan had formed in his mind.

"Is the lamb a little dry, darling?

"No, perfectly fine Susan, but I've a little work matter on my mind and it's rather taken away my appetite."

***

There was enough information in Zlotnik's envelope to persuade the Old Man to launch covert action against Waters. "If the bugger's working for the Soviets, I want your report as tight as a camel's arse, and I want him dealt with. The PM's had a bellyful of Marjorie Byers and the toffee-nosed prima donnas who work for her."

And now he sat slumped at his desk, squirming at the image of Waters leafing through the stolen file, two years' painstaking bloody work.

He swung an imaginary shovel at Waters' face. Could he kill a man? Ralph had never been tested - did eighteen months' national service in peacetime, just played at being a soldier in Hampshire. Pull yourself together, man.

He left the office around 4pm and had a couple of Scotches in a station bar at Paddington. Two or three trains departed while he was drinking, but by the time he arrived home, the dulling effect of the alcohol had worn off, leaving an evil coating on his tongue and a pile-driver headache. There was half a shepherd's pie in the fridge but he couldn't remember how to turn on the oven. Susan had shown him once. Not his job. Cold dinner, then: It wasn't too bad with a pickled onion. He lay on the ottoman in the sitting room, and poured a big brandy. And another. Three or four glasses later, there was an inch left. Why not finish the whole sodding bottle? He swigged the last mouthful and lit another cigarette. Bugger. Wasn't there some Scotch in the cabinet? But his head was swirling and he'd have to crawl on his knees to get it. Perhaps he should just drink himself to death. Or empty Susan's sleeping pills down his gullet. Would she get his pension if he finished himself off? Note to self, check regulation. Para 26, Clause 92, Footnote xvii, allocation of pension entitlements to dependants in case of pathetic git jumping off London Bridge. He pictured a funeral with no mourners. Raining. The Old Man turns up just as the coffin is lowered. Was he really having these thoughts? A pellet of pickled onion and brandy squeezed itself up his oesophagus and burned his throat.

The house was dark, with only a standard lamp throwing a pool of yellow light in the corner. A night bird cried out nearby, and there was the sudden yowl of cats. Music: Some music would soothe his desolation. The stereo was in reach, and he scrabbled in the rack of cassettes. Satie's *Gymnopédies* - his dear Emma had bought it for him in the days before Waters had poisoned his life. The thought of playing it was unbearable.

He badly needed to speak to Susan in Malta. Bugger the cost of the call. The phone was in reach. It would be early morning in Gozo, but he'd call anyway.

"Operator. Number please?"

Ralph mumbled the international code and the number.

"Country code 356. That'll be Malta, will it, Sir? Hold the line, please."

He cautiously raised himself to a sitting position and closed his eyes for a moment. His head swirled. There was a brief burst of a static-laden voice as an operator somewhere in Europe connected the call.

Cats. There'd been cats outside, but the dogs hadn't barked. Odd. They'd probably let themselves out of the flap and gone foraging.

He heard a grunt behind him and half-turned. His body was snatched upwards and over the back of the ottoman. The phone flew from his hand and twanged across the room on its cable. He was aware of strong arms pinning him on either side, and then the floor slid away under his feet. There was a horrible thump, and then his brain connected with the pain of his head striking a door frame. It was dark - the hallway? - and then he was on the ground, his eyes bound with a blindfold that had come out of nowhere. He spouted vomit and a voice said, "Fuck's sake". His right arm flipped free and he snatched the blindfold away just as the lights came on.

Snapshots flashed before his eyes: A masked man swearing and wiping muck from his hands. A woman in a dressing gown swinging a hockey stick. A man with a balaclava crashing to the floor with blood spurting from his scalp. The hockey stick smashing into an eye socket and then a knee. Someone screaming, "You've fucking blinded me, you mad bitch". Two men scrabbling to their feet, shuffling, cursing, the bang of a door.

Then quiet, but for a squawk from the phone.

"They've gone," Mrs Littleproud said. "I'll make us a nice cup of cocoa."

***

He woke early the next morning and cleaned up the vomit and blood. There was a tooth, attached to a clot of gore stuck to the quilted pelmet above the French windows. The dogs were nowhere to be seen.

The neighbour had been persuaded not to call the police before taking her hockey stick home. Ralph had given her a little lecture about proportionate force: "Mrs Littleproud, I'm afraid you'd be charged with quite a serious offence if we were to make an official report. But I'm very grateful for your help. I'm sure they were just burglars, and they certainly won't be back for more of your special treatment. Ha ha!"

The morning was warming up early: Another blinding day ahead. Damn this heat wave. His head throbbed. The percolator bubbled on the stove. A coffee and a cigarette tamed the menagerie of memories from last night. Good thing he hadn't got through to Susan. What would he have said? "Darling, I'm about to get sacked because I've lost a top-secret file. Bloody nuisance really. Nothing to worry about. I was thinking about killing myself."

He telephoned his secretary at nine o'clock and told her he'd take the day off - strained his back picking up a log in the garden.

"If you don't mind me saying so, Sir, there's an awful fuss here today."

"What sort of fuss, Mary?"

"I'd rather not go into details over the telephone. I just think that you ought to come in, if you don't mind me saying, Sir."

He had no choice. To stay home was to admit indecision and timidity. The correct drill was to face the consequences. Get it over with. Save whatever shreds of his career that might be left. He downed the last of the coffee. It was bitter and lukewarm. He'd drive to the station and take the 10.05.

In ten minutes, he was approximately presentable: Yesterday's shirt, second best suit, a clumsy shave. It occurred to him that he should check whether the neighbour was in good health after last night. He'd normally avoid conversation with her, but he was in her debt.

The door opened.

"What can I do for you, Mr Stonehouse?"

"I just wondered if you, well - after last night, you know."

"I'm perfectly well, considering."

"Well, that's a relief," he said, letting the words hang under her flinty glare.

"Considering events, that is," she said.

"Events? Have there been other events?"

"Oh indeed, Mr Stonehouse. Last Sunday I was knocked over and spreadeagled on the front path by your visitor. I dropped a valuable Japanese flower pot. I took the trouble to secure the premises."

"Secure the premises?"

"The door, Mr Stonehouse. The visitor left it open and I closed it with the spare key you keep under the Peter Pan. I hope you don't think me presumptuous."

"Not at all." He gritted his teeth. So they'd been watching the house, got in when he was walking the dog.

"I'm most dreadfully sorry, Mrs Littleproud. I don't recall having a visitor on Sunday."

"Well, you most certainly did." She crossed her arms and peered into the distance as if she had all day to wait for Ralph to beg for the next morsel.

"I insist on paying for the damaged pot."

"It was irreplaceable."

"Would you mind telling me what the visitor looked like?"

"Young."

"Young?"

"Thin."

"Thin. I see." Ralph said. "Is there anything else you can tell me?" He bit his lip in frustration.

"A young, thin person, carrying a briefcase."

Well, that was something, but it was evident that she was willing to say no more. Ralph wished her a good day. She sniffed and marched down the path.

And who was this thin person? This young, thin person? His heart skipped dangerously. Control yourself, man. It was just some junior criminal, a kid from the Gypsy camp. Logic, think logically. Logic cut in with blood-freezing impact: How did the young thin person get in? How did the thugs get in? There were no signs of forced entry. He went into the garden and sidled around the Peter Pan statue, watching for the twitch of curtains next door. The spare key lived in a hollow rock in its base. There it was, undisturbed in a wrapping of tinfoil. Nobody else had a key except for Susan and Emma. Made no sense, no sense at all.

The ritual of starting the Range Rover and navigating the lane down to the main road yanked Ralph back to normality. The retired surgeon two houses down was washing his Jaguar, and waved at him with a chamois leather. The milk van stopped to make a delivery, the landlord mopped off the tables in the gravelled forecourt of The Dog and Whistle. For a moment, Ralph doubted that last night's events had actually happened. He pulled over and rolled up his shirt sleeve: Ugly bruises in the shape of fingers, no question about that. And the mess of congealed blood and spew had been real; he hadn't imagined gagging while he mopped it up. This was a new reality: Ralph Stonehouse, career civil servant, life buggered up in the course of four days.

Who the hell were the men the neighbour had seen off? Common burglars? But burglars wouldn't quietly let themselves in with a key. No, they had to be connected with the stolen file and pass. Were they trying to deliver some kind of message? 'Keep your distance, Stonehouse'? But what professional agents would scarper after being bashed with a hockey stick by an elderly woman? Yet on reflection, he was shocked by the almost psychotic viciousness of Mrs Littleproud's attack.

He parked the Range Rover at the station. The two men by the news kiosk - were they pretending not to look at him? Was that a clicking noise from the van parked next to him? He half ran up the steps and found a seat on a bench between two pensioners from which he could scan the whole platform.

He made his mind up. He'd confess that he'd taken the Waters file home. Yes, they could sack him, but everybody took files home, didn't they?

And Ralph had made a more profound decision. He would confess that he had lied during his positive vetting years ago. He'd confess that he'd had a homosexual encounter in his teens. He would tell them that Waters had blackmailed him for the last five years. If he was to be drummed out of the Civil Service, he'd take the bastard with him, file or no file. He wasn't a bloody queer anyway; he was married, and there'd never been any problems in the Susan department. A tide of euphoria washed over him; the decision would cast out the ghastly thoughts of ending it all that constantly lurked in his mind. But the tide began to recede; would he have the courage to do what he must?

***

The meeting was in the Old Man's office: All stainless steel and Swedish birch wood. Sir Oliver Mountjoy flicked a stainless-steel desk ornament, and a row of suspended shiny balls clicked back and forth. "My wife bought it at Habitat, I believe. It's supposed to be relaxing." He sighed and asked, "Did you take the file home?"

"Yes, I took it home."

"And it has been stolen?"

"Yes."

"Any idea by whom?"

"I'm told by a young person," Ralph said. "Somebody thin. A lad from the Gypsy camp, perhaps."

The Old Man touched the desk toy, and the balls stopped clicking. "You've buggered this right up, Stonehouse," he said. "Anything to add?"

Ralph hesitated. He couldn't discern what direction the meeting might take next. A good dressing down? Demotion? Was this the moment to try to bluster his way out? He found his courage.

"Yes, I want to confess that I lied in my positive vetting when I said that I had never engaged in a homosexual act."

The Old Man sat up in his seat. "Now, easy does it, Stonehouse. That's a serious admission."

Ralph gulped. He'd gone too far to hold back now. "It was at school. Donald Waters has been blackmailing me for five years."

There was a moment of silence. The Old Man flicked the toy and the balls clacked. "As a matter of fact, we know all about it."

Ralph struggled to understand the words among the clack-clack-clack. "Would you be good enough to stop those balls knocking together, Sir?"

The Old Man placed his hand over the toy.

"You know - about Waters?" Ralph asked.

"We do indeed."

Ralph slumped into the chair. He strangled a hysterical cackle, his mind veering between mortification and rapture. "Do you mind if I have a cigarette?"

The Old Man offered a packet of Player's Navy Cut. The two men lit up, bonded for the moment in a cloud of smoke. What next, Ralph wondered? An apology might be apposite.

"Sir, may I say how deeply I regret my actions, and that I will do my utmost to mitigate any negative repercussions."

"It's a bit bloody late for that, as a matter of fact. Operation Aqua is about to kick off. It's been in the planning stage for months."

Ralph sat bolt upright. Planning stage? Kicking off?

He'd never expected Operation Aqua to take form, to actually happen. His report had provided enough evidence for Waters to be arrested without the entrapment. He'd imagined there'd be a knock on the door at 6am, Waters handcuffed in his pyjamas, escorted to an unmarked van. That was how it would happen in real life. The sting operation was just a bit of window dressing, a hypothetical he'd cooked up to show ... to show what? That he was cleverer than Waters?

"Sir ..." He choked on his words. His cheeks burned.

"And since you're about to ask, there are very good reasons why Waters can't be quietly arrested and charged under the Official Secrets Act. The last thing anyone wants is for documents from your file to be declassified and used in evidence. MI6 are adamant that he be caught red-handed with something criminal we can charge him with."

"But, Sir, why was I never informed?" Ralph spluttered.

The Old Man sighed. "Settle down, Stonehouse. It was need to know - normal procedure for this kind of thing. And in your case, very well-advised given this cock-up. With the file floating around Lord knows where, the whole operation is at risk. The PM's bloody incandescent."

This was humiliating beyond measure. "Sir, you will have my resignation letter on your desk within the hour."

The Old Man started clacking the metal balls again. Clack-clack. Clack-bloody-clack. He placed a finger on the desk toy, looked at Ralph for a full minute.

"You don't get off that easily, Stonehouse. You can still make yourself useful."

"How, Sir?"

"You have a house in Malta."

Ralph nodded.

"You're to travel there immediately." The Old Man passed a document across the desk. "You've had a nervous breakdown according to this, so try to behave accordingly on your way out. Nothing too theatrical. You're on indefinite sick leave, full pay. Await our instructions."

Ralph stood up, muttered thanks, tried to focus his gravelly eyes. He turned to leave, not sure whether to feel relief or despair.

"Before you go," the Old Man said.

"Yes, Sir?"

"About last night at your house. It never happened."

Chapter Five

On the evening Ralph arrived at the farmhouse in Gozo on 'sick leave', a thyme-scented breeze stirred the dust in the rustic lane. Church bells pealed on the dark horizon. A light went on and off three houses along. A dog barked.

He paid the taxi driver and went up the stone stairs to the terrace. The night air was still warm enough to stick his shirt to his back.

Susan stood at the stone balustrade smoking.

"What's going on, Ralph?" The international phone lines had been congested when he'd tried to call her from Heathrow, but he'd phoned her from Valletta airport three hours ago without giving any details about why he was suddenly in Malta.

"I've got something important to tell you."

Her hands flew to her mouth. "Oh God, it's not Emma, is it?"

"No, not Emma."

"What then? Why are you here?"

"Why don't we go downstairs?" He cocked his head at the neighbour's house.

"They're out. We can talk here. Please, Ralph. Tell me."

"You'd better sit down."

He pulled up a chair next to hers and leaned close, speaking in a hoarse whisper. It all came out: Boarding school, Waters, the file. It was against all his instincts and against all his undertakings to Her Majesty's Government, but this was different; he was at an impasse, and if he couldn't tell his wife about the blackmail that had tainted his life for half a decade, who could he tell? The bloody trick cyclists from Personnel? Bugger them.

She listened without comment for twenty minutes, head down, nodding once or twice, never meeting his eye. The light on the terrace was dim, and he couldn't read her expression.

When he'd finished, she sat up straight, and looked up at the night sky.

"I need a drink," she said and went down into the house.

He waited. The church bells pealed again. There was no sound from below. She came back after a quarter of an hour holding a bottle of wine and two glasses. She turned on the outside light, and the yellow bulb threw long smudges of shadow under her eyes.

"Let me get this right, Ralph. You had a fling with a boy at school and you're being blackmailed for it, and you lost a file. I'm struggling with this. There's something missing," Susan said, staring into the dark valley beyond the house as if the answer to the mystery lay deep in the prickly pear and gorse. She took a deep draught of wine and sat down. Her shoulders were stiff, and her free hand gripped the arm of the chair.

"I'm sorry, Susan."

"Damn your 'sorry'."

"Believe me, Susan, I'd be angry in your place."

She turned to face him.

"My place? Sorry in my place? I'm bloody furious, Ralph. Not the file, although I can't believe that you were so careless to get yourself blackmailed. And not the fling; don't all boarding schoolboys do mucky things like that? What I'm damned furious about is that you've kept it all this from me."

Ralph picked at his nails. She'd got it all upside-down. "Can't you see my problem? I'm bound to secrecy. I could go to prison. I had to keep it to myself."

"I, I, I. Why am I hearing nothing but 'I'? Where's 'Susan'? Where's 'Emma'? You fucking bastard. How could you? She flung the glass at the stone balustrade, where it struck the top and showered slivers into the street.

"How could you walk around for five years with that long face and those evasive excuses? How could you act towards me like a damned stick of wood? How could you turn your back to me every night? And poor Emma! That girl's tortured herself wondering why she's displeased you."

"I want to explain, Susan. About Waters."

"Shut up. I don't want to hear about Waters. I want to hear about our family."

"Hear me out, please."

Susan grasped her hair as if to yank it from her scalp. "So there's more? This'd better be convincing. Ha! I've got it. It's men you like, is it? That's what you're really trying to tell me, is it?" She ripped her blouse apart to expose her bra. "This not quite your thing these days? Off tits, are we?"

He jumped out the chair and leaned over her so that she flinched.

"I'm not a bloody homo - you know that. But it's the whole situation with queers. The service is peppered with them. But there's a rule - an unwritten rule, I suppose - that it's never mentioned. You give the right answer when they do your vetting interviews, and that's it. And that's what keeps the whole thing ticking over - a sort of consensus of silence, whether it's a stupid schoolboy crush years ago, or a fellow caught out in a public toilet, or a raving queer with half a dozen rent boys on the go. If Waters got wind that I could expose him as a spy, he'd have brought it all up and I'd be finished."

"That's pathetic, Ralph. You haven't grown up, any of you."

He stood away from her and unbuttoned his shirt. The finger marks on his arm were an ugly black, and there was a large maroon smudge on his side where the intruders had dragged him across something unyielding. He stood under the outside light.

"You talk about grown up? Here's what happened to me when some grown-ups broke into the house. Susan, I was beaten up in our own home the day before yesterday. By my own people."

She looked at the bruises and flinched. "My God, how could they?"

"You see," Ralph said, quietly now. "It's not pathetic when some swine decides to break the rules and talk about it. It's the cardinal sin. Worse than adultery, worse than drinking too much, worse even than being a drug addict. Worse than that bloody Lord Lucan with his gambling."

He sat down and lit two cigarettes, passed one to her. It was an old habit.

Insects were clicking in the night-fragrant brush beyond the lane. A pair of lovers strolled past under an ancient lamp on the wall, chatting in Maltese. There was the crunch of glass underfoot. Their giggles hung in the hot, dry air after they turned the corner.

"I need to tell you something, Susan."

"What else can there be?" She was dabbing tears from her eyes.

"I meant to take my own life if Waters spilled the beans."

She gasped in the darkness.

"You bastard. There's nothing more cruel you could tell me."

"I'm telling you for a reason."

"What reason could there be, Ralph? Some self-indulgent, self-pitying wallow? What kind of man are you? You're like a stranger. Shut up, no more."

"It's to do with Emma, and with you."

She was looking away from him, but he sensed that she was listening, waiting.

"I don't know if I could ever have done it - done myself in - but I kept it in my mind as a sort of contingency, just in case it all came out."

"But how cruel that would have been, Ralph. What a dreadful thing for Emma and me, the people who love you."

He was taken aback. Susan and Emma still loved him? He stood at an abyss staring into the depths of his folly.

Words stuck in his throat, then stumbled out: "But that's the point. I wanted to make you love me less, to protect you in case I had the guts to do it." But as soon as they had passed his lips, he understood the monstrous nature of what he had done: To withdraw from his wife and daughter to lessen their grief if he suicided; to blight their lives with his cowardice.

He got up and stood against the old balustrade. The familiar gritty stone was both a comfort, a token of the good years, and a rebuke to the years he had poisoned. After a little while, he realised that she had gone inside the house.

Mr Buttigieg's voice floated across the yard. His wife answered. It was their nightly ritual of locking-up, rattling of bolts, jangling of keys. The familiar sounds brought him to a place of comfort, a place in the past before this horror broke out. He considered following her to their bedroom, but he had no idea how he might find her and what he should do. No, spare room. Enough for one day. See what tomorrow brings.

***

Next morning, she was gone, and so was the old rusted Mini. She was surely headed for the airport. The Air Malta schedule showed a 1pm flight. He rang the local taxi and got to Mgarr just before the 10am ferry left for the main island. A package holiday party with a mountain of suitcases clogged up the coffee bar counter on the boat. Suitcases! Damn, he hadn't checked if Susan had taken luggage with her. Concentrate! He threw down a strong coffee just as the ferry reached the mainland, and his head began to clear.

In the queue for cabs at Cirkewwa, a voice called out, "Mr Stonehouse!" It was Mr Buttigieg, his neighbour, beckoning from his car with a plump hairy arm.

"Do you need a lift? I'm going to pick up my sister from the airport." Ralph hesitated. If he refused or just asked to be dropped in Valletta, he'd surely bump into his neighbour when he eventually reached the airport. If he accepted, he'd be up for an hour of polite probing in Mr Buttigieg's fruity English. There was no choice.

"Very generous of you. I'm actually going to the airport myself." He'd just have to get his story straight. Mr Buttigieg was a retired civil engineer with a relentlessly efficient memory for facts and their correct arrangement.

They exited the concrete port access road onto the rocky promontory.

"You are meeting somebody, I expect, Mr Stonehouse?"

"Actually, my wife is picking up a friend from the eleven o'clock flight, and after she'd gone off this morning, I noticed she'd forgotten her purse." He patted his trouser pocket.

Mr Buttigieg tutted at least twenty times. There'd be more tutting if he witnessed Ralph imploring Susan not to get on the London plane.

The neighbour nursed the car through the bends at a stately twenty miles an hour. After a while, he said, "Well, I suppose a person would not want to drive home without their purse."

"No, indeed," Ralph said, and turned away to watch the suburbs of Valletta.

"I expect Mrs Stonehouse's friend has visited Malta before?"

Ralph pretended to be fascinated with the view, and Mr Buttigieg completed the journey in silence, other than the occasional *tut* when another car infringed - even slightly - the Highway Code.

As Ralph opened the car door, Mr Buttigieg said, "I hope Mrs Stonehouse had the wherewithal to pay her ferry ticket."

"Wherewithal?"

"Her purse, Mr Stonehouse. She left it behind."

Nosey bugger. "Of course. She always keeps a pound note in her shoe. Bye for now."

Lost for words of advice, Mr Buttigieg nodded to Ralph, checked the handle of the passenger door, engaged first gear, released the handbrake and proceeded towards the car park.

She wasn't in the tiny airport - not the departure hall, nor the little café full of English holidaymakers in straw hats and ugly shorts. He searched the car park for the Mini, and hid behind a van when he saw Mr Buttigieg driving towards the exit. Back in the terminal, he asked at the Air Malta desk whether a Mrs Susan Stonehouse was booked on a flight today or tomorrow. The official called Head Office and spoke solemnly on the telephone for some minutes in Maltese before telling Ralph, "I am sorry, Sir. There is no record of the lady."

Ralph's anxiety faded, to be replaced by peevish self-righteousness; she had no right to walk out without explanation. In the taxi back to Cirkewwa, his mind churned at the bloody injustice of it all - Waters, his exile in Malta, and now Susan's unexplained disappearance. Gone shopping in St. Julians, he supposed, or out for lunch at Sliema.

He skulked in the aft deck to avoid Mr Buttigieg - the irritating fellow would be on this ferry or the next one at 5pm. But at Mgarr, there was no sign of him.

***

The Mini crunched into the driveway in the early evening. By now, Ralph had drunk most of a bottle of the filthy local wine. Waiting under an umbrella on the terrace, he had swung from bitter remorse to anger at himself, to regret and tenderness for his wife. As he listened to her opening the outer door and climbing the stairs, he felt a woozy tug of desire, imagining his hands on her shoulders and her breasts, his fingers exploring her.

Susan came back onto the terrace, stepped up to him and slapped his face hard.

His cheek burned, and his eyelid stung where a fingernail had caught it.

"What was that for?" he asked. She didn't answer, just glared at him.

"Where have you been all day, Susan?"

"Shut up, Ralph. You've forfeited your right to speak until I've had my say. You've stolen five years of our married life because of your timidity and your contorted principles. How do you think I enjoyed those endless days of dog walking and playing bridge with the neighbours, arranging flowers at the church with that simpering vicar and his stultifying women and their jumble sales? And my reward for being a model Berkshire housewife? Making dinner every evening for a misery guts who plonked himself down for the rest of the night with a history book and a sour face. For God's sake, Ralph, we had a life before you crawled into your shell. We did things, went out, talked, had friends around, went to bloody bed more than twice a year!"

She stopped, folded her arms.

"You haven't a clue, have you? I tried, you know, to keep you interested. Looked after myself, dieted, wore make-up, read the kinds of books you liked, asked you questions about your hero Roger the bloody second of Sicily." She was sobbing now. "You ignored me, ignored the wife you made vows to in church. Do you know how many times I thought I'd have an affair? Yes, you can snort with disbelief, but I can tell you that I was an inch away from a fling with Sandy McDonald at the golf club."

She laughed. "Yes, thirty-year old Sandy McDonald with his sports car and his tarty wife. He thought all his birthdays had come at once at the thought of a dirty weekend with a forty-five-year old ex-air hostess. It was to be a *ménage à trois*. Oh yes, he wanted the tarty wife to come too. That's what he wanted, but I told him one thing at a time. Just him and me, but I can't say that I wasn't a tiny bit excited. And do you know what stopped me? Do you know?" She stopped and he heard her breathing hard.

"No," Ralph muttered.

"What stopped me was that I hoped against all hope that you might come back to me and Emma." She turned away from him and leaned on the balustrade.

His lip tasted of blood. "I've told you everything. I've risked everything by telling you. I have come back to you, Susan." He stood behind her and slid his hands over her breasts and stomach.

"You're drunk. Leave me alone. I need to lie down."

***

He heard the sound of the shower at sunset. She came into the big sitting room wrapped in a towel, and sat on the edge of the coffee table. He waited, unsure of how things stood.

She said, "Ralph, I was a bitch walking out like that and then hitting you."

"And I was an oaf."

"Can we have a bit of a truce?"

"That'd be for the best."

He felt the tension in his body relax for the first time in days - or was it months or years?

There was a rap on the front door, and Susan darted into the bedroom to get dressed.

It was Mr Buttigieg, all five foot six of him, in khaki shorts and a freshly pressed white shirt with coarse hair overflowing above the top button. "Good evening, Mr Stonehouse. My wife and I will be honoured if you join us for dinner. We will partake of the Maltese speciality of rabbit stew with peas and garlic. And your dear wife's friend, who is newly arrived - she is welcome, of course."

Susan was suddenly at Ralph's side. "My friend?"

"Brenda," Ralph said, winking furiously at Susan.

"Brenda," Susan repeated.

"She's lying down, quite exhausted from the journey," Ralph said. "May she be excused if she isn't up to it?"

Mr Buttigieg agreed to this proposition, adding somewhat acidly that his sister, also newly arrived, was 'asleep on her feet but nevertheless battling on'. He consulted a large watch. "Shall we say eight o'clock?"

"Perfect."

***

In the early hours of the morning, he fetched a jug of iced water. The salty rabbit stew and rough wine had parched him. They sat up in bed with the shutters open to catch the breeze from the ink-blue where the sea and sky merged. A sliver of moonlight threw her shoulder and breast into contour and he pulled her towards him. They made love, spontaneously, tenderly, without discussion.

Afterwards, she said, "Where do you think the file is, Ralph?"

"Do you want the bad version or the atrocious version?"

"Bad first, I think," she said.

"OK. Somebody other than Waters could have got a sniff of the case I'd built against him; there are always leaks, and London's crawling with spooks and hangers-on. If the operation has actually kicked off as the Old Man said, the activity could attract attention; people have to be recruited, money changes hands, the word gets around, I suppose. Someone could have been watching me, hoping there was something in the house. The Iranians, the Israelis? Who knows? The file could be sitting in Tel Aviv or Baghdad or Teheran with some intelligence boss rubbing his hands at how he can use it to his advantage."

"You said it was someone young who stole it," Susan said.

"A student, perhaps. The universities are full of Marxists and Maoists and anarchists."

"So, sticking with the bad version, what happens next?"

"Anything," he said. He reached for the cigarettes, lit two and passed her one. "Anything at all."

"And the atrocious version?" Susan asked.

"Waters organised the theft, he has the file, and he knows we're on to him. He sabotages the whole operation and buggers off to Moscow, leaving me as the nincompoop who tipped him off by taking a file home."

"And are you banking on the bad version or the atrocious one?"

"I'm not sure. There are other possibilities."

"Worse than atrocious?"

"There's an egregiously atrocious one that's occurred to me."

"Tell me."

"Our own people could have stolen it, Susan."

"The Old Man?" She sat bolt upright.

"Yes, Sir Owen bloody Mountjoy, bless his cotton socks."

"Ralph, it couldn't be."

"Just a theory. Perhaps they wanted an insurance policy in case the operation went haywire. Blame it on Stonehouse, the poor devil who lost the file, had a nervous breakdown and was sent on leave to get better."

She pulled him close and kissed him. "And this is what you do for a living."

Did he hear the hint of a purr?

***

"What shall we tell Emma?" Susan asked the next morning.

What indeed?

He found his mind wandering freely here in Malta, beyond the sealed atmosphere of the Cabinet Office. His daughter flitted ghostlike through his memories and his present feelings: Her junior school days, flute recitals, homework on the dining table; the years when she became a young woman, when the child's face took on unexpected angularities and he saw himself in the shape of an eye and the similarity of a gesture. And then the years when his soul was stained with fear and hatred, when he infected his daughter with Waters' poison. He cringed at what he had done.

He would tell her enough of his story as he could, but not yet. He was still absorbing the enormity of what he had done by telling Susan about the contents of the file. Strangely, his guilt was tempered by a reckless levity in his spirit, as if he had chucked a brick into a greenhouse.

He adjusted his sunglasses against the glare from the sun-bleached stone wall of the farmhouse. The remains of their breakfast were curling in the heat: A crust of bread from the stone oven across the lane, a couple of uneaten grapes, a smear of *gbejna*, the salty cream cheese they sold in the tiny grocer's shop. A wisp of cloud obscured the sun for a few seconds and the electric buzz of a million cicadas subsided. The crack of a small calibre rifle sounded: The local men were shooting birds from the hide in the gully.

"I have to explain to her, at least some of it. I have to apologise somehow. God knows where I even start."

"You're sure she's in no danger, Ralph?"

He didn't answer.

"Ralph, tell me. Is she in any danger from this Waters character?"

"Emma, no, I'm certain of it."

"But?"

He lit a cigarette.

"Ralph, speak to me."

"They've told me she's got to be given the cover story; she's got to think that I've lost my marbles. That's the best way to keep her safe. You'll have to write her a letter, Susan. We have to keep her in London - in the dark - until this is over."

Chapter Six

After she came back from her act of insurrection in Berkshire, Emma pretended to have a bad case of flu, staying in her darkened room and only coming out when she heard Linda leave.

What the hell had she got herself into? She'd done some idiotic things, but this was on a different planet. The standard line in the Stonehouse family was that she was headstrong, impulsive, ungrateful, and that 'there'd be a fall one day'. But a fall from what? From a French live-in boyfriend, a conviction for a pinch of hash, and stuffing up her 'A' Levels? Well, how about stealing a top-secret file and falling into Holloway Prison for ten years? The despair came in waves: For the next few days, she smoked, chewed her nails, cried, slept, and smoked more. The file, stuffed under a pile of cushions, hid like a malignant familiar. Emma averted her eyes from the cushions, and even crossed the room to avoid the spot.

On the third day, she woke very early and crept into the kitchen to make coffee. The corrugated rooftops of the terraced houses stretched into the distance. She opened the kitchen window, lit a cigarette and exhaled into the silent air. A movement caught her view. It was the back of the opposite terraced house, where a girl of her own age smoked at an open window. The girl looked up, caught Emma's eye, and they both withdrew. What had the girl been thinking about? An exam? A boyfriend? Money troubles? There were hundreds like this girl and herself in these North London suburbs, studying, working, going to the same pubs, buying the same records. But Emma wasn't the same anymore. She was a criminal. Cold truth. Her future life would never be like her last week's life. The thing existed. It demanded to be read. She took the pot of coffee into the bedroom and dug the file out from under the cushions.

The cover said it was a briefing paper for Cabinet. Her dad's name was on the cover page. There was a lot of bureaucratic stuff at the beginning - reference numbers, code words, for these eyes only, for those eyes only. Not for Emma Stonehouse's eyes, that was for sure.

The file began with the analysis of the career of a senior civil servant working for something called 'Ealing'. What the hell was 'Ealing'? She'd been to a party at West Acton once and got off at North Ealing by mistake. Keep going anyway.

The Ealing person had a codename - Roughtrade - and his life was carefully unpicked to show that he was a Soviet agent; he'd been long embedded in Britain's intelligence service. Her dad wrote this? She sat back and tried to remember what she thought he did at work. Far-off pictures came back, from the time before things had soured: Daddy coming home in his raincoat and hat, Mum fetching him a sherry. What did you do at work, Daddy? Oh, not much really, this and that. What did you do at school, my darling?

She made a cup of tea and sank deeper into the sofa. The thing read like a spy novel: Controllers in Moscow, information passed through front organisations with links to Czechoslovakia, money handed over on park benches, microfilm in cigarette packets. The author - her dad, she had to remind herself - described how Roughtrade had been under suspicion of Soviet entanglement before, but that no conclusive evidence had been evinced. And then one day a Soviet agent codenamed 'Zookeeper' betrayed him.

'Evinced'. The word pulled her up, and she flipped back to the cover page with R. STONEHOUSE typed in capitals. Yes, 'evinced' would be her dad's sort of word. She felt a funny tremor of pride in what he'd written. From her shaky understanding of what she'd read, R. Stonehouse had *evinced* enough proof to put Roughtrade away for good.

With each page, forgotten strands of her dad's character emerged from between the lines of typing: His way of emphasising a crucial point, the ordering of the known facts, the evaluation of hazier kinds of evidence. Here was the father she'd loved before everything went wrong, the man who'd taught her to play chess, introduced her gently to Bach, guided her through her 'O' Levels, taught her how to write a bloody essay.

There was a long section dealing with Roughtrade himself, based on what Dad would have called 'multiple strands of evidence'. According to Zookeeper, Roughtrade had been groomed by a female lecturer at university, an older woman who seduced him in a hotel room in Maida Vale. Her codename was 'Housewife'. Emma blushed at Dad's coy summary of her 'sexual proclivities'. Roughtrade was smitten with Housewife, 'hooked like a drug addict', Zookeeper claimed.

Emma's tea had gone cold. She put the file aside. How did this Zookeeper guy know all this about

Roughtrade's sex life? Only one way - he must also have been her lover, or at least a confidant. She grinned to herself; she was getting the hang of this. Back to the file.

But who was Housewife? Dad wrote that she was sometimes on BBC radio talk programs, but that was all. Emma imagined her as sleek, dark, fortyish, well-groomed in a kind of eccentric way, foreign accent maybe. Whoever she was, she became a secret mentor through Roughtrade's university days, 'skilfully designing the template for his life', as Dad put it. When he got his degree and joined the Civil Service as a Middle East specialist, she introduced him to a Soviet handler, and the last piece of the pattern fell into place: A junior civil servant with a brilliant career ahead, secretly committed to the Soviet ideal.

Roughtrade travelled a lot in the Middle East. He provided a steady flow of top-secret material to the Russians on Britain's plans and policies in the Arab World. But how did he get into the Civil Service in the first place? Surely whoever did the checking would have worked out where his loyalties were. Dad had the answer (trust Dad!): Housewife had trained Roughtrade in the art of deception. Wow, she was something, this girl!

In the next section, things began to get weird. Emma sensed that Roughtrade was more than just a routine traitor, if such a thing existed; Dad's analysis was strangely personal, as if the man was an old friend - or perhaps foe. She read how Roughtrade had been bundled off to boarding school at five while his parents ran their thoroughbred stables in Ireland. He was clever and secretive; Dad said he 'developed a conflicted sense of where he belonged' but didn't say how he knew. Some junior school reports obliquely mentioned punishment for cruelty to a cat. And then the name Hepworth Castle jumped off the page - Dad's old school! Dad knew Roughtrade! There was a school report that mentioned 'a tendency to manipulate less self-assured boys', but nothing worse.

The final part of this section introduced a new codename, 'Cordelia'. How did they make up these codenames? Cordelia: King Lear, yes, his youngest daughter. But this Cordelia was an Iraqi Communist, for God's sake, and Roughtrade had fallen in love with her in Beirut. Emma's mind spun like a top: Did they have communists in Iraq? Where was Iraq anyway? It occurred to her how completely bloody ignorant she was. Stop. Concentrate.

So Cordelia's father was exiled to Moscow. Something about falling out with the Ba'ath Party, whoever they were. Then Roughtrade and Cordelia get married in Tunis in secret and someone called Abu Ammar turns up. Hang on, that's Yasser Arafat, isn't it?

Emma had a sudden urge to cry. She lay on the sofa cradling the file and wept a thousand tears - for her stupidity, for her loneliness, for her fear, for her lost father. When the tears dried, she foraged in the kitchen. Rice Crispies - that's all there was. There were some sugar cubes pinched from a café; she dropped two of them into the puddle of mush.

The last section of the document went on to analyse an operation carried out in 1973 by Joe Cahill, the leader of the Provisional IRA Belfast Brigade. Cahill had been arrested off the coast of Ireland on board the yacht *Claudia*, which was laden with five tonnes of weapons and explosives from Libya.

At this point, Emma felt her ears redden. What had Dad said when she made her idiot remark about Irish bombs? "You know nothing of these matters." She knew less than bloody nothing. Emma laughed bitterly at the memory of Stash and his revolutionary theory: A fraud and an amateur; it was obvious now.

In the final section, Ralph Stonehouse had proposed an elaborate plan - Operation Aqua - to replicate Joe Cahill's gun-running operation. Except that it was a sting designed to put Roughtrade away. The plan included a fake arms dealer, whose proclivities were even more bizarre than Housewife's.

Her dad wrote this. Her dad. She hugged her knees. No more tears. Anger, shame, God knows, she didn't really know.

Linda was up and clumping around. Emma hid the file.

"You're up early. Want a fried egg?"

"I don't feel very well."

"Suit yourself. Can you wash up if you're not going out?"

***

When Linda went downstairs and the front door banged, Emma went to the kitchen. She stood at the open window eating a packet of salt and vinegar crisps that Linda had hidden behind the washing-up liquid. Somebody was playing a Joni Mitchell record in the flat below. The girl in the opposite house was smoking at her window again, but didn't look across. What, Emma wondered, had the girl been doing for the last two hours? Nothing very momentous, she suspected - at least nothing like seeing your father change from an anally retentive bore to a character from a spy novel.

But it wasn't just Ralph Stonehouse who was transformed. Emma searched her mind to find the words to describe the change that she sensed in herself.

The word 'wisdom' floated across her mental landscape, but it didn't make much sense. She rolled a joint and drifted into a fuggy place where none of it mattered.

Over the next few days, Emma found a hundred tasks to distract her: A letter to Jules explaining things were over between them; obsessive cleaning in crannies neglected by tenants for decades; filing and re-filing her college notes; ironing garments that had never spent a day unwrinkled. But in quieter moments the sole question remained: What to do with the bloody thing? Sometimes, her inner self answered back: 'There's bound to be a copy. Just burn it'. Sometimes another version of herself said, 'Find a way to return it. You could be destroying his career'.

***

On the first Friday after she had stolen the pass and the file, Linda asked her if she was coming to Stash's caravan.

"I've got so much else to do. I'll leave it for a week or two."

"What's eating you, Emma? You look like someone with a guilty secret. Come on, spill the beans."

"Nothing's eating me."

"Fair enough. The kitchen's polished like a bloody mirror. It's turned me right off my food. You've catalogued all the books and magazines, and you've scraped all that shit from under the sink. Sure, nothing's eating you. By the way, if you've got time, can you count all the Rice Crispies to make sure there are none missing?"

"You can be a cow when you want to," Emma said.

"Does that mean you want to let me into the secret?"

Emma needed advice, but who could she trust? It wasn't exactly a 'by the way I've stolen a top-secret document' situation. God knew what Linda might do if she told her about the file; run off to Stash and boast about what a fantastic revolutionary her friend was? She was sure that Linda wanted more than Stash's intellectual favour. The silly fool squirmed in her tight little jeans whenever Stash opened his mouth.

A question occurred to her: What would Dad do in this situation? The novelty of the idea astonished her. She thought carefully. Yes, that was it: Ralph Stonehouse, the familiar stranger, would take a small risk to test the depth of the waters.

"Linda, you remember the insurrection business?"

Linda's eyes widened behind the lenses.

"What have you done, Emma?"

Emma took the pass from her jeans pocket and handed it to Linda. Her flat mate blew her cheeks out.

"Shit, Emma. Who's the guy? Where's it from?"

"I don't know who he is, but it's from MI5 or something like that."

"How did you get hold of it, for fuck's sake?"

"Best I don't tell you."

"We should tell Stash," Linda said.

"No, not Stash. Not yet. Give me time to think about it."

Linda turned the pass over in her hand. She brought the side with the serial number close to her eyes and stared at it for ten seconds.

She's memorising the number, the cow, Emma thought, and snatched it back.

***

After a week of wrangling with the idea, Emma made her mind up to call her father. She waited until 10pm when she knew he'd be home from the office, and went to the phone box outside the betting shop. She didn't want to use the phone in the hallway and have all the tenants know her business.

A harassed-looking woman was smoking and gabbling into the receiver while her small child made finger pictures on the steamed-up glass. Emma smiled at the child, but the woman pushed the door open a crack and said, "Just wait your sodding turn." The gabbling and gesticulating went on until Emma heard, "Well, you're not bloody getting her back," and the woman slammed the receiver onto the cradle.

There was no answer from Berkshire. Half an hour later, she tried again: No answer. By midnight, she'd tried five times. The street was silent and empty. A policeman came up to her and asked, "Anything the matter, Miss?" She shook her head. "Better run on home, then."

There was a heap of mail on the table in the downstairs entrance corridor. It ebbed and flowed each day as the tenants took their letters and tossed out the advertising rubbish. She hadn't checked it that morning. A blue airmail letter peeped out from between a copy of the local rag and a cut-price offer for window cleaning. She sat on the bottom stair and ripped it open, tearing the flimsy paper so that she had to hold the ragged edges together to read it.

Dear Emma,

Just a note to let you know that Daddy is with me in Malta. His doctor thinks he has had a little breakdown because of the pressure of his work, and suggested that a clean break here in Gozo would work wonders. There's absolutely nothing to worry about. In fact, he's on the patio right now with his feet up, enjoying a gin and tonic. He'll be on the mend very soon, I'm sure.

Daddy's not quite up to writing to you himself yet, but he made me promise to send you his love and kisses.
Will write soon with more news.

Lots of love,

Mummy

Emma gripped her calf to stop her heel drumming on the stair. She lit a cigarette to slow the loop of words running through her mind: Have I destroyed my father?

Chapter Seven

Zouzou closed the curtains to shut out the low evening sun. Another July day in London had baked the bricks of the terraced house like a Hovis loaf. The driest summer since 1727, they said.

"See, Pierre. It can't be true. They're actors." On the TV, two men in spacesuits lay in a cramped capsule full of cables and switches. The scene switched to a pulsating fireball. A crisp English voice was saying, "On maximum dynamic pressure". There was a string of beeps and a fainter American voice: "Stage four separatin' ... lookin' reeeal good."

Pierre had got home in time for the beginning of the Apollo-Soyuz launch: Russians and Americans joining up in space? But perhaps Zouzou's Egyptian instincts were right: Propaganda. Who believed what they said on the TV and in the papers? That was a lesson well learned in Egypt: Reading *Al-Ahram* entailed weighing up the written and the unwritten to arrive at some version of the facts.

But this was 1975, and anything could happen, even Russians and Americans in space rockets. Just look at the House of Commons: A female Opposition Leader. And what a woman, this Madame Margaret, with her magnetic stare and regal manner. If he were an older man, Pierre thought ... then pushed the idea aside. Imagine such a woman elevated to such a post in Egypt: Ha! Imagine for a thousand years!

"Zouzou, *habibti*, let's pretend for a moment that we are witnessing an extraordinary historical event." She made a huffing sound. He knew her ways; Zouzou had survived perfectly well by taking a fluid attitude to veracity. What was it she often said? 'Why tell the truth when a lie will suffice?'

Without taking her eyes from the screen, she said, "Pierre, *habibi*, there was a *gawab*. It's on the table." They used Arabic at home, but were discreet outside, speaking English and keeping their identities obscure.

A letter? A letter meant anxiety, trickiness, care to be taken. Other than the gas bill, Pierre never received letters at the flat. His translation business correspondence went to a post office box in Camden.

"It was addressed to you," she said.

"To me?"

She tutted, that peculiar Egyptian way of indicating 'yes'. They were training themselves not to do it; the English took it the wrong way.

"Addressed to Pierre Farag?"

Another *tut*.

"It'll wait," he said, knowing it couldn't. He sat with her and watched the men in puffy white suits operating switches, an outdoor shot of Americans in bright sunlight peering at the sky through sunglasses, and then men applauding in a room in Houston.

"This is it?" she asked.

She'd guessed, of course, although he hadn't told her what the future might hold. But they both knew their life in London was just a stop along the way there.

He turned to look at her. Her short blond crop - Miss Patchett's ugly hairdo - had given way to a sleek mane of black hair. The insipid make-up was gone, and she was a Cleopatra again.

"Yes, this is probably it," he said.

"Open it, Pierre."

He lit a cigarette. She put the Nefertiti ashtray on the coffee table. It had a little plunger that whisked the dog-end into the base of the device. Pierre had spotted it at a second-hand stall in Petticoat Lane. His Aunt Serpouhi in Cairo had an identical model. Often he'd watch the spinning disk, expecting to look up and find himself back at her boarding house in Huda Sha'rawi Street: The gentlemen lodgers eating dinner at the big dining table in the vestibule; a servant bustling in with a dish of *fattoush* salad, the call of the *muezzin* floating above the hooting of cars ...

A plain brown envelope, hand-addressed to Mr Pierre Farag, Flat 4b, 26 Allenby Road, NW1. No sender's address, but that was the English habit: To add one would be to impugn the reputation of The Royal Mail.

Pierre turned it in his hands several times.

"You have acquired x-ray eyes, *habibi?*"

He laughed grimly and slit the envelope with a little penknife he carried on his key ring.

The note within read: 'EALING BROADWAY STATION. JULY 19. 6AM.'

***

When the sun set at last, Pierre poured *karkady* for both of them and opened the curtains. He leaned on the windowsill taking in the cooling air with its faintly metallic ozone smell. The scent of London was a foreign map he'd had to explore from scratch. Or perhaps he'd had to unlearn his map of Cairo first: Frying chickpeas, sewage, donkey shit, mouldering cabbage, cumin – bold, arresting stinks. The nose was subtler here: Impending rain pricked the nostrils damply, pipe tobacco spoke of smoldering rosewood and warm leather. A bare-armed woman's smell when she passed you in the street on a hot afternoon. Charred Mothers Pride on the landing from a neighbour's toaster.

Zouzou turned off the TV and joined him at the window, sliding her arm around his waist.

"What will you do, Pierre?"

"I will go to Ealing. What else can I do?"

***

It was Pierre's second summer in London, and his mind had still not grown accustomed to the far northern arrangement of dusk at 9.30 pm and dawn at 5am. The bitter smell of damp hedges from an overnight shower penetrated the bedroom, but the silvery sun – always low in the sky – warned of another scorching day ahead.

There was a half-typed document curling from the Smith Corona portable with the Arabic keyboard; the fees from translations kept them in food and lodging, but they badly needed a new source of income; Zouzou's singing job barely covered her taxi fares.

Pierre had had a stroke of luck at the start of his career as a translator in London: An advertising agency wanted a translation for the one-word slogan of a famous cigarette brand - two minutes work for three hundred pounds! But that kind of luck only came once. Most of his work was depressing legal depositions or desperate letters of demand needed by the Arabs on the Edgware Road.

Zouzou had money in a bank in Beirut, but a civil war raged in Lebanon.

"I cannot risk travelling there, Pierre. A prison cell would be my hotel," she had said.

A distant cousin from a branch of Pierre's Armenian family in Bourj Hamoud had offered to help extract the funds, but there'd been no news in three months. The Armenian Dashnak party was sure to be pulled into the conflict sooner or later; perhaps cousin Hagop had already been slaughtered in the bloody cross-currents of the war.

Pierre dressed quietly, kissed the sleeping Zouzou, and trotted down the common stair to the ground floor.

Ealing Broadway Station was barely awake at ten to six when Pierre took the steps up to the street. He observed the descending trickle of glum faces: A shop girl doused in scent, an apprentice with acne, a gaunt Sikh, a beaked civil servant in a bowler. These, he thought, were the real faces of Empire, the toilers whose labours had kept half the globe in thrall to men in tropical khaki shorts.

He skulked behind a *Daily Express*, watching the station entrance. A three-wheeled milk float stopped at the kerb and blocked his view. The driver hopped out of the cab and pushed his peaked cap back on his head. He kicked the flanks of his little vessel and turned to Pierre: "Bleedin' battery's flat. Third time this month. Would you credit it? I'm goin' for a cuppa."

Pierre buried his face in the newspaper. He felt a light hand on his shoulder.

"Don't turn around, Sir."

Pierre folded the newspaper and waited.

"Good chap. Now, do you see that car parked by the Wimpy Bar?"

"The grey one?" Pierre asked.

"That's the one. The Rover. Off you go, then."

Pierre got into the back seat of the car. It pulled away from the kerb, drove around the block, and then pulled up back at the station to pick up a man wearing a fawn cardigan over a shirt and tie.

"Good chap. You'd be Mr Rogers, of course."

"In a manner of speaking," Pierre said.

"Smashing." Cardigan Man sat back in his seat and watched the passing streetscape.

"And, Sir, you are?"

"Oh, I'm just organizing transport and so on. By the way, this is for you."

Pierre looked inside the brown envelope and fingered the ten-pound notes. Four hundred? Five hundred? A fortune to an exile with next week's rent hanging in the balance.

"If it isn't too much trouble, would you mind signing the chit?"

After twenty minutes, the car pulled into the graveled drive of an ivy-covered house just beyond Staines. It was a substantial building with ornate brick arches at the front and a modern extension at the rear. Dense hedges stood along the boundaries. The bonnets of half a dozen cars peeped from a wooden garage at the far end of the drive. They got out and the man offered Pierre a cigarette. The driver stayed in his seat.

"There's somebody who's asked to see you," Cardigan Man said.

"Does the somebody have a name?" Pierre said.

"You know him as Colonel Dimashqi."

Pierre's viscera recoiled at the name. He dragged deep on the cigarette and stared up at the windows of the building.

"What is this place?"

"A private hospital."

Dimashqi. He should have killed the swine on that Christmas Eve eighteen months ago. He'd stood behind the traitor on the crowded platform at Ealing, poised to shove him in front of a through train. Dimashqi - the man who had traduced Pierre's father's reputation, had his oldest friend killed, and forced him into exile.

"What does he want of me?"

"To give you information – only to you, he says."

"Why now, and why me?"

"You'd better see for yourself."

The man spoke into a microphone on a pad beside the front door. They were ushered in by a male orderly, who led them through a corridor that seemed to be the spine of the modern extension. Four or five small wards and medical workstations were located along the corridor. No staff or patients were evident.

The orderly stopped them at the last door and knocked. An elderly man admitted them to a ward bisected by a curtain. Pierre could hear a slow, rhythmic humming and an intermittent hiss.

"I'm his doctor. We'll dispense with names. Just do what you have to do."

The doctor pulled the curtain aside.

Pierre gasped.

A green metal cylinder about two feet in diameter and six feet long sat bolted onto a metal frame. At one end, a long metal lever rocked back and forth. It was attached to an electric motor on the bottom of the frame and a black rubber skirt at the end of the green cylinder. A giant green pump. A human head protruded from the other end, resting on a pillow.

"He's awake, I think," the doctor said, and that was when Pierre saw the reflection of Dimashqi's face in a mirror fixed at an angle above the head.

"What is this … horror?" Pierre asked.

"You don't know?" the doctor said.

Pierre shook his head, unable to utter speech.

"We call it a negative pressure ventilator. Most people know it as an iron lung."

Yes, he saw it now: The rubber skirt pushed air into the green tomb and then sucked it out again. Pierre was suddenly aware of his own diaphragm flexing and relaxing, and the thread of air that separated life from death.

There was movement from the head. An elasticated picadil surrounded the neck to make an air seal. Pierre flicked his eyes to the angled mirror, which held Dimashqi's face in disembodied suspension.

The face was grey and deeply wrinkled, the scrappy hair flattened where the head met the pillow.

"My spectacles, please." The voice, in Arabic, was attenuated and hoarse.

Pierre picked up the tinted glasses from beside the head, and carefully settled them on the man's face. His fingers brushed Dimashqi's brow, and he wondered why he didn't flinch.

"There is a smear."

Pierre removed the glasses and wiped them with his own handkerchief, but this time, a slug of nausea hit him as he manoeuvred them onto Dimashqi's face again. He flung the soiled handkerchief to the floor and wiped his palms on his trousers to rid himself of the man's deposits.

The rocking of the lever and the hiss of air filled the room with melancholy.

"Please transact your business," the doctor said. Cardigan Man nodded.

"What do you want?" Pierre asked the frilled head in Arabic.

Dimashqi waited for the machine to begin emptying his lungs, then said, "Incline your ear".

A sliver of rank breath cut across Pierre's nostrils as the lungs emptied in unison with the lever. After another inhalation, Dimashqi said, "I seek your forgiveness".

"Only God can forgive you."

"I cannot ask God's forgiveness until you have forgiven me." The machine sucked air into his lungs again. "I have little time left."

Of course, Pierre thought; this is the Muslim way, everything done in the right order. He shuddered at Dimashqi's fate: Reduced to a gasping head with his useless body trapped in a tube, connected to life by a three-pin plug, calculating his chances of avoiding the fiery crater of *Jahannam* on the Day of Judgement. Who was he, Pierre Farag, to deny the man – however loathsome – his pathetic request?

There was still an oily smear and a fleck of dried skin on the man's glasses. Pierre gently removed them again, picked up the handkerchief and carefully polished the lens. All revulsion and hatred had dissolved in the tiny theatre of grotesque intimacy.

Dimashqi prepared to speak again as the lever rocked back. "I can offer a token of expiation."

"There is no need. You have my forgiveness."

"But still, we live in this material world. We are *bashar*, with debts to pay and accounts to be settled."

Bashar – human? The man had lived the life of a devil. What kind of token could stand in expiation?

"Do they understand Arabic?" Dimashqi asked.

"They may. I'll test them."

Pierre turned to the doctor and said in Arabic, "I'll have your mother's cunt for lunch and your sister's tits for dinner, you donkey". The doctor glared.

"Your pants are undone. I can see your *zubr*," he said to Cardigan Man, who frowned but made no move to check his fly.

The head chuckled and then coughed as the lever rocked to inhale. The motor whirred and the lever rocked back.

"Incline your ear close. They may understand more than we think."

Pierre bent again. He winced at the gush of foetid breath and whispered words. The lever rocked out and in, and Dimashqi spelt out a man's name: *siin, taa, alif, shiin*.

Pierre nodded, stood back and said to the doctor, "The business is done, thank you, Sir".

***

"What is wrong with him?" Pierre asked Cardigan Man outside. They dragged on their cigarettes in the morning sun. He desperately needed a coffee, but not the grey dishwater that Londoners drank.

"A tumour, I believe. Ondine's Curse, the doctors call it. He stops breathing when he falls to sleep."

"How long does he have?"

The man didn't reply to Pierre's question, but said, "Someone will debrief you. You'll be contacted. Don't leave London. I'm off, then. Delighted to meet you".

"Can you give me a lift?"

"A lift? Terribly sorry, but I'm headed for Bristol. But look, hop in and we'll drop you at the bus stop."

The Rover drove off. There was no shelter from the glaring sun at the bus stop. Pierre hailed a taxi. He fingered the envelope of bank notes in the back seat and wondered whose payroll he was on.

Pierre showed Zouzou the money when he got home. She whistled and rolled her eyes: "Another bargain?" They tried three or four hiding places and finally settled on a box of fish fingers in the ice compartment of the tiny fridge.

They spent the afternoon by the Serpentine watching the ducks and the toy sailboats. Office workers sprawled in deckchairs, the men with their shirts off and trousers rolled up, and the women in tank tops and skirts hitched up to the thigh. A tinkling of bells and gongs announced a Hare Krishna procession snaking through the plane trees down to the lake, a bobbing thronglet of faded orange, shaven white heads and beatific smiles. The repetitive chanting drifted up to the park bench, mixed up with the chatter of children and a low jet approaching Heathrow.

"I miss it as I'd miss my own blood, Pierre."

"Miss what, Zouzou my darling?"

"Cairo of course. What did you suppose?"

"I try not to suppose. It's better that way." Where did supposing get his mother's people, the Armenian side of his family? Supposing their middle-class lives in Ottoman Turkey would continue uninterrupted if they ignored the signs around them. And his father – his Coptic father, a fighter pilot - killed in '67 for supposing that the Egyptian Air Force was a match for the Israelis. Supposing didn't keep you alive. You had to live in the moment, act on the signs you saw.

"And America?" Zouzou asked.

They both knew the prospect of America was fading. He'd assumed that there would be a way to get papers. His great aunt Serpouhi had left Cairo for California a year ago, and there had been a rush of suggestions from distant cousins in Fresno and Glendale about how to get their Green Cards. But the suggestions fizzled out until there were just hints of more dire methods, such as driving in from Canada. But where to get a car or a Canadian driving licence? And then what? Mop floors for peanuts, always looking around for cops on the lookout for illegal immigrants? But these problems were no more than flea bites compared to Ealing's stranglehold on his freedom.

And he fretted about Zouzou. While he filled his days with translating mundane documents for tight-fisted clients, Zouzou went for long walks alone, often for hours. If he asked where she'd been, there would be a vague answer – but then Zouzou was vague about everything. Once, to his shame, he had followed her – a skill he'd perfected in his work in Cairo. She had spent a whole morning drifting up to Hampstead Heath, then to East Finchley. The last he'd seen of her was at Alexandra Palace on a park bench, feeding a squirrel.

They talked, mainly about the future, but again in the vaguest terms. Wouldn't it be marvelous if we could live without fear, she'd wonder? Often, she spoke of living in a house surrounded by trees. Once, she spoke of children: "I am thirty-five, *habibi* - the years are passing too quickly."

"Do you not get bored – just walking?" he asked one evening when she came home hot and tired.

"You know how it was for me in Cairo, Pierre. I detest this city, but somehow those aimless footsteps cleanse my soul a little every day."

He thought he understood. Her bargain had been fifteen years of celebrity for her services as plaything to the old men in Cairo and Beirut. Wouldn't he find soothing the shady elms and oaks of Hampstead Heath if he were in Zouzou's shoes? But still, the vision of America danced on a distant, imagined horizon for them both. Zouzou's soul, he knew, would be purified in the golden sunlight of California.

And always behind them was beloved Cairo, with its alleys and churches and mosques and cafes and glitzy night clubs: An old glove of a city that fit the hand like a second skin; a catalogue of memories to prick the senses so that the sight of a robed woman on the Edgware Road or the whiff of a broiled corn cob in Brixton would transport Pierre back to his great aunt's guest house on Huda Sha'rawi Street.

***

The next day there was another letter. Pierre left it on the breakfast table while Zouzou warmed a pan of *fuul*. She spooned a dollop of the earthy stewed beans into two bowls, arranged sliced eggs and shallots on top, and sprinkled the dish with olive oil and lemon juice.

They ate silently. An ice cream van drove past the house playing *Greensleeves. Ding-ding, ding-ding, ding-a-ling-ding-ding.*

"No parsley, *habibti*?"

"The Pakistani shop ran out."

When they had finished, he opened the envelope.

There was a single black and white photograph of Dimashqi's head protruding from the sarcophagus in its elasticated shroud, the mouth gaping in an arrested scream. Pierre passed it to Zouzou. What should he feel? Elation, pity? But there was nothing.

Had Dimashqi outlived their investment in him? Had he refused to give up some grubby secret? Had he been exposed as a double agent?

***

It took them two days to invite him. They were efficient, these British *mukhabarat*. Everything in the proper order, get the fundamentals right. Never mind that the country seemed to be marching in stately fashion towards its own decline: A million out of work, and prices going up every day; Londoners being blown up by Irish terrorists. A country adrift on its own nonchalance. Their English insouciance was stamped on their language – or perhaps their language fed their insouciance: Their stitches in time, their ha'pworths of tar, their watched pots. But the *mukhabarat* - they were another breed.

The letter ordered him to report to the Pensions Review Section at an undistinguished office building in Ealing. He remembered it well as Dimashqi's workplace, the building from which Pierre, with righteous murder in his heart, had stalked the turncoat.

A security guard took him to a foyer on the third floor, where he was given a visitor pass on a lanyard and admitted through a locked door to a very long corridor painted the colour of *baba ghanoush*. Here an expressionless young lady took over, and showed him into a room with two chairs and a table, where he sat for ten minutes alone.

The door opened, and his heart jumped when Margaret Thatcher entered. But of course it wasn't Margaret Thatcher, just an example of the magnificent genus, one of this formidable breed of gimlet-eyed, permanent-waved Englishwomen. He fought the urge to wilt under her unblinking stare, stumbled to his feet, offered a limp hand - which she ignored - and sat down again.

The lady arranged herself in the opposite chair, unsnapped a handbag the size of a kennel, and took out a fountain pen and notepad without once breaking eye gaze with Pierre.

"What did the man in the hospital tell you?" No preliminaries, 'what' pronounced 'hwot'.

"He asked my forgiveness."

"Forgiveness for hwot?"

"For betraying my father and for killing my oldest friend."

She made a minuscule mark on the notepad. The ink was purple.

"And there was something else," she said. It was a statement of fact, not a question.

There was no point in prevaricating. But how did they know? Had they guessed? Was there a microphone hidden in the iron lung? No, Dimashqi would have known. They were guessing.

"He told me about a missing item of great significance," Pierre ventured.

"Item?"

"He used an Arabic word to describe the item. The word was *shanta*," Pierre said.

"Signifying hwot, in your view?"

"I cannot say exactly. A handbag, a briefcase, a satchel, a portfolio, a smallish or larger piece of luggage."

The nickel-plated glare drilled deeper. "We have not asked you here to rehearse *Roget's Thesaurus*. Hwot is your best guess?"

"A briefcase."

"Containing hwot?"

"Documents, I suppose."

"We are not interested in supposing. Hwot were his actual words?"

"His words, translated of course, were 'something big enough to blow the testicles off the rotting corpse of the British government'."

She stared more intensely, blinked, unscrewed the lid of the fountain pen, made another note, looked at it, made a small amendment, and locked eyeballs again.

"Where is this briefcase now?"

"He said it is in the possession of a Moroccan gentleman somewhere in London."

"Name, please."

"Rashid Shukri."

Another note in purple ink, except this time, she wrote from right to left: An Arabic scholar?

"There must be hundreds of men with that name."

"Indeed," Pierre said.

"And you are about to tell us that there is something particular about this Rashid Shukri. Please do not waste our time." Her pronunciation of the Arabic name was perfect.

"He used the word *a'war*. It means one-eyed."

"We know hwot it means," the lady said. "Is there anything else?"

"Nothing else."

"Why did the man ask to speak only to you?"

"I presume he wished to confess to me," Pierre said.

"We require a better answer."

"I have none," said Pierre, "But I have a question for you."

The lady raised one eyebrow a sixteenth of an inch. "Ask your question."

"Was he tortured before he died?"

Her neck flushed below the line of make-up. She stood up and said, almost inaudibly, "We are not to be played with," and left the room, leaving the faintest aura of lavender and coal tar soap in the air.

Left alone in the room, Pierre slumped back. He was damp under his arms. After five minutes, Cardigan Man came in.

"All set, then, Sir. Your task is to find the Moroccan gentleman for us. Keep a record of expenses. Call us weekly on this number." He slid a piece of paper across the desk. Pierre nodded and the paper was withdrawn.

"Why did you have to kill him?" Pierre said.

"Haven't a clue what you're on about, Sir."

Pierre dived into the first pub he saw, swigged a double brandy, smoked two cigarettes, and ordered another brandy. He had no doubt whatsoever that the woman with the stare regarded the one-eyed Rashid Shukri as a complete fabrication. And she'd be quite right.

Chapter Eight

Pierre Farag had spent much of his thirty-eight years negotiating the frontiers between the numerous languages he spoke, for which he thanked his Armenian mother; it was in the blood of her people, ranged as they were for nearly two millennia across the lands of the Middle East and Asia Minor; and more recently flung starving and beaten from their heartland.

Between the huffing strokes of the iron lung, Dimashqi had spelt out an English name in Arabic letters: *siin taa alif shiin* - 'stash'. The man Pierre should find, he had gasped, was a *khunfus*. He lived in an *'arabah* in Will-izz-den.

So, Pierre deduced, the person he sought was a Mr Stash. And a *khunfus*? A 'beetle', of course - the Arabic slang for 'hippy', and Mr Stash the hippy lived in Willesden. But he lived in an *'arabah*? Pierre envisaged a wagon or a van of some kind. But it was something to go on. In his Cairo days, somebody from his network would have found Mr Stash in hours; but in alien London it would take longer.

How much did the people from Ealing know? He pondered this mystery as he made a glass of mint tea. Zouzou had gone out, and he sat at the window looking down at the street, already baking at ten in the morning.

Did they already know the location of the stolen briefcase and were they using Pierre in some obscure double bluff? Indeed, was there a briefcase at all? Worse still, was Dimashqi's performance in the iron lung just that - a performance? Was he, as it appeared, a defector who had turned on his new masters? Or was this an evil dish cooked up from British duplicity and Egyptian bald-faced guile? Oh, the tricks of *la perfide Albion*.

He had no doubt that he would be tailed as he searched for the man who nobody believed was Moroccan nor named Rashid Shukri, so he decided to see how easy they'd be to shake off. One morning, he strolled down Kentish Town Road towards the canal, stopping occasionally to light a cigarette or tie a perfectly well-knotted shoelace. It was hot and sunny. The pavement of the dead straight road left him entirely exposed. The tail became obvious quite quickly - an older man in a blue striped business shirt carrying a shopping bag. Pierre crossed the Regent's Canal bridge and ducked into the doorway of the mock-Tudor pub on the corner of the towpath. He lit another cigarette and scanned the street: The tail man was gone. He looked again. But how? Did the man have wings?

What would he have done in more familiar territory, he pondered? If he lost a tail so easily in the crowded streets around the Cairo Museum, what would his next step be? For a moment, his confidence evaporated. Playing cat and mouse in this city of unbroken pavements and locked doors rattled him. He conjured up the words of his old friend and mentor Major Ahmad Fawzi, who had taken his last breath just eighteen months before: "My boy, think like an Armenian. Sideways, upside-down. All the angles". Pierre's confidence stuttered back. Poor Fawzi, dead at the hands of Dimashqi's thugs.

He trotted down the steps to the towpath and walked quickly eastwards. Three men with fishing rods sat on canvas stools, ten yards apart: Together, but separate, this was the way with these English anglers. One of them reeled in a tiny grey fish. "First bugger this week," he said to nobody in particular. Pierre bent to inspect the catch, surreptitiously looking back down the towpath: Nobody. There was a bridge ahead and a stretch of empty towpath with no places of concealment. He walked more slowly now, scanning the next hundred yards. Then, a flash of colour: Blue. The man was standing on the bridge as bold as a brass coffee pot, looking directly at Pierre.

And so the chase played out for the rest of the day. Pierre tramped the streets, scuttled into Tube stations, hopped onto buses, hid in pub toilets. Not only was he followed with dogged efficiency, but they made sure that he knew. It was a game he'd played in Cairo once or twice to get his quarry off kilter so they'd make a mistake: Let the poor sap know they were being tailed until they did something desperate.

***

He arrived home fidgety and preoccupied.

"If you don't relax, I will sing off key tonight," Zouzou said.

"I don't know what you mean, *habibti*."

Zouzou rolled her eyes.

"We are two sides of one coin, Pierre, my heart."

When she called him *'albi* - 'my heart', Pierre knew to pay close attention. He couldn't hide his feelings from her if they buried him inside the Great Pyramid of Cheops.

"I was followed, the entire day."

"They watch our every move, Pierre."

Zouzou didn't sing off key at the Orient that night, but Pierre was distracted, studying the faces in the gloom and watching Cash-in-Hand John for any discreet nods or hand signals. On the Tube trip home, he sat staring at an advertisement for Polo Mints while he tried to use his peripheral vision to spot the tail among the oddballs and drunks in the carriage.

**

"Zouzou," Pierre said the next morning. "You love to walk, don't you?"

"I walk, certainly. But do I love to walk? I would go mad if I did not walk. Your question, *habibi*, makes no sense."

Of course it made no sense. Pierre was desperate to set the world right for Zouzou. She had, after all, placed her trust in him, left Egypt with him for an uncertain fate. She had given him her pure love after the years of her foul bargain with the senior military man in Cairo, trusted him to find a way to make new lives for them in California. His obligation to her was beyond measure, as was his desire to keep her from harm. But he was in a jam.

"Zouzou, there is something I want to ask you."

"I think I might know what you are going to ask of me," she said.

How could she know? He had hardly formulated the question himself. He opened his mouth.

"Hush, Pierre. Do you remember when you followed me to Finsbury Park and Alexandra Palace? I know that you did it out of love and concern. You were easy to spot, by the way."

Pierre swallowed Zouzou's remark like a fishbone. Easy to spot?

"Why bring this up?" he asked.

"It's not unconnected to the question you want to ask me," she said.

"I can't see the connection. But, Zouzou *habibti*, since you mention it, I followed you because I wanted to protect you from ..."

But the words faltered. Protect her? Protect Zouzou Paris, the woman who had spent her years as an actress being guarded by paid strong-arm men? Protect Zouzou, who had endured and survived being a single woman in a world of powerful men? The woman who, through all that time, had guarded her dignity and her virginity?

She looked directly into his eyes, and said, "What were you doing on Tuesday?"

He blurted out some words: "I had some business."

She held his gaze: "Business on the canal with a man in a striped shirt? The business of men?"

He blushed and looked down. What was she saying?

"I followed you. I saw what happened - the man in the striped shirt. You couldn't shake him off."

"Why did you follow me, Zouzou?"

"I suppose I wanted to look after you - to protect you, if you like."

Pierre was dimly aware of a kind of epiphany welling in his spirit. How could he have missed her on the canal? But then, yes! He had a faint memory of a dark shape. A smudge. A woman, robed and scarved. He had dismissed the figure as insignificant, the background in a painting. And as he raised his eyes to face her, a strange and beautiful idea struck him.

"Yes, now you see it, *'albi*, we are partners," she said. "Partners in everything. A woman and a man. We protect each other."

Pierre could find no words. A huge single sob welled up from nowhere and spilt over.

He allowed himself to be enveloped in her arms, and felt the tears on her face mingling with his own. Her hand snaked up his spine to his neck and she pulled him into a passionate kiss.

She released him and sat back. There were tracks of mascara down her cheeks. He watched her in wonder. She was truly lovely, truly strong, this raven-haired partner of his.

"Now, Mr Rogers," she said in English. "Tell me what we are looking for. I shall be the best streetwalker in London."

***

The plan was straightforward. Pierre would systematically search an area far from Willesden, making it appear that he was moving in on his quarry. He would attempt to evade his followers even in the knowledge that these crafty Londoners knew the territory better than he did. Zouzou would continue her random wandering, but she would haphazardly include Willesden along the way.

"Do you think they will catch on?" Zouzou asked.

"It depends on how good an actor you are."

"Then you can be sure that nobody will know what I'm doing."

Pierre wished he had his wife's confidence. He studied the *Mini A-Z* and chose Peckham as the bogus search area. Peckham: It sounded quaint and refined.

On the third evening, Pierre plodded home to Camden. Curse this charmless Peckham with its litter-strewn streets, dusty brick walls, and mean-faced shoppers with their fussy wheeled shopping baskets! His endurance was reaching its limits. How many housewives could he accost with, 'Excuse me, Madam, but I've forgotten the house number of Mr Shukri?' How many more times could he observe some innocent front door from the cover of a parked car or a side alley? How many times could he be told to 'sling yer bleedin' hook' by a suspicious pensioner? How many more of those execrable British 'cuppas' could he drink in cafés that stank of bacon and the sour HP Sauce they smothered on their food?

But tonight, Zouzou was sizzling with news.

"It was pure chance, *habibi*. I spotted what the English call a 'caravan' in a front garden."

"And what is this mysterious vehicle?"

"It's a little house on two wheels."

He clapped his hand to his brow. Of course! Pierre had seen the odd caravan attached to a car: An ingenious invention that allowed whole families to avoid the cost of a hotel. Was this the *'arabah* that Dimashqi spoke of? There was, after all, no exact word for this kind of 'caravan' in Arabic.

"Go on."

"Well, there were actually two caravans, side by side, each with curtains at the window. I walked past and then went around the block, and almost bumped into a *khunfusa* coming out of the garden where they were parked."

"A female hippy, you mean?"

"Yes, it was obvious that the poor woman needed a visit to the hairdresser," Zouzou said.

"And what else was there about her? Apart from needing a hairdo?"

"She wore very thick leather sandals and was dressed like an Indian peasant - long scarves and bits of coloured cloth. She had two small children with runny noses and horrible manners."

"Did you say anything to her?"

"Not a word, except of course 'sorry' because I bumped into her and made her drop her bag."

"Did anything fall out of the bag?"

"Just a packet of lentils."

Could this be the wife of the *khunfus*? But wait, would a *khunfus* have a wife? What about free love? Would the members of his commune not couple at random? Pierre had no real idea of the habits of hippy life.

But someone had to go back at night when the whole nest of beetles would be gathered together. Not Zouzou - he couldn't expose his wife to danger. He, Pierre, would have to throw off the men who followed him. But how?

"*Habibi*, I forgot to tell you. I'm doing the nine o'clock show tomorrow night. The regular band have an early *gig*, and they're taking my spot later."

Gig? Pierre shuffled the English lexicon in his head and couldn't come up with a match; another new word. But Zouzou was on to something: She had taken the nine o'clock 'gig' a couple of times before, and if - as he suspected - the Ealing people had been watching him for some time, they would assume that he was in the club until midnight: An ideal time to slip out for a clandestine visit to Willesden.

***

Zouzou stepped into the spotlight. She had adjusted her *décolletage* to demand total attention from the audience. Pierre nudged a couple of bank notes into the manager's palm. Cash-in Hand nodded towards the back entrance, and Pierre melted away.

The car was waiting by the purple *DUREX* sign. Pierre knew the driver only as Yahya, recommended by an acquaintance in one of the coffee shops on the Edgware Road where the Middle Easterners met to lament their various species of exile. A telephone call to a Yemeni had arranged it.

The street was busy - mostly excited suburban lads out for a razzle, Pierre thought. He latched onto the end of a group who were weaving towards Yahya's car, then broke away, slipped into the car and lay on the back seat, watching the street lights of Soho float by in the darkening sky.

"If I'm not back in half an hour, you can go," Pierre said to Yahya when they arrived in Willesden. The man nodded and parked fifty yards past the two caravans. Pierre patted his shirt pocket for his ID; it might give him a few seconds in a tricky spot. He ducked behind a brick pillar at the sound of thumping music. Two scruffy youths came towards him, shouting to each other over the sound of a big portable cassette player. Pierre withdrew into foliage that smelt of dog turds. The scruffy youths passed by, and the street was empty again.

The two caravans almost filled the tiny front garden amid a tangle of weeds and rubbish. The one on the right was dimly lit behind the windows. The caravan to the left was more brightly lit. The dimmer *'arabah* looked to be the best to start with.

Pierre put on a black woolen balaclava and sidled up to the caravan, pressing himself against the aluminium siding. He moved his head millimetre by millimetre until he had a view through the gap where the curtain almost met the window frame. The *khunfusa* lay in candlelight on a mess of cushions, suckling a dirty-looking toddler. An older child played with a cat. A flimsy-looking table bore a miscellany of pans and bowls and food packets, as well as a kerosene stove and kettle. So, was this Madame Stash, or one of the *Mesdames* Stash?

The quiet of the evening was broken by the metallic whine of an approaching train on the track behind the house. Pierre crept to the second caravan and braced himself to observe.

The vertical gap between the curtain and the window frame was narrower, so that Pierre had to sway from side to side to scan the whole interior. A Tilley Lamp hung from the ceiling, flooding the four walls with an intense white aura. Its gentle hiss was just audible, and there was a faint kerosene smell from the ill-fitting window. At the next sight, he almost jumped away: A ginger-haired caveman sat against the wall, trouserless, with his legs wide apart.

Oh, no!

He looked away, then looked again at the awful spectacle of a young woman's fist pumping the man's pale stalk in its bush of orange. The snub-nosed girl knelt awkwardly at the caveman's side, and seemed to be squinting. Mr Stash - for Pierre was convinced he had found his quarry - was frowning at the pages of a book as his devotee laboured at her task. The cover of the book bore a portrait of Lenin. Then the man put the book aside, indicated to the girl some adjustment to her stroke, and leaned back.

Pierre closed his eyes. There was a faint groan. Through slitted eyelids, he saw that the girl had put on thick-lensed glasses and was now on her feet. She opened the door of the caravan a crack, and Pierre heard

the *khunfus* say, "Linda, get my wife to make me a cup
of tea, and bring me a bit of that nice cake". The door
of the caravan was on the far side from Pierre's vantage
point; he could remain unseen and learn more.

Mr Stash put on his trousers and sat on a wooden
wine box, which seemed to be the only variety of
furniture in the *'arabah*. He bent over so that the view
from the window frame was obscured. Pierre's foot
found something hard - a brick. He raised himself and
leant to the left and the right, scanning the scene. Stash
was writing, apparently making a fair copy from a page
of scribble. He folded the sheet and slipped it into an
envelope.

The brick wobbled and Pierre stifled a curse as his
foot threatened to give way. But at the same instant, the
girl with the thick glasses shouldered the ill-fitting door
open with a metallic creak. Pierre saw her hand Stash his
tea and cake. Without looking up, the caveman gave her
the envelope and said, "Usual drill. Off you go".

A hundred yards along the road, the girl stopped to
take out a cigarette. She jumped when Pierre, unnoticed
behind her, flicked his Zippo alight with a clack.

"Who the fuck are you?" Her voice quavered.

He flashed the ID card - twenty pence worth of rub-
on lettering, the royal crest cut off an envelope and
gummed on with school glue.

"Excuse me, Miss. Special Branch. I've got some
questions for you."

"Oh, shit."

"Just routine enquiries, Miss." He had learned this
phrase from watching *Z-Cars*.

"Oi, why have you got that funny accent if you're
from Special Branch?"

No idiot, this one. Think fast.

"I am seconded from Interpol in ... Geneva. And I am armed." He patted his jacket pocket. The girl began trembling, her breath coming in panicked gasps. Pierre hesitated. After a year and a half in London, he was still unsure of how British people reacted under pressure. The girl's fear seemed excessive. The mention of a gun? Of course, their bobbies carried mere truncheons.

He steeled himself, and said, "The paper, please, and your full name and address. Then you can go."

The wretched girl handed him the envelope.

"Who were you going to give it to?"

"Nobody."

"Nobody? Do you always give envelopes to nobody?"

"I give them to a man in a shop," she said.

"What shop?"

"A second-hand shop in Holloway."

"Its name?" Pierre took out a small notebook.

"Lumley Antiques." Her voice wobbled.

"Your friend Mr Stash, does he deal in stolen goods?"

"What?" she said.

"Do people bring stolen things to him?"

The girl's eyes were leaking tears behind the milk-bottle glasses.

"Oh fuck," she said.

"Come on, Miss. Does he deal in stolen things?"

"He's getting a card. A card in a plastic holder. Like an identity card," she moaned.

"And who has this card?" Pierre asked.

"My friend Emma. The girl I live with. She's going to give it to him."

"No stolen bag, or briefcase. Nothing of that kind?"

The girl shook her head and said, "Just fucking let me go."

He bridled at the word. In Cairo, his friend Mark Bellamy had taught him the basics of English swearing, but he found its artlessness unappealing. These words were on the lips of every young person! But then what sort of young person was it who would involve herself in the distasteful scene in the *'arabah*?

"Just give me your full name and address, Miss, and you may go."

She hesitated. Pierre reached towards his jacket pocket for a cigarette, and she flinched. He heard footsteps and turned. It was Stash, forty yards away and meandering towards them on unsteady legs.

"Now, before he sees you," he said.

The girl blurted out her name and address, and ran off.

Stash was closer now.

"It's a fine evening for a stroll, Sir." Pierre said.

The *khunfus* seemed to lose focus, and walked past Pierre, humming an indistinct tune. What to do? Follow him? But the boom of music heralded the return of the two youths with the giant sound box. Pierre backed into a scrap of hedge that was shaded from the streetlamp by a parked van. The men passed Stash and the music faded as they walked on. But the *khunfus* had stopped to talk to a man on a bicycle, who had appeared from nowhere. The rider leaned the bike against a fence and drew Stash into a front yard. Pierre observed the shadowy motions of some exchange, and then Stash emerged. He stood under a streetlamp, checked the contents of a small plastic bag, and - apparently satisfied - began to wander homeward.

Now, where was Yahya the driver? On cue, the parked car made a U-turn and pulled up next to Pierre. Yahya gestured at his watch.

It was time to talk to Zouzou.

***

Pierre poured two glasses of Armenian cognac, which he'd bought in a shop that sold Soviet products and souvenirs near Russell Square.

"It's a code of some kind," Zouzou said. She was in a silk dressing gown, and Pierre ached to peel it off her voluptuous body.

Stash's paper lay on the kitchen table. On it were written lines of capital letters in groups of five.

"I've seen writing like this before. Yes, it was in *I Married A Spy*. I played the girlfriend of an assassin, and I discovered his secret messages under the floorboards. I remember someone on the set saying that the Arabs invented this way of writing in code."

Zouzou was right. He'd learned this at school. It was coming back to him. Of course. It was Abu Al-Kindi in Baghdad a thousand years ago.

"I have a library card."

Pierre looked at Zouzou. He was used to her unpredictable remarks, but knew by now that they usually presaged something important, later if not immediately. He raised an enquiring eyebrow.

"There might be books that tell you how to break the code. You were a wizard at mathematics at school," she said.

"But that could take days, Zouzou. I need to be doing other things - going to the addresses the young lady gave me."

"You call her a 'young lady'. From what you've told me, I'd call her a *sharmouta*!"

"Nevertheless, I don't have time for code-breaking."

She gave him a look that reminded him of his great aunt Serpouhi when he had forgotten her birthday.

"Oh yes, I see," he said. So, it was to be the Camden public library for him. They were, after all, a partnership.

And then the silk gown slipped away and he no longer cared.

Chapter Nine

Pierre heard the key in the downstairs door, and Zouzou's steps on the stair. He turned off the television and let her into the flat. It was close to midnight. She collapsed on the sofa.

"Pierre, *habibi*, I am exhausted and my head is cracking. I will tell you everything in the morning." There was to be no argument.

"Shall I bring you a drink?"

"I'd like some *karkady*, my heart." There was a new package of dried hibiscus flowers he'd bought on his last visit to the Edgware Road. He steeped the petals in hot water until the liquid went a light cherry colour.

"Rub my feet, please Pierre. Oh, yes, perfect - like that." She lit a cigarette and sipped the hot drink.

"What did you do while I was out?" she asked.

What did he do? Watch *Benny Hill*, *Dixon of Dock Green* and *Panorama* and worry his heart to a frazzle, that's what. It was foolish to let her go to interrogate Emma Stonehouse in Holloway. But what choice did he have?

"I worked on deciphering Mr Stash's document." He detested lying to her, but the truth was he'd given up on the cipher. He knew by now that it was a simple substitution cipher, with the ciphertext alphabet shifted forward by a five-letter word. But what was this slippery utterance? He suspected that it began with an 'O'. But what would Mr Stash have chosen? Not *onion*, not *opine*, not *oakum*, not *omega*, not *ocean*, not *olden*. There were hundreds of them, thousands if he was wrong about it beginning with 'O'. Just yesterday, he had discovered the word *oleic*, and rushed to set up the plaintext and ciphertext. The foolscap sheet lay at his elbow on the sofa:

abcdefghijklmnopqrstuvwxyz
oleicabdfghjkmnpqrstuvwxyz

But the first line yielded rubbish: OJJKN KPNQR BMKKH SSNUS MADSRMF. And why shouldn't it be rubbish? *Oleic* indeed. What would a Marxist like Stash know of a colourless, odourless fatty acid? Indeed, could he be sure that Stash, and not the recipient, had devised the ciphertext?

"Is it going well, this deciphering?" Zouzou gave him her penetrating look. It was hopeless to resist. He confessed: The problem, he explained, was that with little knowledge of the motifs of Stash's life, it was impossible to know what word or name may have popped into his head.

"Remind me. What do we know about him, Pierre?"

"Well, he is a communist of some kind, and an adulterer. He is duplicitous but he is also charismatic. Believe me, *habibti*, I have turned my brain inside out and back again."

Zouzou took another sip of *karkady* and turned towards him.

"Didn't you say that he bought some drugs in the street?"

A smudge of dawn arose in a corner of Pierre's mind, then a brighter outline emerged, and suddenly it was there picked out in lights of almost blinding intensity.

"Opium," he whispered.

***

"You first, Zouzou, if you aren't too tired," Pierre said the next morning. She had been complaining of exhaustion for the last week or so; perhaps the onset of autumn would revive her. He lifted the brass *kanaka* from the stove just as the coffee froth reached the rim. The folded foolscap sheets lay on the table, ready for him to reveal the message he had spent the early hours deciphering. But he must first hear Zouzou's account of her work last night.

"This Emma was terrified, the poor lamb," she began, "Even though I told her that I was enquiring about her television licence. Can you believe that the English have little vans that patrol the streets checking whether people have paid for the *ijaza* to watch the television?"

"Go on," Pierre said.

"Yes, terrified. And quite lost, it seemed. Once I was inside the flat, I told her I was looking for my friend Linda, as you and I agreed, but she was suspicious of course. 'What kind of friend? Linda never mentioned you to me,' she said. I said Linda had told me about Mr Stash, but that made her even more agitated. I asked if I could smoke and we both lit up, and that calmed her down a bit. Well, by now I was starting to get the idea of this whole undercover business. All I have to do, I thought, is gain a little bit of her confidence, and then prod a bit further."

"And what did you do next?" Pierre asked.

"You'd have been proud of me, *habibi*. I said, 'Emma, let me tell you the real reason I'm here'. She looked as confused as an ant and said, 'First it's the television licence, and then you're looking for Linda. What the 'f' is next?' The poor innocent, but I must say, the language of these young people is absolutely filthy."

Pierre was of course captivated by Zouzou's narrative style but wondered if he dared hurry her up a little. He tried a querying lilt of one eyebrow.

"Yes, of course, Pierre, I am coming to it. 'I am a little like you, Emma,' I said to her. 'I am a woman trying to survive in a world of rapacious and overweening male persons.'"

Overweening? Pierre had a faint recollection of the English word. Male persons? Did that include him?

Zouzou switched back to Arabic: "My husband, I told her, was a brute. I could tell - it's a woman's instinct, you see - that she had been ill-used by a man. So, there was a spark of interest from little Emma when I said that. You see, Pierre, I gained a little more of her trust."

"And what is your brute of a husband accused of?" Pierre asked.

"I couldn't think of anything fast enough, but I did say that I loved him nevertheless and that I wanted to help solve his problem. 'What problem?' poor Emma asked. She's pretty, but skinny like all these English girls: No meat on her, thin hair. But a well brought-up girl, I believe, despite her dirty language, which I expect she learned from some lower-class friends."

Pierre concentrated on Zouzou's words; there was gold in here somewhere.

"Well, *habibi,* her question set my mind spinning like a dung beetle on its back. And then it hit me. 'My hubby works for a certain government department,' I said,

'And I am not at liberty to tell you very much more. But he is searching for a particular lost item'. At this she burst into tears. I gingerly put a hand on her shoulder and the poor creature threw herself into my lap and wept for a full minute."

Pierre was agog. "Darling," he said, "You are a genius."

"Please, Pierre, save your praise until I have finished. And some coffee, please. Now, where was I? Oh, yes: 'What sort of lost item?' she asked when the crying had stopped. 'Documents,' I replied. She straightened up with her eyes as wide as a fish. Her face went dead white and I feared she might faint. Then I saw her relax a little; she had overcome the shock and was beginning to think sensibly. She asked me where I was from."

"What did you say?" Pierre asked.

"Syria."

"Why Syria?"

"Why tell the truth when an untruth will suffice?" Zouzou replied. "She asked me what language they spoke in Syria, and I said Arabic. Then she wanted to know if that was the same language they speak in Libya. Well, now I was getting excited. I knew she wanted to tell me something, so I just sat and looked at her with a solemn and sympathetic expression. I remembered I'd played a female judge in *Justice or Death* and I had to give the chief witness a look like that, until he broke down and confessed."

"And did Emma confess?" Pierre asked.

"Even better, my heart," Zouzou said. "But let me finish. Just as I thought she was about to reveal everything, there were footsteps bounding up the stairs and the door crashed open. I leapt up - the police, I thought - but it was another young woman, yowling like a hyena and her little face all red and puffy."

"Was she wearing glasses?"

"Yes, thick like the bottoms of medicine bottles. It was that girl, the one ..." and here Zouzou made a flicking gesture with her wrist, "the one you saw with the *khunfus*."

"Linda."

"Yes, Linda. And she kept howling, 'He's dead, he's dead,' over and over until I slapped her face."

"You slapped her?"

"Yes, it's the only thing for hysteria. She settled down, at any rate. By now, Emma had gone utterly white and was trembling. She asked Linda who was dead, and Linda said, 'Stash, strangled in his caravan,' which set her off howling again. Emma told me to wait, and took Linda to the bedroom. I could hear muttering, and then Emma came back. 'Linda said she's never seen you in her life,' she said. I replied, 'But she knows my friend from Special Branch. Go back and ask her'".

Pierre held his hand up. "Zouzou. Just stop for a moment, please. Is there any of that Armenian cognac left?"

"It is only breakfast time, my love. Perhaps an aspirin?"

"Yes, that will be fine, Zouzou. I just need to think for a moment." Pierre stared ahead, willing the fragments of the story to connect in the way of a child's well-loved jigsaw puzzle.

Zouzou handed him a glass of water with the aspirin still sizzling. He felt the tiny bubbles on his face, the astringent solution on his tongue, the undissolved grains bitter in his throat.

"By the way, was *opium* the key? Did you decipher the letter?" she asked.

Pierre gestured to the papers on the table. Zouzou read aloud:

"ALL MEMBERS COMMITTED TO ACTS OF INSURRECTION. ACCORDING TO MY INFORMANT BRITISH STUDENT EMMA STONEHOUSE HAS STOLEN IDENTITY PASS FOR SECRET ESTABLISHMENT IN WHITEHALL. HAVE NOT SIGHTED PASS BUT INFORMANT GIVES SERIAL NUMBER 7272445BX AND IDENTIFIES HOLDER AS POSSIBLY STONEHOUSE'S FATHER. IRISH MEMBERS BUCKLEY AND O'DONNELL UNLIKELY TO CARRY OUT MILITANT ACTION. SUGGEST THEY ARE ON FRINGE OF IRA SPLINTER GROUP BUT TOO NERVOUS TO COMMIT. NEW ZEALAND WOMAN ANN SCOTT UNKNOWN QUANTITY BUT HEAVY DRUG USE SUGGESTS FANTASIST. MY INFORMANT LINDA RISDEN UNLIKELY TO COMMIT MILITANT ACTION. MY LAST ENVELOPE SHORT TEN POUNDS. PLEASE MAKE UP SHORTFALL NEXT PAYMENT AND BE INFORMED THAT I REQUEST INCREASE OF FEE TO ONE HUNDRED AND FIFTY POUNDS PER MONTH CONSIDERING ADDITIONAL RISK."

"So the *khunfus* is a police informer," Zouzou said. "Squashed like a cockroach."

Pierre was suddenly deflated. It was just the same, wherever you went: Deception, subterfuge, dishonour.

London was no better or worse than Cairo. He closed his eyes and lay back on the sofa. He felt Zouzou settle on the cushion next to him. She stroked his hair and said, "Don't despair, *habibi*. You will overcome all obstacles. I have had complete faith in you since the day you came to me in Cairo. Do you remember?"

Of course he remembered. He'd been escorted to the apartment of Zouzou Paris by two of her hired meatheads, wondering whether he'd end up gutted in an alley. The 'national bitch' they called her - Egypt's most notorious actress, her celebrity liaisons smuttily hinted at by the glossy magazines, the screen idol lusted after by teenagers and old men alike, and held in secret admiration by women - pious or otherwise: Zouzou Paris, who, in her private chamber had wiped away her makeup and levered off an enormous wig of lustrous black hair to reveal his childhood sweetheart, Aziza Faris. Of course he remembered the gentle girl descended from a Circassian slave, who he'd loved since holiday nights around the brazier on the beach at Agami while their parents grilled brochettes and laughed over bottles of Stella beer.

"You've done a wonderful job, Zouzou."

She said nothing, pulling away from him.

"*Habibi*," she said. "I am trying so hard to help you. I know you are proud of my clever work, but playing tricks on little Emma rots my soul. It is not worthy of me, if you see what I mean. This is a man's work, to deceive and to hoodwink. Please tell me that it will not be much longer."

"Just a little more, Zouzou. We are reaching the end. Now, please finish your story."

She sat up very straight, smoothed the silk dressing gown, and breathed calmly for a few seconds.

"Well, as I said, we were interrupted by Linda, but when Emma came back in, she was holding a big envelope."

Pierre seized her wrists. "Where is it?"

"You're sitting on it."

He leapt up and snatched the cushion from the sofa. There it lay. Why hadn't she mentioned it earlier? But then, Zouzou worked to a logic of her own; it just wasn't the same as his, the man who had been 'turned in on himself' until she had breathed human warmth into his soul. He had no right to question her methods.

"She gave you this?"

"She was desperate to get rid of it, as if it had come from Satan himself," Zouzou said. "I feel the same; I don't want to see the horrible item again."

Pierre slid a sheaf of papers from the envelope. The words 'TOP SECRET, Cabinet Office, Joint Intelligence Office' danced across the foolscap sheets.

Further into the papers was a document in Arabic. He scanned the words *al-jaysh al-jumhuriyyi al-irlandi* and the handwritten signature *Mu'ammar Gaddafi, Leader of the Revolution*.

His stomach turned queasy. The Irish Republican Army? Muammar Gaddafi? If this wasn't worth two US passports, then nothing was.

The entire file took him an hour to read. As he finished each page, he detached it from the binder clip and passed it to Zouzou, who shook her head and muttered *maa shaa' allah* from time to time.

At last they sat back. Pierre carefully slid the sheets back into the file.

"This name - Roughtrade - who can it be?" Zouzou asked.

"I've no idea," Pierre said, too quickly. "It doesn't matter who he is. They evidently sprinkle these code names around like rice at a wedding. The file is a mere commodity, something to trade for our freedom."

Zouzou looked at him darkly and he glanced away. Roughtrade, he had deduced, was none other than Donald Waters.

There was an Instamatic camera in the sideboard drawer, still wrapped in its packaging. He'd bought it to take snapshots, but Zouzou said she had no wish for mementoes of London. He arranged the documents on the bed: The front page of the file, another page in English, and the one in Arabic. And next to them he placed the photograph of Dimashqi's death face. He overlapped the file documents so that only half of each page was visible, then leaned over the bed and snapped three times. Next, he drafted a message:

READY TO NEGOTIATE. LEAVE REPLY MIDDAY AUGUST FIVE IN SAINSBURYS BAG NEXT TO RUBBISH BIN BY LAKESIDE CAFE ALEXANDRA PALACE

He then enciphered the message on a single sheet of paper using the *opium* key:

AMOUY SKJMB KSDOS MPMOV MQMLG YHDUU OYOTB TRSAD RMDJR ODJRP TQYRP OBJMX SSKQT PPDRC PDJPY GOFMR DUMIO AMOGM XOJUQ OLOGO IMOOPI

The Yellow Pages yielded the address of Lumley Antiques, which Pierre wrote with his left hand on an envelope.

"Zouzou, do you have a pair of thin gloves?"

She looked for them while he rewound the film in the camera.

"Excellent. Now, please open the camera and put the film into this envelope." He folded the message, tucked it into the envelope, and sealed the sheet of paper and the film within. There were some stamps in the drawer. He took a guess and stuck on four of them.

"It's called a 'dead drop' in English," Zouzou said.

"What is?"

"The rubbish bin at Alexandra Palace. I learned about it when I was in *Spies Need Love Too*. The script writer and the director had a big argument about the right expression for it in Arabic, so we used the English word."

"Well, in that case it will be 'dead drop'."

Zouzou stretched out on the sofa and yawned.

"I'm starving, Pierre, my heart. It's not far from lunchtime. I'd love a Wimpy and chips."

He frowned at her. He'd seen the English seated before these Wimpies through the window of the 'Bars' where they were purchased: Flat anaemic buns containing a strip of grey meat, next to desiccated yellow potato chips.

"But you've never had a Wimpy."

"I have - once, when I was out walking. It was insipid. I loathed its meanness."

"But you want one now, Zouzou? Wouldn't you prefer a chicken Vindaloo and some Bombay Duck or perhaps a little kofta with tabbouleh? We could go to the Edgware Road."

"Pierre, indulge me. Only a Wimpy will do."

While she dressed, he unscrewed the fascia of the electric bar heater, carefully lowering it until it hung from the wiring. The file just fitted next to the fake passports in the names of Clive Rogers and Victoria Patchett. I'll have to find a new place when winter comes, he thought, screwing the component back in place. Winter? No, he couldn't tolerate another winter here. It must be California.

"Well, that's done, Zouzou. Let's go for lunch."

They sat opposite one another nibbling the Wimpies without enthusiasm. Zouzou put her bun down. The air smelt of cooking oil and the sickly men's scent Pierre had learned was called *Brut*. The ketchup bottle was an oversized plastic tomato with a trail of dried sauce blackening on the side.

"I'm sorry, Pierre. I cannot eat any more of this. I'd like to go home and rest."

They stopped at the Post Office. 'What English rat will it flush out?' Pierre asked himself as he poked the envelope in the slot of the red post box. He lingered for a few seconds to mould his fingers around the royal insignia of Victoria Regina that stood proud in British cast iron. And it was then that it occurred to him that Emma could be in great peril; the rat, whoever it was, knew that she had stolen an identity card that might belong to her father, and could be a step away from knowing about the file. Although he hadn't met Emma, Zouzou's pity for the frightened girl had stirred in him a sense of obligation. It was nobody's fault but her own that Emma was involved in this grubby business; but if the file was to be his and Zouzou's emancipation, then he owed the girl something. The thought of Emma sharing Dimashqi's fate was unspeakable.

When he and Zouzou walked home arm in arm, it seemed to him that Zouzou's fingers gripped his sleeve more tightly than usual. He said nothing but wondered if she too had Emma on her mind.

Chapter Ten

After the woman had left with the file, Emma sat smoking at the kitchen table, willing her mind to stop lurching from one awful scenario to another. She put her hands to her ears to block the stream of sobs pouring from the bedroom.

The noise stopped and Linda shuffled into the kitchen, her face shiny with snot and tears.

"What the fuck's going on, Emma? What are we going to do? And who was that foreign woman?"

"Stop snivelling and tell me what you saw. What happened to Stash?"

Linda took off her glasses and rubbed at the smears with a tea cloth.

"It was horrible, really horrible. I've never seen a dead person before." There was another gale of sobs. "His face and tongue, it was all fucking purple and there was some kind of flex around his neck."

"A flex?"

"Yeah, like on a toaster." Sobs again. "And the worse thing ..."

A huge inhalation of breath presaged another gush.

"The worse thing was ... he'd wet himself." Here, she broke down completely. "And I just ran off and left him there."

Emma grabbed her by the shoulders and shook hard. "Where was this? In the caravan?"

Linda nodded.

"What were you doing there? We only go there on Friday nights."

No response. So, it was confirmed now. Linda was sneaking around to Stash's for sex, while the Earth Mother cared for his runts in the caravan next door. Emma suddenly realised how Linda revolted her: Wiping her eye muck on the teacloth, the ostentatious *fucks* in every utterance; and now a sordid tryst with a conman. A dead conman.

A bolt of an idea struck her. "Linda, did you tell him about the identity pass?"

The sobbing girl sank sideways. She wailed, "Oh fucking shit, Emma, it was your fault. If you hadn't shown me that pass ..."

A fruit machine in Emma's brain began to whirr and click, faster and faster: Her father sick and ruined; the Syrian woman; the file; Stash strangled. And the spinning stopped abruptly as an idea clicked on like a switch: She was in mortal danger. From whom or what, she had no clue, but a dead acquaintance and a visit from the weird Syrian woman added up to something terrifyingly outside her experience. Christ, why couldn't she have left well alone? If Stash wanted them to play trainee terrorists, couldn't she just have sprayed 'IRA rules' on a wall? Wasn't it obvious he was a fraud, putting on that sacrament nonsense? Just a drugged-up pseud getting his kicks out of a bunch of idiots.

The Syrian woman loomed on the edge of her thoughts: An enigmatic and bizarre figure, at once threatening and empathetic, as if she were acting from a memorised script. And her appearance: Voluptuous almost to the point of plumpness, glossy jet hair, eyes bruised black with a pound of mascara. Her English, Emma recalled, had been jagged, as if the words were forced through a cheese grater.

When Linda went back to her room to work on her sobbing, Emma packed a rucksack. There were five twenty-pound notes in a hidden tobacco tin, as well as enough hash for a couple of joints. She hesitated over the little chunk of brown paste, and then crumbled it into the toilet; she was in enough shit already.

Her passport should be in one of the knee-length purple suede boots she never wore.

It should be.

It wasn't.

Yes, she'd found another place, she remembered. Under the edge of the rug in the bedroom. No, no, not there. Christ, where was it?

There were stumbling sounds on the stairs. Linda had reached the phone in the downstairs hallway.

"Yeah, course it's a fucking emergency ... yeah, police ... what? ... someone got killed ... Willesden ... no I'm in Holloway ... just fucking listen, will you?"

It was dark outside. Emma's bike had a rack big enough for the rucksack. She wobbled out of the alleyway and headed south. She'd have to come back for the passport. There was barely any traffic on Chelsea Bridge. Emma passed the spot where the kindly taxi driver had helped her, and felt a tug of regret in her heart for the lost years. The man had said he had a daughter her age. He probably told her silly jokes and she brought her boyfriend around and they watched TV, drinking beer and eating crisps. Wasn't that what happened in ordinary families? Not in hers. But why couldn't she have thought beyond her own bloody sorrows?

Couldn't she have made the slightest effort to imagine what was in her dad's mind?

The squat was in darkness when she parked the bike next to the corrugated iron flap. It was past midnight.

She pulled back the flap and hissed, "Kit". A strong smell of hashish and fry-up told her that somebody was awake, but nobody answered. She saw a spoon on a string and tapped it on the iron sheet. "Kit, it's me, Emma."

A girl's face appeared behind the flap. She was one of the northerners who had tripped with them at Southwark.

"Hi. I need to crash - just for tonight. Is Kit here?"

The girl led her by torchlight through the ruined ground floor of the large Victorian house, and up the stairs. A door opened into a big bedroom - the one she'd slept in after her bad trip - but now it was lit with candles, and Kit's friends were reclining in a circle on pillows and sleeping bags. A couple of joints were circulating in opposite directions; *Dark Side of the Moon* was playing on a cassette player, and Kit was frying sausages on a Primus stove.

Bodies shifted apart to make a space, people said, "Hi," or gave little waves. No questions asked. One of the joints arrived at Emma's place and she dragged deeply and swapped it for the joint coming the other way. Everybody laughed. The area of brain behind her forehead tingled like a sherbet fountain. She giggled. Kit handed her a sausage sandwich. She took a bite and passed it to the person next to her and everybody laughed again. The person with the sausage sandwich gave her a chocolate biscuit. The northern girl seated across the circle smiled and Emma smiled back, and then the giggling came uncontrollably and there was sausage on her chin and chocolate on her lips and an impossibly tranquil feeling of belonging with her beautiful stranger friends. But a new voice deep in her mind urged caution: *Keep your head, girl, stay detached. You're not like these people. You're not like anyone you know.*

***

At the beginning of August, Ralph received an electricity bill and a letter in an envelope bearing the words *Sptar San Luqa* - St. Luke's Hospital.

He'd been in Gozo more than a month now with nothing to do but 'get better' and worry about Emma. He was past fretting about his career, and had adopted a fatalistic attitude to the future. After all, once you'd lost top-secret documents, confessed to blackmail, and told your wife what you did for a living, things couldn't get worse. He took to muttering, 'Bugger 'em'. No word from the Old Man: Perhaps events had moved on at Whitehall, a new strategy was in place, Stonehouse was parked in Malta until things were sorted out and he was invited back. Perhaps.

Each morning, he and Susan walked up to the café in the village, where they drank coffee with condensed milk in the dense shade of the honey-coloured sandstone buildings on the south side of the square. The creamy facade of the Parish Church rose in gaudy triumph over the village, all colonnades and rosettes and carved saints: The most religious people in the world, the Maltese. They'd done a survey to prove it, Ralph had read in the *Times of Malta*. There was always a blessing going on; police horses, motorbikes, football teams, anything. If it moved, there would be a ceremony to bless it. Really quite commendable - a people who knew their roots, who had a compass to guide them. A good place to be buried, he sometimes thought.

When the sun rose above the square, they would drive the old Mini the two miles into Victoria and buy the few provisions they needed in the open-air market near the Citadel: Tiny capsicums and contorted tomatoes grown in rock-hard fields fertilised with rotted seaweed; dwarf potatoes of earthy sweetness; a shiny fresh fish - *lampuka* or *awrata*; a slab of bread that could break your teeth; a bottle or two of the local white wine that was so rough it had to be mixed with lemonade. In the afternoon, they escaped the sun and rested inside the thick walls of the farmhouse, sometimes making love under the ceiling fan. I'm changed forever, Ralph thought.

Despite his confession, there was a wariness in Susan's attitude to him. Although she gave herself to him, something - he couldn't say what - was held back. One day, late in the afternoon, he woke just as she stirred, and muttered, "You're a bastard, Ralph".

It was no holiday; there had been no word from Emma or from The Old Man. Each day, the texture of their reconciliation frayed a little until they repeated the same answerless questions: 'How much longer should we wait to hear from her?', 'What do you think Whitehall is playing at?'

Ralph folded the letters and stuffed them in his shorts pocket. They put on their sandals and hats, and strolled up the lane past the crumbling sandstone walls. Susan walked up the hill ahead of him, and he watched with lazy pleasure the summer dress clinging to her thighs. An old woman came out of the stone oven - a cave, really, where a red-faced family baked rough, yeasty bread that was sold out before it cooled. Here and there, a kitchen chair stood in the shade and a cat glared down from behind a clump of prickly pear.

Ralph bought a *Times of Malta* from the grocery shop on the square. Dom Mintoff, the new man, had been cosying up to Gaddafi again. What was he thinking of, the Prime Minister of Malta signing agreements with that Libyan clown? And the rallies! Mintoff brought the workers out in Valletta for political meetings that went on for four hours or more. Like bloody Cuba!

"Was there any post, darling?" Susan asked. Darling: He was still getting used to it, getting used to touching her with affection, to kissing her when they woke, even if there was economy in her embraces.

"Just this - from that rat-hole St. Luke's." He handed it to Susan. It was probably a circular for a charity do. The old hospital was falling apart. She took a sip of the thick coffee and dabbed her lips with a napkin.

"Dear Mr Stonehouse," she read, "Please make yourself available at the Psychiatric Outpatient Unit for assessment. Goodness, Ralph, they've made an appointment for next week. For an initial assessment, apparently".

"Does this mean I'm officially mad?" Ralph asked with an uneasy laugh.

"This is serious, Ralph. Maybe they're beefing up your cover story. You haven't exactly been behaving like a nutcase. Who knows who might be watching you?"

"A hidden camera in the stone oven? A man in a trench coat at Ramla beach?"

"Mr Buttigieg tapping out Morse Code messages to his Ukrainian handlers?" Susan said.

It wasn't a joking matter, but that was what the English did when they were in a spot, wasn't it? Make it a bit of a lark.

Ralph knew that nothing happened in little Gozo except for extravagant religious processions, brass band contests, tombola and football. But, he thought, the main island of Malta was a different story. The unravelling of a corner of the Empire was taking place before their eyes, as Mintoff snipped the links with Britain. The Republic of Malta had been proclaimed nine months ago, and the Maltese labour unions were rampant. There were Libyans strutting in and out of Luqa airport with fawning Maltese officials in tow. The gossip among the expatriates was that Mintoff would take their holiday properties away. They'd heard a rumour going around that an Australian celebrity had already been kicked out. Anything could happen here.

"So, should I go?" Ralph asked. He had no option, he was sure.

"Don't be silly, darling. Of course you should. Someone in London has gone to a lot of trouble to organise this. I'll come over with you on the ferry. I can drop you off and do some shopping in Valletta."

***

Emma's watch said 9am. The room in the squat smelt stale. Her eyes were sticky and she was dying for a drink of water. She padded across the empty sleeping bags to the doorway where she remembered there was a bathroom. Running water? Yes, but cold - there was no electricity connected. Nobody around: Of course, they all had jobs, these free spirits.

The euphoria of the night had evaporated. This was Emma, Emma in a bloody terrible jam, not fake-Trotskyist Emma, not stoned-out-of-her-brain Emma, not Daddy's troublesome daughter Emma. This was a real-life nightmare version of Emma who had demolished her father's career and caused Stash's death. She splashed water on her face. No towel. No soap. The water tasted slightly metallic. Her face looked ratty in the speckled mirror.

And then it came to her: The passport. It was taped to the back of the bed. If only she'd remembered in those few minutes when Linda was calling the police.

London to Dover? How far? A hundred miles? More, less? Two days on a bike, more since she'd lose a morning cycling back to Holloway for the passport. It was stupid, hopeless. Better to ditch the bike somewhere south of London and hitch. Was it the A2, or the A20? Christ knows. Grab a free Esso map from a garage, that's what she'd do.

She was sweating and breathless when she parked the bike a hundred yards from the house in Holloway. There were no police cars, nothing unusual - just the normal smattering of pedestrians, motorbike riders, and delivery vans. Linda wasn't at home. Emma had the passport untaped in a second and hurtled down the stairs. Don't run in the street; don't make yourself noticeable; walk steadily, don't look around.

The combination lock on the bike wouldn't open. She knelt on the ground, reset it to zero and tried again: Jules's birthday, 3004. The metal tongue withdrew from the barrel and the wheel was free. But someone was leaning over her, too close to her, somebody with black hair and a heavy perfume, almost animal in its intensity.

"Miss, you are in terrible jeopardy." It was the Syrian woman.

"Leave me alone. Get out of my way. I'll call the police."

The woman stooped down next to her, straining against her tight skirt. She looked like a prostitute, Emma thought. Prostitute's shoes. No, not a prostitute, not the right word. Something else.

"Do you want to protect your father, Miss?"

"What do you know of my father?"

"Please, come now to meet my colleague. Walk in front of me with the bicycle."

"Fuck off and leave me alone."

"That word is not worthy of you, Miss Emma. Please come."

"What if I don't?"

"You will come. Look, he is in that café across the street."

A man seated at a table in the window made a beckoning gesture. Emma parked the bike without locking it and followed the Syrian woman. The café was half-full of shoppers drinking tea and workman eating fried breakfasts. They sat down. The man shook her hand and said, "I am Pierre Farag. I want to help you. You can trust me. You have met my wife Zouzou, of course."

Emma looked from the man to the woman. She was beautiful in the way of a blemished orchid; he was olive-skinned, dapper, with keenly intelligent eyes. And there was some singular quality in his expression, something that convinced her that he could be trusted.

"You read the file, of course?" he said.

"Who are you? You're not police."

"We are Egyptians. We do not belong here. We need to speak to you about your father, in order to assist you both. You will understand from the contents of the file - even if you did not comprehend it all - that you are in dire need of help." Who was this Pierre Farag, talking like a dictionary and imploring her to listen? And how come the Syrian woman was suddenly Egyptian?

"Two cuppas, was it?" The man from behind the café counter put two cups on the table, slopping the tea in the saucers. Emma caught a glimpse of a dark shape - a truncheon - under the man's jacket, and then the workmen and two of the tea-drinking ladies had surrounded the table and somebody was intoning, "Mr Pierre Farag, I am arresting you for entering the United Kingdom with forged documents. Anything you say will be ..."

Zouzou shrieked and clapped her hands to her chest. She gasped and drooled, keeling sideways to the floor, where she writhed, her blouse buttons ripped apart and her skirt around her thighs.

The man with the truncheon was kneeling over her in a second. "Stand clear! Heart attack! Give the lady some air," he shouted. Zouzou moaned and dribbled while other police knelt to help. The husband Pierre sat impassive among the pandemonium, but momentarily caught Emma's eye. He winked. She ran outside, leapt onto the bicycle and plunged into the traffic. After half a mile she slewed into a side street, and looked up and down to make sure nobody was around. Her father's pass was still in her Levi jacket pocket. She wrapped the lanyard around the pass, and poked it through the iron grid of a drain in the gutter.

***

In a film, Emma thought, there would be a plain-clothes man who steps forward just as Customs and Immigration has stamped your passport. 'Not so fast, Miss,' he would say, showing you a document headed 'Interpol'.

But not at Dover. Emma was just another student hopping across the channel for a hitching holiday. The stamp thumped down on her passport with barely a glance from the uniformed official, and the same happened at Calais except the official hat was different.

She took a train to Gare du Nord, and found a cheap hotel room. Next morning, the Metro took her to Porte D'Italie, where she remembered from a previous hitching trip that there was a motorway ramp just south of the *Périphérique*. The plan was simple: Hitch through France and Italy, hop over to Sicily at Messina, down to Catania to pick up the Malta ferry.

A woman of her mother's age picked her up at the ramp, and they sped through Orléans and along the dead straight two-lane road that pierced the forests to the south. Emma chatted to the woman - her name was Solange - in 'A' Level French. She was always surprised how it just clicked in: All those hours chanting irregular verbs in first form paid back.

They stopped for lunch at an ordinary-looking café at Vierzon, where Solange conferred with the waiter in detail about the menu. She seemed - Emma thought - not unlike her mother: Fastidious, thoughtful, conservative. Watching the French woman eat her tiny lunch, it occurred to Emma that her mother's air hostess figure must be the consequence of strict dieting, not that she'd ever taken any notice of the size of her meals. But for whose sake did Susan Stonehouse diet? For sour Ralph Stonehouse? Was it possible that there was intimacy between them? What on earth went on in the privacy of their marriage? She recalled the 'sexual proclivities' Dad had described in the file. Did Mum and Dad do those things? When she giggled out loud, Solange smiled at her quizzically.

She asked Solange if she were married, hoping her phraseology was right; did you ask this kind of thing of an older woman in France? The woman smiled and replied in rapid French, which Emma didn't understand, except for the first time Solange used *tu* and not *vous*. Emma smiled back and wondered if she'd made a gaffe.

The French woman called for *l'addition* and made a little shooing gesture when Emma took out her purse. Emma turned over the edge of her napkin to conceal a spot of sauce on the tablecloth. Just like Susan Stonehouse.

They spoke little during the final half-hour of the journey, while Emma absorbed the moving panorama of French cars with their snub noses and boxy angles. One of her lecturers had a Citroën 2cv -the height of chic in London right now - and smoked *Gitanes* cigarettes during tutorials.

Once, she dozed off and awoke with a cry when she saw that they were speeding along the wrong side of the carriageway.

The woman dropped her at Limoges, where she spent the night in a youth hostel. A Kombi stopped for her on the entrance to the A20 - a couple of New Zealand boys with identical waist-length hair and tie-died T-shirts, heading to Turkey. The Kombi throbbed with Lou Reed and Dr John. They stopped in a lay-by near Grenoble for the night. The boys opened cans of baked beans and luncheon meat, which they ate cold with bottles of beer. The cold beans were hideous, but the New Zealanders slurped them down without blinking. Emma had never met Kiwi travellers before; certainly, they spoke English but there was a wildness about them, as if they belonged on the far lip of the world. They set up a tent and offered Emma the bed inside the van. She lay awake for a long time in a sleeping bag, which had a sweet, unwashed smell. Sounds of lovemaking came from the tent, cries of incomprehensible endearment in dense accents. Funny, she'd been to parties where couples were screwing behind sofas, but it was weird to be so near to men having sex. Thoughts of Jules intruded as she drifted in and out of sleep; his hands on her, his lips. A noise woke her in the early hours - an animal in the bushes nearby? The Kiwis having a cigarette? For a long time, she lay watching the trees swaying outside the Kombi's back door. When she finally fell back to sleep, her last thoughts were of the Egyptian man in the café winking at her while his wife thrashed about on the floor.

She parted company with the New Zealanders at Milan, and arrived at Catania two days later. The ferry to Malta left the next day, so she booked into a hotel for the night. At a post office opposite the hotel, she used her ragged Italian to send a telegram to the farmhouse in Gozo. The restaurant had horse on the menu. Why not? She'd dropped acid, stolen a top-secret document, absconded from England. Eating horse was nothing.

Chapter Eleven

Pierre, a man formerly 'turned in on himself' knew how to suppress his feelings, but the officers facing him were world champions. These English: Their emotional range started at 'faintly displeased' and ended at 'slightly gratified'. The officer with a face like rice pudding was marginally more animated than the ginger one, who recited Pierre's movements for the last week, stopping after each event to raise an enquiring eyebrow. When Pierre nodded his agreement, the pudding face blew out his cheeks and made a note on a pad.

He was astounded by how much they knew - all the way back to the tail by the canal in Camden. He was deflated by the realisation that his Cairo skills were worthless in London. Where was his *shabkah* when he needed it? The Cairo doormen, the ex-crooks who owed him favours, the officials glad to earn a bit of *baqsheesh* for massaging the rules? Pierre had no network here in London. They'd run him around like a three-legged cat. There was no point in denying any of it - Zouzou's discovery of the caravan, Pierre's efforts at decrypting the message, the interrogation of Linda and Emma.

"My wife, where is she?"

"That would be your common-law wife?" Ginger said. Disgusting oaf! Pierre suppressed his indignation at the insult to the woman he loved more than anything under the sun. Their blessing by a priest in the drafty Gothic church in the French countryside may not have been an official marriage. But common-law? There was nothing 'common' about his courageous partner Zouzou.

"She's being seen by a doctor," the other one said. Her heart attack charade had been momentarily convincing. But knowing the English, they couldn't be too careful. 'More than my job's worth to lock the lady up till she'd seen the medic,' someone would have said. Wearing your Jobsworth hat, they called it.

When they'd arrived at an anonymous-looking building somewhere in Central London, Pierre and Zouzou had been separated. Lord knew what story she was telling them. Not that it mattered any more. They had nothing to bargain with.

Or perhaps they did. The interrogators had made no mention of Dimashqi. Where did the dead Egyptian fit into the puzzle? And was it possible that they knew nothing of the grisly business with the iron lung? Or was their silence just another crafty ruse?

While he pondered this, Ginger produced a document and slid it across the desk.

"Please sign ... here." He jabbed a pink finger at the papers. "And initial here and here and here." Pierre scanned the sheets. It was a record of the interrogation expressed as a statement by Mr Pierre Farag. All prepared in advance.

"What if I refuse to sign?"

"We'll sign for you." Ginger demonstrated with a biro on a cigarette packet.

Pierre shrugged and scribbled where the finger pointed.

"One more thing. Where's the file?" Ginger asked.

What was the point in holding back?

"Inside the electric heater, with our false passports."

Ginger frowned at his colleague. They bent over a typed page, Ginger running his finger over the lines.

"An electric heater, you say?"

Pierre nodded

"Nothing about an electric heater here."

The two men stood up and left the room.

Alone, Pierre sat dejected and defeated. There was only one prospect for him and Zouzou: Deportation to Egypt, arrest by the *mukhabarat* at the airport, Zouzou carted off to a stinking female prison, he to a cell full of murderers at Tora Farms Jail. And then months waiting for some kind of hearing for an unknown offence, postponed again and again until they were forgotten for the lack of influential friends. But Zouzou, the fallen star - surely she would be spared - plucked out of detention by a rich old fellow who'd offer her a bargain she couldn't refuse. But would such bondage be more palatable than prison?

The door opened and a man well past his middle age entered and sat opposite Pierre.

"I'd like to speak to my wife immediately."

"Your wife," he said, "has given us a statement that would best be described as a load of codswallop".

"I expected nothing less of her, Sir."

The man sighed. He had the air of a person worn down, a man who was beyond the possibility of being animated. "Extraordinary woman, your wife. The amateur dramatics had my men fooled."

"My wife is no amateur, Sir. When can I see her?"

"Patience. First we have an offer to make to you."

An offer. An offer he couldn't refuse, like all of them when you were in a corner. How he yearned to be in California, the imagined paradise where they would lead lives unencumbered by their histories, free of the dealmakers with their tawdry bargains.

"Tell me about your offer."

"Have you ever been to Libya?" the man asked.

"I saw the border when I was on national service," Pierre said. He had a sick feeling that he knew the direction of the interview.

"Have you had any involvement with senior people from Libya? Army people, government, oil industry?"

Pierre thought carefully. He had met the odd Libyan over the years. Clumsy fellows, not the type you would dine with. Rolling in cash. But what could you expect? The Great Leader, or whatever he called himself, was a pompous primitive bobbing on an ocean of oil. They said he lived in a tent protected by female African guards with whom he engaged in unspeakable acts.

"No, nobody crosses my mind."

"So," the man said, "if you found yourself in Tripoli, there's no chance that somebody would recognise you?"

Pierre tried to move his lips, but somehow the connection between thought and speech was severed. Libya? Who would voluntarily travel to that sandblasted hell?

He managed to croak, "I am unknown in Tripoli."

"Very good. Next question: Have you any experience with boats?"

"Boats?"

"Coastal shipping. Have you been involved with cargo ships, in the Mediterranean for example?"

Ships? The only time he had been on a ship was when he and Zouzou fled Alexandria on the *Syria* in 1973.

They had watched Soviet missiles being offloaded on the quay as the decrepit tub chugged out of the harbour, and although he seldom prayed, he had knelt in thanks when they reached Piraeus. He shook his head.

"Not to worry. Never too late to learn, eh?" the man said.

"Could we please get to the point?"

"I am getting to the point." The man stopped to gaze out of the window. Was this part of their training? Leave the victim to stew in ignorance?

Whatever had fascinated him outside evidently passed from view, and his eyes slowly turned back to Pierre. "Yes, we want you to impersonate somebody. An arms dealer. In Libya. Do the job properly, and you and the missus get new papers. You can go anywhere as long as it's not Great Britain."

"May I smoke?"

He nodded. Pierre lit up. His life was as transient as the smoke that curled from the tip of the cigarette. A gust of wind and it was gone. But impersonate an arms dealer in Libya? Disguise was part of his professional repertoire, but he'd never get away with this.

"I won't do it."

"I think you will. Given your wife's condition, surely you must think of the future."

"My wife is perfectly well."

"So the doctor has told me."

"Then what is this 'condition' you speak of?" Pierre half-rose from his seat. What double-speak was this? Zouzou was perfectly well, but with a 'condition'?

There was a long silence as the man stared at Pierre in a puzzled manner. Pierre stared back. Condition? Think of the future? Had the doctor found symptoms of some congenital disorder that might manifest itself in years to come? Zouzou ill? How could he bear it?

"She's expecting, man. You surely knew?"

Pierre's jaw went slack. Expecting? Expecting what? A message? A gift?

"Twelve weeks bloody pregnant," the man said, exasperated now.

Pierre nodded dumbly at this bolt of lightning. Fool! The idiocy of a man 'turned in on himself'! It was clear now: Her fatigue, the nonsense at the Wimpy Bar, the recent softness in her embraces. Confusion gave way to desperation. "I must see her."

"Ah, well, that's where there'll be a bit of difficulty."

"I demand to see my wife," Pierre shouted, now springing fully to his feet.

The man stared up at him. "You're not in a position to demand the right to pass wind, let alone see the missus. Now, be a good chap and sit down."

He squeezed back hot tears. By God, could Albion's dogs be more perfidious than the specimen sitting before him? Could they be baser than this nondescript English savage with his custardy cheeks and a heart blacker than Satan's?

"You see," the savage said, "Your wife is now part of my offer. Get the job done, and you get her back. And passports. And papers for America. Happy families". He sat back and made a popping sound with his lips, a full stop to end the conversation.

***

'RAF Brize Norton', it said on the road sign. Pierre was thus delivered into the next stage of the life designed for him by the mandarins of Whitehall. Mandarins! Such an appropriate word for those inscrutables.

The plane left late in the evening. He was sat towards the front end of a jet airliner apparently owned by the RAF, next to the broad-shouldered man in uniform who had escorted him by car from London. The badge on the man's sleeve said 'MP'. The back half of the plane was filled with mothers and chattering children.

"Who are they?" Pierre asked the military policeman.

"Wives'n kids," he said. Yes, Pierre remembered: The British Army shipped their soldiers' families around the world. A group of them had been evacuated from the Canal Zone in '51.

"Where are we going?"

"I am not at liberty to say." But Pierre knew.

The children and their mothers soon nodded off. The military policeman looked around and, satisfied that nobody was watching, took a paperback from his pocket. Pierre peeped at the cover before he shielded it with his hands: *Showgirls in Trouble.*

Sleep. Perhaps sleep would quell the rage. But it was hopeless. If he could not sleep, then he must control what he could control - his seething thoughts. He slowed his mind to a crawl and carefully moved things into compartments: Pregnant Zouzou here, Libya there, Donald Waters in another box, California over there. He reserved a special box for the events of the coming days.

He had no choice but to comply with the mandarins. The details of Operation Aqua were etched in his mind: The voyage to Libya, the deal between Gaddafi's people and the Irishmen, and the sting that would put Donald Waters in jail.

The plane full of jolly wives'n kids was, without doubt, heading for Malta, where Operation Aqua was to begin two days from now, and where Pierre was to play the part of the arms dealer Cornelius Lamine.

***

The honey-coloured city of Valletta took shape from the dun land mass of Malta. The ferry blew a jolly hoot. Emma leaned on a rail and watched the church domes and spires sharpen into focus.

Mum would be there to meet her, she was certain. Perhaps Dad would be well enough to come over from Gozo. She wondered if the Mini was still working. Her parents always bickered over it; Dad said it had another fifty thousand miles in it, but Mum said it was a deathtrap. On the way home, they'd chug up the hill to the village and then down the ridge to the street leading to the farmhouse. She imagined making tea in the flag-stoned kitchen; there'd be a hot loaf from the stone oven, and later a couple of bottles of white wine with lemon pop, Dad basting rabbit on the barbecue.

Don't be sentimental, she told herself. Just because she'd seen another side of her father in the poisonous document she'd stolen and given away, it didn't mean anything had changed. She'd get the same cold shoulder, and her mother would scuttle around keeping up the happy-families facade.

No, the only thing that had changed was Emma. She'd grown up, she'd learned things she shouldn't have. She'd glimpsed a secret world. The rest of it - college, politics, music, drugs - was just a flimsy wrapper.

The water between the ferry and the wharf boiled as the deckhands braced themselves for contact between steel and timber. Stocky Maltese men with hairy arms and kinked black hair lugged barrows and crates back and forth. The passengers surged for the gangplanks and the customs shed. Emma took out her passport and shoved to keep her place in the rowdy queue. An official thwacked a stamp into her passport and she was through the barrier, looking right and left for her mother. A cardboard sign - EMMA STONEHOUSE - bobbed above the heads. She waved and the man holding the sign caught her eye: Dad had sent a driver! She pushed through the crowd.

**

"We'll have breakfast on the ferry," Susan said. The drive from the farmhouse to the ship terminal at Mgarr was no more than fifteen minutes; Ralph could wait for his coffee. Susan had dressed up for the day trip, he noticed, and she looked delectable.

Their habit was for Susan to drive while Ralph surveyed the bald hills and church domes, pointing out landmarks and lecturing her on Malta's place in the Kingdom of Sicily.

"Poor Gozo," he said. "Unloved and desiccated. Did you know that the whole island was enslaved and shipped to Libya in medieval times?"

But Ralph's heart wasn't in it today.

Susan caught his mood: "Darling, you haven't mentioned King Roger the Second once this morning," she said, shimmying the Mini into the double line of cars and trucks waiting to board through the roll-on-roll-off gate of the ferry.

"I was thinking about Emma. What she might have made of the letter," Ralph said.

"It's been a month since I wrote. Why hasn't she replied?" Susan said.

"You know Emma. She's not the world's most active letter writer. And all she knows is that I'm taking it easy after a bit of a turn."

Susan gave him a doubtful look and nudged the Mini up the ramp into the car hold. They took the steel staircase to the upper deck, where passengers were queuing for coffee and pastries to get them through the stately forty-five-minute trip. The rocky hills and church domes of Gozo receded, and the passengers' attention shifted towards the mainland in the distance ahead. The sea was glassy and the sun was warming the morning air.

They rolled off the ferry at Cirkewwa and drove slowly through the seaside towns - Mellieha, St. Paul, Bugibba: On their left the sea sparkled all the way to Sicily. On their right a landscape of concrete sheds, paddocks, prickly pear and cottages straggled towards the dry inland hills. The traffic thickened in the charmless outer suburbs of Valletta: Heavy trucks with a military-surplus look belching black smoke, buzzing motorbikes, 1950s buses, Minimokes loaded with blistered tourists.

At St. Julians, the vista took on the look of the French Riviera, and then they were in Sliema with its yachts and restaurants and pricey villas. The last traces of concrete gave way to sandstone and marble as they drove into Valletta.

"It's a tiny jewel, this city," Susan said. "Naples in the palm of your hand." She squeezed the car into a space outside a miniature hardware store that would have looked old-fashioned in 1950. A handful of stringy boys played soccer in the marble streets while carved Virgins looked down from crumbling nooks and lintels.

"Nervous?" Susan asked.

"Not in the least," Ralph said.

"See you outside the cathedral at twelve-thirty?"

"Perfect. We'll have a look at the Caravaggio and then grab a bit of lunch. But just in case I'm not there by one, go home on your own and I'll take the bus back to Cirkewwa." He kissed her and headed off on foot for Pietà.

Bloody nonsense, the whole business. Psychiatric assessment? People like him just didn't get mixed up in that sort of thing. You pulled yourself together if you went a bit wobbly. Not that he was in the least wobbly, of course. All of this was part of his cover. But what if the psychiatrist wasn't in on the game? What if there was to be some probing about his feelings, about his past? On the other hand, what if they really wanted to find out if he was a homo? You never knew what they might dig out of you.

By the time he reached the hospital gates, he was damp with sweat, and the warm weather wasn't solely responsible.

St. Luke's was a shambling complex of blockhouses and chimneys on a hill above the harbour. When he eventually found the psychiatric outpatient unit, he was fifteen minutes late. The tiny waiting room was full of distressed-looking individuals, some apparently stricken with deep gloom, and others staring blankly. He presented himself to a woman in a white coat at the counter. She looked startled at his name, and immediately made a whispered telephone call. A nurse ushered him down a corridor and into a consulting room containing a hospital bed and a chair.

"Please take off your shoes, lie on the bed, and wait for Doctor."

The hands on the wall clock crept forward five minutes. Ralph fought to calm his rising pulse.

Somebody in a white coat came into the room.

Ralph turned his head. It was a tall man, young, craggy film-star type.

"Don't get up," he said, taking the chair in a professional manner. Crisp white shirt, tartan tie, mirror shine on his black shoes. "How are we, Mr Stonehouse?"

"We? I'm not royalty."

"And I'm not a doctor."

"So who are you, then?"

"You can call me Mills." Cut-glass accent, a man trained to command. Who the hell was this Mills?" Guards officer turned spook?

"I suppose you're not going to enlighten me further, Captain Mills?"

The man laughed. "Good guess, Mr Stonehouse. Actually, it's Lieutenant, Royal Navy, retired, but that's between you and me. Can we get on with it?"

A decent chap by the look of things. Fingers bloody crossed. "So, you're not going to ask me whether I'm in love with my mother or when I stopped wetting the bed?"

"Well, I might do, just for form's sake." Mills made notes on a pad. "There we are. Not in love with mother. Bedwetting ceased at three years. Satisfied? Now settle down and listen. As far as you're concerned, I'm a doctor attached to the British High Commission."

"Ingenious," Ralph said. "And I'm a British nutcase for you to practice on."

"Your description, Stonehouse, not mine. But your mental deterioration is integral to the plan."

"Plan?" Ralph was still lying down. "Can I get up?"

"No. Somebody might come in. Try to look the part, man."

"So, what is the plan, exactly?"

"Just bear with me. The good news is about your lost document. It's been found," Mills said. Of course it had been found; the bastards had probably stolen it themselves. No point in asking for the details; they had everything sewn up tight as a duck's arse. Better tread with care. Ralph breathed slowly to quell his pounding heart.

"So, who stole it?"

"That's all I can tell you."

"Thank the Lord," Ralph said, calm now. The details didn't matter. Operation Aqua was intact. Waters would be picked up somewhere between Malta and Libya, charged with gun running and spirited back to London, just as Ralph had proposed. But what had Mills meant about Ralph's mental deterioration being integral to the plan?

He swung his legs over the side of the bed.

"Lie back down."

"Get stuffed."

"Suit yourself. It doesn't matter to me whether you receive this news lying down or standing on your head."

"What news?" He prepared himself for the worst. "It's Emma, isn't it? What's happened to her?"

"Emma - oh, the elusive daughter. Don't worry about her."

"You mean you're keeping tabs on her?" Ralph asked, but Mills ignored him.

"The plan," he said, "is that you will command Purple Phase."

Purple Phase? Yes, he remembered. When he'd designed Operation Aqua, he'd named the various phases with colours. The arrest of Waters at sea was called Purple Phase.

"No, no. I'm a senior civil servant, not a military man. I don't command things. This is preposterous. I must protest."

"But you know everything about Aqua. It's your baby." The posh lout raised a rakish eyebrow in an unconvincing attempt at camaraderie.

"Bugger you and your damned plan."

Mills's face hardened. "You'd prefer five years behind bars for leaking a top-secret document? Who'd keep an eye on that rather tasty wife of yours? I'm partial to a bit of the older woman myself actually."

Ralph lunged at Mills. Couldn't help it. Stupid, but what could a man do? Mills spun him around and held him in a bear hug. He felt the big man grinding his crutch into his backside. He struggled to be free but Mills grasped him harder, grinding and panting. "Yes, I'm getting a feel for lovely Susan. I bet she loves it from behind. You too, I've heard."

"All right. Let me go, you swine." It was useless. This Mills was a brute with twice his strength and the personality of a Rottweiler. God knew what horrors he'd performed in his service career. The bastard knew no boundaries. The best thing for himself, Susan, and - he shuddered - Emma, was to play along.

"What do I have to do, then? This commander business?" Ralph forced himself to breathe calmly.

"That's better. What do you have to do? You'll be on board the freighter. Cornelius Lamine will disembark off Libya and return with the arms. You'll take over from there. You'll rendezvous with Donald Waters and make sure he's detained. You'll have *carte blanche*. If you need to eliminate him, that's up to you."

A bubble of confusion forced itself into Ralph's mind. He tried to read the handsome bastard's face, but the eyes gave nothing away. Grey-green. Glass marbles. Cold.

"I beg your pardon. You mean as in 'eliminate him from our enquiries'? He can't be eliminated - he's it. He's the one we're after."

"Are you being deliberately obtuse, Mr Stonehouse?"

Ralph tried to rewind the conversation in his mind.

"Do you mean what I think you might mean?" He heard his own voice, dry as ash, but oddly dissociated from his voice box.

"Yes. If you mean what I think you mean. You're going to kill him if necessary," Mills said.

It was some kind of secret joke. Ralph threw his head back and laughed, expecting him to join in. But he didn't.

There was a nervous knock at the door and a nurse peeped in. "Shall I bring the medication, Doctor?"

"All under control, Sister. I'll call if I need help."

He addressed Ralph. "I'm sure we don't want a tranquilliser, do we?"

Ralph stared at him. How would he - could he - kill someone?

The truth seeped into his mind. Of course - he was mad. That's why he would kill Donald Waters. Deranged with vengeance. That's why the nurse would come back with a syringe if he made a fuss.

He choked back a wedge of acid vomit. "This makes no sense. I'm a desk and committee man. You can't make me kill someone." A last protest, for form's sake, but he and Mills knew the game was on.

"Go home to your farmhouse and wait for instructions." Mills stood up and left the room. So this was what it'd come to. Ralph Stonehouse shitting his ruddy Y-fronts because of an overgrown boy scout psychopath.

There was a toilet along the corridor. Ralph locked himself in a stall with puddles on the floor. He lit a cigarette, smoking until the nausea was quelled.

He sat, immobile and stunned. It vaguely occurred to him that his socks were wet. Outside the stall, men entered, coughed, urinated, whistled, washed hands, farted, exited. The cycle was repeated - he didn't know how many times. The gurgles of flushing and the clatter of a hand towel dispenser provided a jagged backdrop to his desolation. Somebody knocked on the door and asked if he was unwell. When he didn't answer, the lock was turned from the outside, and a kindly attendant with large eyebrows led him into the corridor and down to the reception where the same roomful of sad individuals sat waiting. "His shoes," the receptionist said, and the attendant went back to the room to fetch them. The woman made a whispered telephone call, and after a few minutes a taxi driver came in and beckoned Ralph to follow.

"Where to, Sir?"

The windscreen of the taxi was festooned with dangling crosses and Madonnas.

"Sir, where to?"

Ralph looked at his watch. There was time to meet Susan at the Cathedral, but he needed to unscramble his thoughts. He needed a place to think.

"Take me to Rabat."

"Rabat? You are sure? It is quite far, Sir."

The taxi bumped its way along the corrugated roads, skirting Valletta and then turning north into the dry inland. After half an hour, the high walls of the old city loomed up from the fields. Ralph paid the driver.

He wandered through the streets and alleys, staying in the deep shade of the honey-coloured chapels and storehouses built for the old Knights of Provence, Auvergne, and Aragon.

There were some tourists of the more cultured variety than the sunbathers from Croydon and Hounslow who packed the beach resorts. A middle-aged American couple in professional-looking walking gear stopped to ask him to take their photograph. French students sketched the baroque church of St. Paul with its three bone-white facades and the fresco of Christ above the middle arch.

The sky was a dome of pitiless blue. Ralph sat in a nook of shade and lit a cigarette.

"Mr Stonehouse." He squinted at the figure standing with its back to the sun. It was Mills, in a Panama hat.

"You followed me here?"

"A precaution. That's all."

"A precaution against what?" Ralph asked. "Do you think I'm going to leap off the battlements?"

"Something like that, perhaps."

"You're a fool, then. I'm not going to top myself because of a scheming prat like you. Just bugger off."

***

When he got back to the farmhouse, it was already dark. Susan sat upright on a chair, her face strained and pale.

"I'm sorry. There was a hitch," he said.

She handed him a slip of paper. It was a telegram, sent from Catania the day before.

ARRIVE VALLETTA 1130 TOMORROW STOP LOVE STOP EMMA STOP

"She should be here," Susan said. "I phoned the port. The Catania boat arrived on time. If she'd caught the bus to Cirkewwa, she'd have got the ferry over here by two at the latest."

"How many more ferries are there tonight?" he asked. There were three, the last one arriving just before midnight. He knew the schedule as well as she did.

They drove the old Mini to Mgarr and stood on the balcony of the Gleneagles Bar overlooking the terminal. Inside, the TV was showing a soccer match, and a couple of expats were playing darts. Ralph brought out two brandies. The lights of the nine o'clock ferry twinkled a mile away.

"Here, this'll settle your nerves."

A little knot of taxis and cars waited just outside the wire mesh gates. Men yawned and stretched and jangled their keys under the floodlights.

Emma wasn't on the nine o'clock or the ten-thirty or the eleven-forty-five.

"Something held her up," Susan said as they drove home. "She must have met a friend and decided to stay over."

"She's her own woman," Ralph said. "She'll turn up tomorrow."

They tossed and fidgeted under the ceiling fan. Ralph fell into a shallow sleep but woke suddenly to see Susan at the window staring into the night. It was 3am.

"They've taken her," she said.

"Taken who?" But Ralph knew. Emma was the security against him packing his bag and disappearing.

"What did those bastards tell you today?"

"Among other things, they may want me to kill Donald Waters."

Susan stared out for a full minute, then fell to her knees and wailed, "My poor girl, my poor, poor girl".

Chapter Twelve

The man holding the sign with Emma's name waited by a small black car. Emma got in the back seat. Nice of Dad to arrange a pick-up. They must have had something important to do that they couldn't get out of. After all, her telegram wouldn't have got to Gozo until this morning. Or perhaps Dad was unwell. Her elation at being on the sun-drenched island dimmed at the thought of what she might learn at the farmhouse.

The car was old and smelly, and the driver wasn't too fragrant either.

"Right-ho, Miss. We'll be off then." The voice was British - Birmingham? Emma was never very sure about accents north of Watford. Unusual, though. Wouldn't a hire-car driver be Maltese?

"Did my father's office send you to pick me up?" Somewhere in Malta, there'd be an 'office' that Dad was connected with. Perhaps the Embassy? Or was it a High Commission? Since they'd turned Malta into a Republic and brought in the new guy Mintoff, things were changing. Dad was always grumbling about 'the beginning of the end', but didn't the Maltese have a right to govern themselves?

The driver grunted something and the old banger slewed out of the carpark. Emma wound down the windows and let the hot wind, scented with wild thyme and exhaust fumes, blow away the man's sweat smell.

But after ten minutes, she became uneasy. On her last few stays in Gozo, she'd taken a hired scooter over to the mainland and buzzed around, visiting the little harbour towns and remote beaches. A sign pointed to Birzebbuga. Wasn't that south of the airport? Maybe not, the town names were so confusing, and sometimes you found two villages with the same name. But if she was right, the ferry terminal at Cirkewwa was to the west, not south.

"Is this the way to the Gozo ferry?"

"Short cut, Miss."

"Short cut to where?"

"Where we get the ferry from, Miss."

She remembered. There was another ferry to Gozo, a bigger vessel. It went a couple of times a week from somewhere else on the main island. Funny way to go, but the man seemed to know what he was doing. Bloody hell though, he really ponged.

She lit a cigarette, but the hot wind blew ashes into her eyes. When she wound up the window, the sweltering stink was unbearable so she opened it and tossed the cigarette out. It danced and sparked in a hot eddy for a moment and then darted up and away.

There was a sign for Marsaxlokk. She could see the enormous power station a mile or two ahead. They must be almost at the pretty harbour with its fish cafés and tiny painted fishing boats.

Something was wrong. Horribly sodding wrong. There was no ferry from Marsaxlokk. People came here to eat fried snapper and drink Heineken, not get on a bloody great steamer.

"Let me out!"

The man grasped the steering wheel more tightly. He accelerated, lurching around bends so the tyres ground against the car's undercarriage. Blue exhaust smoke swirled inside the cabin. Emma was thrown from one side to another, bashing her shoulders on the door handles.

"Stop, you bastard." She squeezed her shoulders between the front seats, shoved her knees against the back seat, grabbed the handbrake and yanked it upwards. The man grasped her hair, but let go as they slewed sideways. He got the bucking car under control with one hand, and walloped Emma's back with the other. She slumped, gasping for air.

When she opened her eyes, they were approaching the village. In the heat of the day, shutters were closed and the streets deserted. A woman in black waddled out of an alley holding a pan. Emma shrieked, "Help," but the old crone just emptied the pan and waddled back. The driver expertly threw the car into a warren of alleys until they came to a dead end. He jumped out and lugged Emma from between the front seats.

"Stand up!" She stood, swaying. He forced a huge black wrench against her face. Something gave way in her mouth, and then there was the taste of blood. The pain flooded her brain and spilled into a rage so intense that she slashed at his face and eyes.

But he had her pinned to the cobblestones in a second, stuffing a foul rag into her bleeding mouth, and then rolling her over to swiftly tape her wrists together. He opened the door of one of the dilapidated sheds that lined the alley, dragged Emma inside and stuffed her into a wooden crate. The lid banged down and she felt herself hoisted up and carried precariously down some steps. The crate was splintery and dark. She was slammed down onto some sloping surface. There was the hum of a motor and the unmistakable movement of a small boat breasting the ripples of calm waters.

***

It was Emma's third day in the cabin, and by now she knew every rivet in the steel walls. There was a wobbly card table and a cupboard with a few greasy plates and cups. The single porthole was covered on the outside, and a yellowish light bulb gave the cabin a sickly air. Opposite the steel entrance door, there was an alcove with a bucket. Although there were air vents in the ceiling, the cabin was hot, and she spent the days in her underwear, dressing only when the Pig came to bring food and water and empty the reeking bucket. She rationed the water, drinking first and cleaning herself with what was left.

In the hours she spent alone, the fear gave way to a nerve-numbing boredom. Trails of hope wended through her thoughts like the smoke from a joss stick: Hope that Dad's work would have people looking for her. Surely they would have searched the island by now and figured she was on a boat. But how many boats were moored off Malta? Hundreds, she supposed. And how many had left Malta since she'd disappeared?

She knew now that she was part of something much bigger than stupid bloody Emma pinching a file. Whatever the something big was, there were powerful people involved. British people. But still, they looked after you in Britain. Someone was out there searching, she was sure. Calm professional men, men like her dad.

The last of the bloody fags had gone and she was working on her cuticles. They were bleeding. Stop! You'll get infected fingers. She'd had it once, her index finger swollen like a sausage. No antibiotics here.

Sometime in the early evening - she'd forgotten to wind her watch, but a crack of light around the window gave a clue - there was the bump of the dinghy on the hull, followed by the scrabbling of feet on the ladder. She quickly put on her clothes.

The Pig had a routine: He'd clang on the outside of the steel door with a big spanner and yell, "Stand by the bucket!" Then he'd unbolt something outside and swing the steel hatch inwards.

"Arm up!" He stepped inside and handcuffed her wrist to the pipe. His face was pink, the large nostrils almost vertical. A tuft of stiff ginger hair stood to attention below his lip. She was inwardly terrified and utterly vulnerable whenever he entered, waiting with dread for a caress - or worse - from his hairy fingers. All she possessed to defend herself was her stare of utter scorn.

On the first day, she'd asked him what was going to happen to her; there'd been no answers, and the pain in her upper jaw told her not to push him too far.

But the Pig must be under strict orders not to sample the goods, despite the filthy yearning in the pink-rimmed eyes.

He swept the dirty paper plate, the food wrappers, and the empty drink cans into a plastic bag, and went outside on deck. Emma smelt the sweet caress of the night air as the fug in the cabin dissipated. The Pig came back in, slapped a box of provisions on the table, and chucked the emptied bucket on the floor. Emma looked up at him, querying with her eyes: There was a double ration of Sprite, cold Cornish pasties and bananas. She started at the sound of another voice outside, a woman's voice. The Pig went out on deck again and came back wrangling a handcuffed figure over the steel coping in the doorway. There was a cloth bag over the head. He unlocked the cuffs and shoved the newcomer past Emma. The shrouded figure tripped and cried out with a woman's voice as it hit a steel bulkhead.

"Move a fucking muscle, and you get this again." He jammed the huge black spanner against Emma's face with one paw while he unlocked the cuff with the other. A rotten meat smell hung around his armpit.

He was gone in seconds. The door clanged shut. Emma helped the slumped figure to her feet. She carefully removed the cloth bag.

It was Zouzou, spluttering and unsteady.

"Are you hurt?"

The woman spat out something red and stared into her palm with astonishment.

"He knocked my tooth out."

"Join the party," Emma said.

"I am not in a mood for parties," she said. She undressed, looked around, and hung her clothes on a wire coat hanger. She lay on the lower bunk and fell asleep immediately.

"And goodnight to you too," Emma said.

The cabin was heating up, and she took off her own clothes.

The woman fidgeted and flailed under the grubby sheet. She often talked in snatches, sometimes in English, sometimes in French, but mostly in what must be Arabic. Emma watched her for a while, but felt uncomfortable sharing her mutterings, even if most of it meant nothing. She climbed onto the top bunk and lay still, counting rivets. The muttering stopped. Emma drifted in and out of sleep.

After six or seven hours - Emma could only guess at the time - Zouzou rolled off the bunk and stood up wrapped in the sheet.

"Where are your clothes, Miss?" she said.

Emma laughed. "It's too hot in here. I just get dressed when the Pig comes in."

"*Il-khanzeer*," Zouzou said.

"What does that mean?"

"It is the Arabic for 'pig' of course."

Of course. Obvious really, Emma. This woman had some sodding attitude.

Zouzou tossed the sheet on the bed and flapped her hands as if to waft away the smell.

"So, we are robbed of our modesty as well as our freedom."

"And our teeth. At least one each." The swelling in Emma's jaw had subsided, to leave a throb of pain and a deep hole where a canine tooth had been knocked out. But Zouzou had a nasty lump on one side of her top lip.

"A tooth is the smallest of my problems."

"I suppose so," Emma said. "Look, there's some food."

Zouzou poked at the cold pies with a red polished fingernail and shrugged. "I prefer to fast. But you, my sister, you are a thin girl. And this food is perhaps more to your taste than mine. Please." She gestured as if she were offering Emma a splendid feast.

Emma picked at a corner of a stale cake, stealing a look at Zouzou, who had taken one of the battered steel chairs. Drowsy mahogany eyes, a strong nose, dense glossy black hair. She was luxuriantly generous in her build, and her olive skin was exquisitely smooth. A Pharaoh's queen in bra and pants, Emma thought, not a prostitute.

"Why are we here, Zouzou?" she asked.

"Here, sister? Here on this boat? Here on this earth? Can we ever know God's will?"

"That's not what I meant." Emma didn't want a philosophy lecture, just some information.

"I detest boats," Zouzou said.

"I beg your pardon?"

"I was an actress, you know. In Egypt and Lebanon. I had to go to many parties on yachts in Beirut." Zouzou stopped and sighed. "So many actresses, so many men with creeping hands. You see, sister, I cannot think of a yacht without remembering the caresses of those old fellows."

What was this woman? Emma wondered. She might as well be from Mars, for all the sense she was making in her jagged accent. Perhaps a more direct approach was called for. A bit of straightforward English treatment.

"Listen, Mrs Zouzou or whoever you are, you'd better start talking sense if we're going to get out of this bloody boat. And it's not a yacht. As far as I can tell it's a small cargo ship."

Zouzou cast a limpid glance at Emma. "You are a good girl, Emma. I can tell. But you are impetuous. Of what should I talk? Of cruel men and suffering women? Of my husband, who is my heart and my soul? Of the day when I will pass on from this world? Of the price of oranges and peas? Of puppy dogs, of goldfishes in their glass balls?"

"Bowls, not balls." This wasn't working. Emma opened a can of orange pop and passed one to Zouzou. They sipped in silence. The ship rolled slightly - the wash from another vessel? Some local sailor passing close by with no inkling of the two imprisoned women?

Zouzou cleared her throat. "I will tell you my story, but it begins a long time ago, far beyond the *khanzeer*. And you will have to be patient."

Now Emma was puzzled. Was Zouzou going to pour out her life story? Was this some kind of *Arabian Nights* performance? Why couldn't they just discuss the immediate problem of getting off this fucking boat?

"Do not worry about how we will flee this vessel," the Egyptian woman said, apparently a mind-reader. "I have a plan. You may find the details unseemly, but it is a sure method."

That was that, then. Problem solved. Emma calculated that the *khanzeer* - such a better word than 'pig' - wouldn't be back for ten hours or so. Let the woman tell her story, then. There was damn-all else to do. Who cared if she wanted to spill her private business?

Again, Zouzou seemed to have read Emma's thoughts. "I have lived for a year and half in London using another woman's name. I have no friends save my husband. I have nobody else to talk to, *ya'ni,* woman to woman." She wrung her hands and looked at Emma with forlorn eyes. "Sister, my life is lonely."

The raw admission brought Emma to her feet. She leant to hug Zouzou, but the woman gently pushed her away. "I do not want your sympathy, merely your attention. Sit, please, and listen."

The story began in Alexandria: An idyllic childhood, with loving parents. Her mother, she believed, was descended from a Circassian slave, not that Emma knew what a Circassian was. It was on holidays at a resort near Alexandria that Zouzou met Pierre when she was fourteen. The two families rented adjoining villas for the summer. But when she was eighteen, her parents were killed in a car accident, and with no aunts or uncles, she passed into the protection of a friend of her father.

"A peculiar variety of friend," she said darkly, describing how the man had helped her into the film industry, where she became a plaything of his business friends. "It was sordid and exciting at the same time. The attention of rich men made me the envy of my fans. But while they envied me, they hated me too. It is the fate of women like me."

"What did you have to do for these rich men?" Emma asked, realising how gauche the question was as the words left her lips.

"I am not a courtesan, sister."

"I never thought you were ..."

"Your thoughts are written on your face. But you are shocked. You - a London girl with your free love and drugs. Now it is my turn to shock you."

What bloody revelation was she going to dish up next?

Zouzou drew herself up and spoke to the ceiling. "I remained a virgin until I was thirty-three."

A giggle bubbled up in Emma's throat, but a glance at the woman's face checked her; Zouzou wasn't joking.

"How? How could that be, Zouzou?"

"A woman can learn tricks. Men are like children - easily fooled. You see, young Emma, the intimate world is a theatre where the actors believe what they persuade themselves to believe. A man may gorge on mango when all he has been given is boiled carrot."

She was right. French cock: The nice girl from Berkshire in a Jean-Luc Godard movie.

"And your husband Pierre - he was the first?"

Zouzou nodded and continued: Mistress to a powerful old man, the threat to her life from a married general with a guilty secret, her reunion with Pierre and discovery that he had become a private investigator. She told of a plot Pierre had been mixed up with in Cairo around the start of the Yom Kippur war a year and a half before, and how they had been forced to flee Egypt by ship. She spoke about California, where she and Pierre would discard their past lives.

"It sounds like something from a movie," Emma said.

Zouzou smiled grimly. "Now, sister, it is your turn to tell your story."

Story? But Emma had no story, at least nothing approaching Zouzou's adventures.

"I'm just a student. I've got a mum and dad, and I've made a big mess just recently. That's all really."

"Is there a fiancé?" Zouzou asked.

"A fiancé? We don't really have them anymore. You just live with someone. But, yes, there is someone, sort of. Or was. A French guy."

"And do you have dreams, sister? Dreams for the future?"

"I did, but they're all gone down the drain. I wanted to work for Amnesty or the BBC or the United Nations or something." She was suddenly overwhelmed with despair and began to cry. But as she fished around for something to wipe her face with, a deep clang reverberated through the boat.

"*Il-khanzeer*," Zouzouz said. "Have you ever acted in a play, sister?"

"I was in *The Crucible* at school."

"Very well, follow my lead exactly," she said, taking her clothes off the wire hanger and placing them on the upper bunk. She bent the wire, opening the hook slightly wider, then slid the hanger underneath the clothes. "Now sit on the bed and be ready for your role."

The great spanner clanged on the cabin door. "Arms up! Backs to the wall."

Zouzou shouted, "Yes, we have done it," and knelt in front of Emma. The plump Egyptian woman smothered her, forcing her lips on her face and caressing her neck and thighs. "Make groans, like me," she said. Emma copied Zouzou's passionate moaning. The door clanged open. She felt the cushiony softness of breasts and realised that Zouzou's bra was off her shoulders. Then she felt her own breasts fall free under Zouzou's searching fingers. They squirmed and moaned as the fresh air penetrated the cabin.

"Fuckin' 'ell." Peeping around Zouzou's head, Emma saw the Pig goggling slack-mouthed at the scene, the spanner dangling from one limp hand and the cuffs from the other.

Zouzou slowly turned from the bed and stood to face the man, her full breasts obviously paralysing his brain. Emma caught her coquettish grimace, and heard her say, "You like what you see? Look, Sir, there is more. Come stand by me, Emma."

The man looked down as Zouzou hooked a thumb into the elastic of her panties. Emma copied. The Pig half-whimpered, half-giggled - a kid loose in a toyshop.

Zouzou hissed, "*Ya khanzeer!*" He glanced up, confused. Zouzou plunged two red-nailed fingers into his eyes. He squealed and his palms flew to his face. The actress drove a knee between his legs. He expelled a *whoomph* from his lungs and collapsed.

"Emma, the handcuffs." Emma darted behind the man and grabbed the cuffs. Her heart beat as if it would explode; the tiny cabin resonated with the *khanzeer's* curses and a stream of nasty-sounding Arabic from Zouzou. She inserted the hook of the coat hanger in the man's nostril. He screamed. With one hand over his damaged eyes and one on his crutch, he rose to his knees like a broken puppet as Zouzou slowly raised the hanger.

He let go his crutch and flailed with one hand, still covering his eyes with the other. The fist whacked Emma and she fell, and then it caught Zouzou's arm, jerking the hanger sideways. As he screamed at this new insult to his nostril, Emma jumped up and flicked the cuff onto the wrist and over the pipe. Zouzou dropped the hanger and the *khanzeer* launched punches in every direction.

He stopped and opened the eye that seemed to be working, squinting in terror at the half-naked she-devils who panted and glared just out of reach of his fists.

Emma and Zouzou grabbed their clothes, stepping into them as they exited the cabin, and avoiding the whirling fists.

"Wait," Zouzou said, and darted back into the cabin. Emma watched her pick up the bucket of human waste and jam it over the Pig's head. But the man's flailing foot caught Zouzou caught hard in the stomach. She went down with a howl of foul-sounding Arabic and crawled to the doorway. Emma dragged her onto deck and slammed the door shut.

They lay panting. It was night, warm and balmy. The lights of Marsaxlokk twinkled in the distance. There were cigarettes and a lighter in a bag the *khanzeer* had left outside. Emma squatted on the steel deck, her mind tumbling the flashes of fists and screams and blood and breasts into a dizzying maelstrom. She fumbled with the cigarettes, dropped one, took another and put it to her lips. The smoke quelled the maelstrom, and she asked Zouzou, "Where did you learn to escape like that?"

There was a wail of 'fucking bitches' from the cabin.

"I remembered it from *Gangsters in Love*. It was in the script, but the director cut it out because it was too violent."

"You mean the coat hanger?" Emma asked.

"No, I made that up."

"And the - you know - me and you on the bed?"

"You said you had acted in plays, sister. Now *imshi*, let's get away."

Emma shimmied down the rope ladder, checking the dinghy with a torch she'd taken from the *khanzeer's* bag. She'd used an outboard before, and this was a simple one. The engine caught, buzzed ready for action.

The ladder swayed, and she heard sobbing above.

"Sister, I am frightened of the water." In the torchlight, Zouzou hung, immobile.

"Come down gently, I'll catch you. Look, it's just ten feet."

The Egyptian woman snuffled. Emma held the ladder steady. A roar of anger from the cabin burst the peace of the night, and metal clanged on metal.

"Hurry, Zouzou. He's bashing the pipe with the spanner."

Emma heard Zouzou utter something - the word *Allah* was in there somewhere - and felt the ladder jerk twice. She reached upwards with her hand, felt a foot, and then collapsed as Zouzou's body dropped on her.

The clanging had stopped. Emma wriggled out from under Zouzou, untied the painter, gunned the outboard motor, and slewed the little boat towards the harbour. Looking back, she saw the outline of the *khanzeer* on the deck against the night sky. Something flew into the night. The shit bucket hit the coping of the dinghy and landed next to Zouzou, who was curled up like a foetus.

The dinghy seemed to crawl across the water, with the lights of the shore barely increasing in size, but at last - maybe after half an hour, Emma thought - they were among the moorings and the fishing boats, each with a staring eye painted on the prow. It must be late - even early morning - because the tiny harbour was deserted when they bumped up against a set of steps cut in the stone wall. A few streetlamps shed yellowy light on the quay. The seaside restaurants were closed, with their chairs stacked on tables. A cat chewed at fish guts spilling from a black rubbish bag, then glared at the intruders.

Zouzou was quite recovered once she stepped out of the dinghy. "I'm hungry," she said.

"Tough luck," Emma said. "We've got to get to Cirkewwa. If we walk up to the main road, we can hitch a lift."

"What is Cirkewwa?"

Before Emma had a chance to reply, car headlights dazzled them. A vehicle approached and parked, and the lights were turned off. The car was black and shiny with an official metal badge on the front grill. Dad had sent someone to rescue her!

"Emma Stonehouse? Thank God I've found you." A figure stepped from the car. He strode into the light, an apparition of clean-cut British manhood. Oh God, please let this be real. Rescued by a real-life James Bond. I'm in a story. It'll all fade in a second.

But it didn't fade. She could smell his aftershave. He was real. She wilted in front of the apparition; her hair was greasy, she stank. There was something on her jeans she didn't want to know about.

"Sir, kindly identify yourself," Zouzou said.

"Mills, Madame. Brian Mills. British High Commission."

The sound of an outboard motor nudged into the silence of the night, then cut out.

"Where's my dad, Mr Mills?"

Emma caught a foul waft from somewhere close. She spun around to face the *khanzeer*, who crouched with fists ready to strike. His right eye was a butcher's shop.

"Run, Emma," Zouzou yelled.

Brian Mills turned on the *khanzeer*.

"Back in the boat. I'll deal with you later." The man with the ruined nose made protesting noises. Emma thought she heard, "Yes Sir, no Sir, three bags full". A punch was thrown in the gloom. "Useless prick!"

"Emma, come, we have to hide," Zouzou hissed, dragging Emma into the shadows.

"No, Zouzou, my dad's sent him." But Zouzou yanked her along the quay and shoved her off the stone steps into a fishing boat. She pulled a tarpaulin over themselves and jammed a hand over Emma's mouth.

The noise of struggling subsided. "All under control, ladies. I've tied him up. Let's get you out of here."

Then there was the buzz of engines, shouts in Maltese. Zouzou relaxed her grip on Emma. They peeped over the gunnels. A dozen motorbikes were circling, headlights flashing randomly, beer bottles smashing, Brian Mills bellowing. A gang of riders circled Mills with their bikes, taunting him, choking him in a cloud of blue exhaust smoke. More bottles flew, more glass smashed. Then the boys were gone, a cloud of angry wasps flitting away from the dock and up the hill until they were gone in the night.

Emma and Zouzou edged themselves under the tarpaulin again.

"Who are those devils?" Zouzou whispered.

"Just village boys. They ride around at night. We got lucky."

"Emma, where are you?" It was Mills.

"Say nothing," Zouzou whispered.

"Why?"

"Who do you trust right now, Emma? Him or me?" She was right. No contest.

Mills's voice drifted from nearby and then far away. "Emma, I need to take you to your father." For ten or fifteen minutes he patrolled the harbour front calling her. Suddenly he was a step away from their hiding place. From the bumps and scrapes, he seemed to be checking inside the nearby fishing boats. Emma caught the tang of his after shave. She and Zouzou lay rigid. Mills had stopped moving. But then a rough Maltese voice yelled, "Hey, you. This is private property. Bugger off!"

They heard a car door slam, the sound of an engine starting, the car pulling away.

Emma drew close to Zouzou under the tarpaulin and asked, "Are you OK, sister?" The Egyptian woman murmured something and squeezed Emma's hand.

***

They slept under the tarpaulin, wrapped together against the cool pre-dawn air. At first light, there were voices on the waterfront, and Emma nudged Zouzou awake. As the Egyptian woman rolled over, her blouse rode up and Emma saw a huge yellowish-purple bruise at the base of her ribs. They slipped over the gunnels onto the quay, and ran crouching among the stacked restaurant chairs and umbrellas until they were clear of the boatmen.

"There's a bus stop just up here," Emma said. She patted her shirt pocket. Her passport was still there, along with a few Maltese lira she'd slipped inside it on her last visit. They started up the hill.

"Where will we go?"

"To my parents' house of course."

"Your parents?"

"They have a holiday house here in Malta. It's on Gozo, the next island. My dad's there. He's ill. He's having a break."

"No, not there."

"Why not, Zouzou? That's the safest place we can go to."

"It is the most dangerous, surely."

Emma looked at Zouzou. She was a woman with a story, someone who'd seen it all. The woman's face had a canniness, a depth of street wisdom, that Emma had never seen among her college friends in London. Those twits had seen sod all.

Zouzou was right of course. Walking into her parents' farmhouse would be plain bloody stupid. They hadn't been at the dock to meet her. Who knew what the bastards had done to Dad and Mum?

"I have to talk to them, though."

"Of course, but first we need to find a safe place, somewhere we can rest and plan."

It sounded reasonable. But there they were, two sitting ducks at the bus stop out of Marsaxlokk with the dirty clothes they stood in, a handful of change, and the sun coming up. And who knew when the *khanzeer's* boss might come looking for them, if that was who Brian Mills was? She wondered what she'd do if Mills pulled up and offered them a lift. She didn't have an answer.

An ancient bus puttered towards them, a comical little thing with gleaming red paint and sparkling chrome trim.

"Hang on. I know where we can go."

***

Zouzou said nothing on the bus trip, but as they entered Valletta, she gasped at the Baroque churches and the carved saints and lintels and Virgins.

"They could bury me here," she said.

"What do you mean?"

"I cannot exactly say. It is like an enchanted graveyard. It is exquisite and macabre all at once."

"I don't know about that. Anyway, here's the bus terminal," Emma said. "We've got to change buses."

They took another toy bus, and when they stopped half an hour later in the suburbs of Valletta, the sun was halfway to the zenith. Emma headed for a street of two-storey villas shrouded in bougainvillea.

"This is the one," she said, leading Zouzou through a shady slice of garden at the side of the house.

"Who lives here?"

"Stephanie. She's German, no Swiss maybe. Her dad's a diplomat or something, I don't know. He lives in the main house, but she's got the flat downstairs." She tapped on a glass door. There was a shuffling inside, and a waif-like girl opened the door. She was wrapped in a sheet and had a freshly lit cigarette between her lips.

"Emm! Wow! What's happening? You haven't been around for a year or more." The girls hugged.

"Hi Steph. I'm in really deep shit. Can I crash for a couple of days with my friend?"

"Wow! What a blast! Yeah, of course. My dad's away in Zurich or Stuttgart, I don't fucking know. You guys look like you need a coffee. Come in. Hey, I've got some good shit. Shall I roll a joint?"

"Just coffee, Steph. Just coffee. Look, this is my friend Zouzou from Egypt."

The girl stared at Zouzou. "*Eine ägyptische Göttin*," she said.

"What's that?"

"A goddess. Your friend is an Egyptian goddess."

***

Stephanie went upstairs to the main house and came down with men's dressing gowns. Emma and Zouzou took turns to shower and Stephanie dumped their filthy clothes in the washing machine.

"Do you have any money?" the girl asked. Emma shook her head.

"Take this. My dad leaves it around everywhere." She took a handful of notes from her pocket - francs, marks, guilders and a few English pounds. "I have to go out now and get some food. You can change the money at the bank tomorrow."

There were a couple of foam mattresses in the sitting room. Emma closed the blinds and the two women lay down. Zouzou began to breathe heavily, but stopped and said to Emma, "Your friend, what kind of girl is she?"

"She's not really my friend. She's a sort of lost person, I suppose."

"Lost?"

"Maybe 'wild' is a better word. She takes a lot of drugs and steals from her father."

"Does she love him?" Zouzou asked.

Emma thought for a moment. "Of course. She must, mustn't she?"

"Sleep well, sister,"

"Why do you call me 'sister', Zouzou?"

"It's what we say in Arabic."

"And how do you say 'sister' in Arabic?"

"You say *oukhti*."

"Goodnight, *oukhti*," Emma said.

"You see, you are fluent in Arabic already," Zouzou said. Her breathing roughened and she was asleep.

***

Emma woke with the sun in her eyes. Zouzou was gone, but she could hear women's voices in the shower area. She rubbed her eyes. These were anxious voices. She jumped to her feet.

Zouzou was sitting on a plastic chair with a blood-soaked towel between her legs. She was grey and sweaty.

"I get my father's car," Stephanie said. "She needs a doctor."

"*La, mish 'awza duktuur*," Zouzou said in alarm. Emma didn't need to know Arabic to get the idea - no doctor.

She crouched beside the groaning woman, trying not to look when she took the sodden cloth away. She eased a fresh towel into place, then wiped the trickled blood from Zouzou's legs with a flannel.

"Listen, sister, I'm not going to let you bleed to death. You're going to hospital. We'll work out our story when we get there."

Stephanie backed a big white Opel into the side passage. Emma draped Zouzou with dressing gowns and guided her into the back seat. She sat in the front but stretched her arm over the seat so she could grasp Zouzou's hand.

"There's a big hospital just outside Valletta, St. Luke's. Maybe twenty minutes," Stephanie said, launching the car into the narrow street.

***

"You can see her now."

Emma followed the matron into a long ward of beds occupied by women. Behind a curtain, Zouzou lay, her colour returned.

"Who dis?" Zouzou said to the nurse.

"She is the lady who brought you here."

"But she's ..." Emma stopped, thought, looked to Zouzou and read the message in her eyes.

"Do you know her name, where she is from? We cannot get a sensible word from her. She seems not to speak very much English," the matron asked.

"I just came across her in the street. I thought it looked like a hit-and-run. Then somebody came past in a car, and we brought her here. I'd never seen her in my life."

"Where I am please?" Zouzou asked.

"You are in a hospital. What is your name, Madame?" the matron asked.

"J'ai oublié."

"She says she has forgotten, Matron. I think she is French."

"Oh my. This is highly irregular. You see, she doesn't know where she is or what her name is. There will be a police officer here soon. He will want you to make a statement."

"A statement?" Emma asked.

"Miss, the poor lady has been injured. We must furnish all relevant particulars to the police. And there is the other matter."

"The other matter?"

The matron took Emma aside and whispered, "She has lost a baby." And then, in a voice so faint that it barely disturbed the air, "Perhaps an abortion."

They turned back to Zouzou, who was making damaged cat sounds.

"She is raving, you see, poor soul," the matron said.

Emma looked at Zouzou. The Egyptian woman paused her moaning and said, "*Oukhti - imshi.*"

Emma turned and ran through the ward, along the corridors, out of the front door. She kept running, weaving through the buildings, left, right, until she saw the main gate. A taxi drew up, but the driver waved her away. Sod him. And at any rate, what was she going to pay him with? Guilders? Belgian francs?

She started walking towards Valletta, head down. There was nowhere to go but the farmhouse in Gozo.

Chapter Thirteen

All Pierre saw of Malta was the view from the back window of the van they bundled him into. And since it was the middle of the night, the vista didn't amount to much - the airport, headlights and the occasional crumbling wall picked out for a few seconds and then gone. There was no seat in the lurching van, so he sat on a flattened cardboard box and braced his feet against the wheel arch.

He'd always been curious about Malta: There'd been a Maltese colony in Alexandria, industrious people who quietly made money and cosied up to the British. They'd been kicked out after '56, taking their funny language with them - a sort of mangled Arabic mixed up with Italian and God knows what else.

They arrived at a little harbour full of fishing boats bobbing under the moon, and the van driver led him to a dinghy tied up in front of a closed-up restaurant. He saw now that the man wore an eye patch and had a hideous wound to his nose.

"Where are we going?" There was no answer.

"I demand to know where we are going."

"Get in," the man said, brandishing a wrench big enough to unbolt the turret of a tank. No point in pushing the point, Pierre told himself. He'd push it later in his own fashion.

They puttered out from the harbour. The night air was gently warm and carried the smell of diesel and seawater. A dark mass ahead materialised into a ship about the size of two or three London buses. As they rounded the stern, Pierre picked out the name WARDA on the hull. He climbed from the dinghy up a ladder to the deck of the vessel, and the driver pushed him through a steel door into a cabin. There was a rumble of machinery somewhere deep below them.

A strapping fellow with film-star looks sat at a card table inside the stifling cabin. The driver motioned Pierre to a camp stool, and stood glowering at him.

"Where is my wife?" Pierre asked. The driver tensed his fists and glowered even more darkly. The seated man gestured to him, and he stepped outside, clanging the steel door behind him.

"Your wife is in good hands."

"I want proof. Without it, this goes no further."

"That's what they say in the movies, but it doesn't work like that in real life," the man said.

"How does it work, then?"

He seemed to be arrested in indecision for a few moments. Evidently making his mind up about something, he took an envelope from a briefcase and withdrew two dark blue passports. Opening them to the photograph page, he held them up for Pierre to see. He and Zouzou stared out. Their new surname was 'Roman'. Clever - a name like that could be from anywhere and nowhere. His kind of name.

"You see? Do the job, and you get the passports and your wife."

Pierre shrugged. "What next, then?"

"That's more like it. Here's what will happen, and you'd better listen carefully. The master of the *Warda* will make a heading for the Libyan coast. He'll moor three miles offshore. You'll be transferred to a Libyan naval patrol boat and taken to Tripoli. It'll be nighttime. You'll be in the role of Cornelius Lamine, and don't damn well slip up. Give the wrong information and they'll have your guts for garters."

"Garters? Guts? What is that?" He knew the revolting expression of course, but he needed time to think.

"You'll be in the shite. Up a gumtree. Arse in a sling."

"Yes, yes, in a tremendous pickle. I have the idea."

"That's the ticket. Now, you've read the stolen file, of course, so you know what's expected when you meet the Great Leader."

"The great who?"

"This isn't Twenty bloody Questions. I'm talking about Gaddafi."

"Gaddafi?" Pierre's stomach swayed. "There was nothing about Gaddafi in the file. I thought Lamine was meeting somebody from the Libyan Ministry of Defence."

"Change of plan. We've had word that the Colonel is taking a personal interest in this. It's a matter of trust, perhaps. He wants to get the *bona fides* directly. Once Gaddafi's satisfied the arms are going to the IRA and this isn't a sting operation, you'll be taken back to the *Warda*."

"Yes, I remember the details. The Libyan patrol boat will transfer the arms to the *Warda*, and we will then proceed to a rendezvous off Gozo. At that point, my job's done, and you'll get me off the ship."

"Good man. You remember the *bona fides*?"

"As I would remember my own name."

"Good luck, then." The man offered Pierre his hand. This wasn't an *au revoir* - more likely a final farewell.

Someone slammed and bolted the door. Pierre looked around the cabin. There was a bunk, some bits of furniture and a dented bucket in the corner. A bent coat hanger swayed from a pipe. He looked closely. There was dried blood on it. He shuddered. The fragrant *Warda*, he thought - the Arabic for 'rose'. Some scratch marks on the wall caught his eye. He lit his Zippo and peered closer. Yes, it looked like Arabic, scraped into the thick paint: It said, perhaps, *uhibbak ya Boutros* - 'I love you, Boutros'. And the date scratched below - one day ago. She always wrote his name in Arabic as 'Boutros'. 'I refuse to write 'Pierre' in Arabic,' she used to say, 'It looks like 'beer'. He peered closer; the *k* was at a funny angle with a stroke missing, and the *s* - well, if he was honest it could be just a squiggle. The more he stared, the more it looked like random scratching. Fool, delusional fool! But when he drew back - yes, surely it was a message from her!

He wept. There was hope. But was there? What mystery did that macabre coat hanger hide?

Pierre composed himself. The door clanged open. A Chinese-looking man in vest and shorts stepped in holding a pair of handcuffs.

"We go Kapten," he said. Pierre let himself be shackled to the man's wrist. The deep rumble he'd heard earlier suddenly increased to a booming growl, and there was the thrashing of water below. The ship was in motion.

"Cigarette?" he asked the crewman.

The man - Pierre saw that his skin was leathery and his eyes faded - manipulated two fat cigarettes from a packet with one hand. They stepped out onto the deck and lit up. Pierre inhaled the hot smoke and smelt the crackle of burning cloves.

"Good?" the crewman asked. Pierre nodded and took a deep drag of the volcanic cigarette.

"Indonesia cigarette," the leather-skinned man said.

"You - all Indonesia?" Pierre guessed his English was poor.

"Ya, all Indonesia." The man grinned a mouthful of brown tombstones.

"You how many Indonesia?"

The man held up five fingers, then made a fist and held up his index finger: "One Pilipin."

"Boss Indonesia?" Pierre asked. The man frowned. Try again: "Captain Indonesia?"

"Kapten? Kapten orang Denmark."

So here were some crumbs of information: Five Indonesian crew, one Filipino, and a Danish master.

He groped his way towards the front of the ship between the steel walls of the superstructure and the coping, the Indonesian leading the way. Light spilt from a doorway ahead. There was a steel stairway. Pierre and his jailer climbed the stairs and he found himself in what must be the bridge. A bulky man with a ginger beard stood over a control panel, staring through the window at the dark sea and eating a sandwich containing hot meat of some kind. He turned to Pierre and looked down at a document.

"Your name?"

"Cornelius Lamine."

The master peered at the document.

"OK. It iss you. Sorry, I must ask you stay in cabin and not spik to crew."

The smell of the meat stirred Pierre's empty stomach. What did they call the eating quarters on a ship? Ah, yes, he remembered.

"Please, where is the mess?"

"I give you bloody mess if you ask too many smart question. Now bugger you off."

He was locked up again, but after half an hour another leather-skinned man brought a pan of rice and curry. It was spicy and delicious. He lay back and waited for what fate would bring next.

***

Memories of Zouzou washed over him. He recalled her face, her expressions, her skin. A voice deep in his psyche told him that he would never see her again. Another voice rose up: 'Yes, yes, you will be reunited. You are two sides of a coin. You cannot be separated.'

Sleep overtook him, Zouzou faded, black oblivion.

When he awoke, he rose from the mattress and cracked his skull on the upper bunk. There was a circle of sickly light from a blocked-up porthole. The door was still bolted. He lay down again, all sense of time and place lost. The steady rumble of the engines and the rolling of the ship were his sole point of connection with God's Earth. 'God'? Where had he got that notion? Despite the ancient and intricate rites of his two faiths - Armenian Apostolic on his mother's side and Coptic Orthodox on his father's - Pierre had no conception of a living God. He was a practical man, a man who made his own way, a man who made his own decisions, who depended on nobody. But Zouzou had penetrated the shell he had built around his emotions - and perhaps his understanding of his place in the now and the hereafter. He recalled the rainy day in France when she had asked a rural priest to marry them. Not without *les certificats*, the priest had said with regret. But he had performed a blessing under the gaunt beams of the church, and the couple celebrated with a cognac at a windswept cafe, served by a girl in wellington boots. God's Earth: If not God's, whose Earth was it?

He must have slept more because there was suddenly a clang and a man's silhouette against the open door. Dusk? Dawn? The man handed him a can of curry and rice.

Pierre made some gestures: "Eat outside?" The man shrugged and let Pierre pass.

"Not run, Mister."

The air was cool and salty, and there were flashes of brightness on the dark rushing waters. He could make out the smudge of coastline and the lights of a ship perhaps a mile away. The fading light told him the curry was dinner, not breakfast. The ship was slowing.

Another crewman appeared with a food canister, squeezed past them and slid the bolt on a door five yards further along. A man stumbled out of the cabin, brushed the crewman aside and dry-retched over the side.

"No food?" the crewman said.

"No bloody food, you stupid wog," the man said. He was fortyish, English.

Wogs, we're all wogs to them, Pierre thought. The man caught Pierre's eye. They stared at one another for a moment. The door slammed shut.

The sound of a high-pitched motor cut across the rumble of the ship's engines. A crewman tossed a rope ladder over the side. There were shouts and torch flashes. The Danish master came down from the bridge, looked at Pierre and jerked his head towards the ladder. Men in combat uniforms reached up from an inflatable dinghy to help Pierre down the ladder. He collapsed into the well of the boat. The motor roared and they were charging across the sea towards a pitching naval vessel, with the *Warda* fading into the night.

"Blindfold him," one of the men said in the barbarous Arabic the Libyans spoke. Strong arms pinned him into a sitting position and a mask was pulled over his eyes.

"No harm meant, brother," somebody said. "It's for your own good."

***

The farmhouse was closed up when Emma dragged her feet along the gravel pathway late in the afternoon, but a line of washing told her that her parents would be back. She'd changed a few of Stephanie's francs at a kiosk in Valletta to cover her bus fare and the ferry ride to Gozo. Despite Zouzou's warning, where else could she go? She'd run out of choices.

The spare key was under a pot of geraniums set into a niche in the wall.

"Miss Emma."

Shit. It was Mr Buttigieg.

"Your parents did not mention that you were expected." He let the comment hang. "Mrs Buttigieg will be delighted to invite you for a glass of lemonade."

"Lovely. We'll catch up." She clenched her teeth and worked the lock in the heavy front door. Mr Buttigieg gave up and crunched back to his garden.

The old house enveloped her in a sense of belonging as she prowled the rooms: The high-ceilinged sitting room with the saggy paisley sofa; her father's books on a funny old coffee table made from driftwood; her mother's faint perfume in the big bedroom. She made a snack from *gbejniet* and tomatoes and washed it down with a can of lager. The bed was made up in her old room. She pottered around, picking up familiar things left behind after her last visit. A *Rolling Stone* magazine with Crosby, Stills, Nash and Young on the cover, a stupid Moroccan leather bag that had stained her white Levis blue, a clay statue of Venus she'd made in Art at school. The bed beckoned. She lay down and drifted in and out of sleep until she heard the Mini pull up outside below her open window.

"You are no doubt tickled pink to have Emma here for a holiday," boomed Mr Buttigieg from his garden path.

"Emma? No, Emma's not here." It was Mum. Then, "Oh my God, do excuse me," and she burst into the house and into Emma's arms.

***

They wept briefly in keeping with the conventions of their background. Susan dabbed her face and made tea. Questions tumbled over answers: We weren't expecting you: I just needed a break. What about college; a few weeks away from the books won't hurt. So lovely to see you. Is Daddy better now; back to his old self, really.

"Where *is* Daddy?"

"Gone to do some work."

"What work?"

"Oh, just something for the High Commission."

"When's he coming back?"

Susan fiddled with her teacup.

"Mummy, when's he coming back?"

Susan held her head in her hands.

"Darling, he's in the most awful trouble. I can't tell you what. He's been gone three days. But, you know Daddy - he's strong, he'll be fine."

"It's this Libya business, is it?"

Susan stood rigid, her mouth open.

"Mummy, I know all about it. It was my fault."

Susan slumped into the old sofa and stared at the floor while Emma told her tale.

They took an hour to compare stories. Susan held nothing back, not even the fact that Ralph may have to kill somebody. When Emma confessed to stealing the pass and the file, she flung herself on the sofa and covered her face with her hair.

Susan kneaded her daughter's shoulders. "It was stupid, but you can't be blamed. Daddy tortured himself with this nonsense about you-know-what. It's inexcusable that he let you blame yourself - and that I didn't realise what was going on."

"Mummy, we're in terrible trouble. What are we going to do?"

Susan laughed in a loose, panicky way that Emma had never heard before. "You know, darling, I've spent years playing the Home Counties housewife. I was bored to death in that bloody grave of a house, but I stuck to my duty. I used to spend hours polishing the furniture and thinking about the BOAC days - hotels in glamorous places, cocktails and swimming pools, handsome pilots. Duty! Duty to my poor blackmailed husband. Duty to my class, duty to my ordained role as a subservient woman. Oh, yes, you're surprised. You should see your face! But I read all your books - the feminist ones."

"Why didn't you tell me? We could have talked, made some sense of each other's feelings."

"Perhaps, Emma, but it's not what we do, is it? We're English. And what was I supposed to do? Announce to Daddy over the Sunday roast that I'd burned my bra?"

"I hate being English sometimes."

"Shall I tell you something, Emma? I hate it nearly all the time."

A silence fell between them.

"Emma, your friend in the hospital. What will happen to her?"

"Zouzou? I don't know. I'm worried sick about her."

Susan got up and took a telephone directory from the bookshelf.

"Yes, here it is." She dialled a number.

"Hello. This is Mrs Shields from the British High Commission. Please put me through to the director of the hospital immediately."

Emma sprang from the chair and stood close to her mother, her ear to the receiver.

There was a series of clicks and then a man's voice. "This is Mr Caruana. Mrs Shields, how can I help you?"

"Am I speaking to the hospital director?"

"I regret to say that the director is on leave. I am acting in his stead."

"Well, you'll have to do. We believe one of our citizens may have been admitted to the hospital earlier today. We understand that she may have been assaulted and had her passport stolen. Our office is preparing an emergency travel document so that we can fly her home tomorrow if she is well enough. Can you please check whether she is at the hospital?"

"And the patient's name?"

Susan put her hand over the receiver, and Emma whispered, "Aziza Faris". Her mother repeated the name. Would Zouzou have eventually given them her name, or come out with some nonsense?

"A British citizen, you say, Mrs Shields?"

Emma held her breath as Susan coolly said, "Just between us, the person I speak of is the distinguished British-Pakistani author Aziza Faris. She is on a lecture tour with the British Council."

A moment's hesitation. "Of course, Mrs Shields. Please hold the line."

"Mummy, who is Mrs Shields? And what's this distinguished author business?"

"Haven't a clue, darling. But he swallowed it. Probably hopes he'll get on the High Commission garden party list. Now you said your friend was play-acting."

"Yes, groaning and raving. Goodness knows what tale she spun them after I Ieft."

There were more clicks. Mr Caruana had returned.

"Mrs Shields, we have an unidentified patient who is to be discharged in the morning, but there are some difficulties of a bureaucratic nature. She does not seem to speak English."

Susan covered the phone. "What does she look like?"

"Thirties," Emma whispered, "Voluptuous, olive skin, dark eyes."

"Mr Caruana. She is a well-built youngish lady of the Mediterranean type, and she is suffering from amnesia."

"Mrs Shields, might I ask what post you occupy at the High Commission?"

"I'm afraid that is confidential, but I should stress that His Excellency is keen to have this situation resolved as soon as possible. I will be at the hospital first thing tomorrow to sign the relevant paperwork."

"Under the circumstances, you are assured of the discretion of myself and the entire establishment, Mrs Shields."

"You are a treasure, Mr Caruana. His Excellency will be informed of your cooperation."

Mr Caruana made some noises that sounded like a cat licking cream from his chops. Susan put the phone down.

"Time for a drink."

**

Emma watched her mother grapple the wheel of the Mini as they bumped onto the roll-on roll-off ramp. She barely recognised the Susan Stonehouse she thought she knew. Her mother was tough, resourceful, courageous. Why hadn't she noticed? But, then why hadn't Susan tried to break through the wall between them? Why couldn't she have just bloody well opened up? But she had opened up in her own Susan Stonehouse way: The Family Planning leaflet, letting Emma hitch back to England. The more she thought, the more she recalled faint signals, little gestures. Stupid bloody Emma had been too self-absorbed to appreciate them.

They parked the Mini in Floriana half a mile from the hospital, and took a taxi. Emma waited outside with the driver.

Susan and Zouzou emerged after ten minutes, trailed by a middle-aged man in a double-breasted suit and bow tie. The Egyptian woman was gesticulating and declaiming while the man nodded, apparently in admiration or perhaps awe. She could sell the Pyramids to the Pope, Emma thought.

"I will speak of the wonderful hospitality of Malta in my next interview for *Paris Match*, your Lordship," Zouzou said, as Susan shoved her into the back seat of the taxi.

When they returned to the Mini, Susan turned on the ignition, made to put the car in gear, but suddenly slumped over the wheel. Her body shook with silent sobs. "Ralph, Ralph, where are you, for God's sake?" she murmured.

Zouzou leaned from the back seat and massaged her shoulders, saying something soothing in Arabic. Emma

197

waited and said nothing. Her mother's mood would quickly be concealed under a bright smile. It was their way.

Within the hour, they were back on Gozo and heading for the farmhouse.

"Emma, when we get there, you divert Mr Buttigieg, and I'll sneak Zouzou in through the side gate."

***

"Bloody wogs." Ralph curled up on the bunk. The seasickness was even worse now the ship had stopped to disembark the so-called Cornelius Lamine - yes, it had to be him. Two days of hell. A wave of nausea rippled from his guts through his chest and up to his throat, triggering a throat-ripping spasm. Nothing left to spew.

Bastard Mills. Lieutenant bloody smart-arse bastard Mills. You don't have a lot of choice, he'd said at the second visit to the hospital. We've got your daughter. No need to tell the missus. There's an ambulance outside to take you to the seaside for a boat ride. Come on, on your toes.

Ralph combed his sluggish brain for the details of the plan he'd meticulously constructed in the two years before he'd lost the file. Against all standards of professional courtesy, someone had decided to activate Operation Aqua without consulting him.

Yes, he remembered the drill: The *Warda* would soon crawl westwards at three to four knots - hugging the Libyan coast as far as the border with Tunisia, and then turning north. It would then make a slow clockwise circle to return to Tripoli twelve hours later. The circuit would be repeated until the Libyan port authorities signalled the master that the entirely hypothetical Cornelius Lamine was ready to rendezvous. The Libyans would transfer Lamine and the arms shipment to the *Warda*, which would head north to rendezvous with a yacht off Malta - a yacht carrying Donald Waters and a bunch of IRA impersonators. A Royal Navy patrol boat would catch them in the act of loading up the weapons. The whole gang would be arrested and taken to Malta. From there, the fake IRA men would slip across to Sicily.

All fine. Except that someone had changed the plan so that yours bloody truly Ralph Stonehouse was on the *Warda* with instruction to knock Waters off.

The boat stopped wallowing. The engines increased speed and they were moving.

Chapter Fourteen

Familiar sights assailed Pierre on the drive from the port into the centre of Tripoli: Palm trees, men in military uniforms, a shrouded woman hurrying into the shade of a doorway, white Italianate buildings. The cars were newer than in Egypt, the traffic lighter, and everywhere there were huge portraits of their beloved Colonel with his unhinged donkey stare. The sound of sirens was deafening; no wonder, the big American car being in the middle of a wailing convoy of ten or twelve jeeps and small trucks.

Pierre's stomach curdled at the thought of coming face to face with Gaddafi. He couldn't do it, even with the aliases and disguises that were the tools of his old trade as a private investigator in Cairo: Pierre, the man known as Boutros to his Coptic relatives and Bedros to his Armenian family. The man known as Pierre to those with no business to know him better; let them puzzle over his origins and his frenchified name.

But play charades with Gaddafi? God help him.

"Not far now," the man on his left said. Ali, he'd introduced himself as. Private Secretary, Revolutionary Protocol Department, not that such a title meant anything to Pierre. Ali was nervously courteous, trying out a few honorifics - 'Your Excellency', 'Your

Eminence', before settling on 'Professor Cornelius'. He chain-smoked in the big American car, ignoring the irritated huffing of the military man on Pierre's right. This one wore aviator glasses and a peaked cap weighed down with half a kilo of scrambled egg. Pierre couldn't work out his rank. If Gaddafi was a Colonel, did that mean nobody else could be higher than a major? Did they have generals and brigadiers? Whatever this fellow was, he wasn't important enough to tell Ali to put his cigarette out.

The car glided along the Corniche with the blue of the Mediterranean to one side and a parade of modern blocks on the landward side. They turned off into a knot of ornate Italianate buildings. "*Place d'Algérie*," Ali said with pride, as if he'd built it himself. The donkey-face portrait stared out towards the desert from rippling banners.

"All Libyans in our *jamahiriyah* are enjoying housing and cars and higher education since the Guide smashed the Western oil monopoly," Ali said through a blanket of cigarette smoke.

Jamahiriyah? Pierre had seen this newly mangled word before - Gaddafi's coinage to convey the idea that the masses ruled Libya. It would mean something like 'crowdocracy' in English, he supposed. And Gaddafi himself was merely the 'Guide', helping the crowds along.

They stopped outside a modern building of astounding ugliness. It was as if a giant laundry rack had been welded to a biscuit tin. The convoy turned off into a parking area. Inside the building, Pierre was led past an empty marble reception area to a suite of luxurious rooms.

"We will call you in the morning for your meeting, Professor. Ring if you need anything," Ali said. The door lock clicked decisively as he left. Pierre flopped on the bed, got up, prowled the suite, tried the bathroom taps, looked out of the window into an internal yard full of parked cars, all new and shiny. He was hungry. He picked up the phone.

"Hello, I'd like some food."

"What do you want, Sir?" A male voice, rural-sounding but polite.

"What do you have?"

"Everything, Sir."

"A grilled lamb cutlet. And a green salad."

"Is that all, Sir?"

Pierre hesitated. Cornelius Lamine was supposedly partial to liquor. But this was Muslim Libya. Would Lamine assert his indifference to religion by ordering alcohol?

"A glass of wine. French. Your best, please."

"At your service, Sir."

There were packets of cigarettes in every room: Kools, Benson and Hedges, Lucky Strike. A smoker's feast. And whiskey. Johnny Walker Black Label, a bottle on the buffet, another by the enormous bed.

Pierre lay back on the silk pillow with a stiff drink and a Lucky Strike. Luxury in the midst of hell; Gaddafi's reputation for cruelty and capriciousness was well-known among the Edgware Road Arabs.

Zouzou floated into his thoughts, but the agony of separation was too sharp. He pushed her aside. Plenty of time for Zouzou when he'd escaped from this nightmare. A son, even a daughter, America, golden days ahead. But now Gaddafi.

"Room service." The door clicked and a an anxious-looking man in a red fez wheeled in a trolley. He skillfully served the cutlet and vegetables, placed a vast napkin on Pierre's lap, and stood to attention.

"And the wine?"

The waiter looked twitchy. A good Muslim this fellow, obviously hoping he could leave the handling of the liquor to the infidel. He made a move to the offending object, found a corkscrew in his pocket, and gave the bottle a good shake.

"Never mind, brother. Leave me the corkscrew."

The label said, *Château d'Yquem 1937*. Pierre took a mouthful of the lamb and raised the glass of Sauternes to his lips.

The door flew open. It was Ali, red-faced and sweating.

"Professor, the Guide has arrived from the desert. He will see you at Bab El-Aziziya now. Please, you will feast later."

The convoy had reformed outside the building. Now, Pierre was squeezed between Ali and a bearded man in a woolen robe, a white headscarf and soft leather pointy slippers. He swallowed the last morsel of his first forkful of lamb. The glorious bouquet of the wine was a whisp of memory.

Dusk was falling. The convoy moved off, shrieking its way through the suburbs. After a few kilometres, a vast wall loomed in the night. Great watchtowers and thick cables lined the parapets. Beyond the wall there could be seen floodlit buildings. The sound of a marching band floated in the night air, and then rifle shots. They drove for a kilometre or more alongside the wall as far as a gate manned by armed soldiers. The car stopped for a brace of camels led by two melancholy-looking robed men. One of them caught his eye. What message was in that look? Dante's words came to Pierre's mind - he'd read the English translation of *The Inferno* as a teenager - 'abandon hope all ye who enter here'.

The convoy peeled off, and the American car approached the gates, where it was subjected to an elaborate security check - a mirror on a pole to inspect the underside, strong lights shone into glove boxes, tapping things under the hood. Pierre was ordered out. Torches were trained on his face, papers consulted, phone calls made. At last they were allowed to drive into what appeared to be a walled town with a floodlit football field, villas, bunkers, a parked helicopter. Ali pointed at another checkpoint.

"We will stop here and walk to the *khaymah*". *Khaymah*? A tent? But yes, everyone knew that Gaddafi lived in a Bedouin tent.

The American car drove off leaving Ali, the robed man and Pierre at a black and yellow striped barrier, guarded by four young African women with glossy lips and bursting military blouses.

"You see, Professor Cornelius, how the revolution has liberated our sisters," Ali said. He didn't sound convinced.

The man in the robe snorted and pushed past the women, muttering something that sounded like "whores".

"Who's he?" Pierre asked.

Ali ignored him.

"How come he goes about as he pleases?"

"He is a cousin or uncle of the Guide, I'm not absolutely sure. But see, we will approach the tent." The African women shrugged and got out their lipsticks.

Before them was a paddock, lit on the perimeter by floodlights. A complex of three or four tents lay at its centre outside the wash of electric light. A group of men, some in suits, some in uniform, hung about in the dim light coming from the entrance of the largest tent. Pierre tripped on something - a thick cable that snaked through the paddock to the tent, from which came the unmistakable sound of an air conditioner.

A uniformed man broke away from the group and beckoned to Ali, who trotted over. There was some gesticulating, briefly raised voices. Ali came back, sweating and jittery.

"A thousand apologies, Professor Cornelius. The Guide is unavoidably detained for the next hour. You will rest in your quarters until I come for you. You will be provided with all the comforts you desire."

Pierre's quarters lay in the basement of a long concrete building within the walled compound of Bab El-Aziziya. It had massively thick walls, more of its structure below the ground than above. Bombproof? Nuclear attack-proof? Who could tell in this paranoid world? As he followed Ali through the neon-lit underground corridors, he could almost smell the stench of fear and suspicion. Corridors led off the main thoroughfare. From one he thought he heard a shout of pain, from another the giggling of women. Singing from behind one door - snatches of a revolutionary song. A large, armoured door slammed shut just as he caught a glimpse of some kind of communications centre with TV screens and racks of radio gear. He'd never suffered from claustrophobia, but the walls of this place stifled him - or was it perhaps the mingled aura of raw power and crushed hope that filled the air within?

His 'quarters' were less than luxurious: No windows, a scarifying air conditioner, and third-rate hotel furniture. The door was left unlocked, at least, but there would be a guard or two posted outside. More whiskey bottles, more Lucky Strike cigarettes. Boxes of Toblerone. Pornographic video tapes.

Yes, now he remembered Cornelius Lamine's taste for whiskey from Ralph Stonehouse's file. In the hours before he'd been put on the plane to Malta, he'd refreshed his knowledge of the fake arms dealer's profile: Born in Casablanca in 1940 to a Rumanian mother and Jewish Moroccan father, both killed in a car accident when he was ten years old. The father's family had sent the orphaned boy to relatives in Cairo, where he attended St. Anthony's Anglican School in Heliopolis. He enrolled at Cairo University, but dropped out in his first year, disappearing from the official records. Johnny Walker, that was Cornelius Lamine's weakness, that and an unquenchable appetite for sexual violence. He operated in the shadows, arranging convoluted arms deals and assassinations with no allegiance to a particular group: A true freelance. Only one photograph of him was supposedly known. And there was so much more in the file. How in God's name had this stuffed shirt Ralph Stonehouse created such a phantom?

An hour passed, and another. A knock on the door. A waiter with a platter of fried chicken and buttery rice. More *Chateau d'Yquem '37*. Pierre took just half a glass: Sublime, but no refill. It wouldn't do to face the Guide tipsy.

By midnight, he was lolling with fatigue. The bed beckoned. He was cold. The throbbing aircon was stuck on 18 Celsius. He turned out the neon light, got under the bed covers fully clothed. Muzzy thoughts, drifting, jerking, drifting again, then blessed sleep, sweet sleep.

"Professor, if you please." Pierre juddered awake. A young woman's voice, hand tugging at his trouser zip. Damn Cornelius Lamine with his appetites. Damn this gift from the management. Dare he refuse? He rolled over towards the wall, made elephantine snoring sounds, muttered some nonsense and played dead.

There were two woman.

"I can't wake him."

"Thanks be to God. They say he likes to use a strap."

"Try waking him again. It's a strap here or a beating from Umm Yusuf back in our quarters."

"I'll take a slap from Umm Yusuf any day. And at least she doesn't have a *zubrah*."

"It might be a Christian *zubrah*. It's probably not circumcised."

"Ugh. Let's go."

The healing balm of sleep returned, punctuated by dreams of Captain Mills beating him with a swagger stick on a ship, and then he was searching for his old friend Fawzi in the City of the Dead in Cairo, but Zouzou was crying through the window of a London bus ...

***

Morning, he supposed. His watch said 6am, but who knew what time zone it thought it was in? There was silence in the bunker, just the shuffling of boots outside the room. A rim of neon light snapped on around the door jamb. A voice. Ali's voice.

"Is he awake?"

"Don't know, Sir."

"Rouse him. We leave for Sirte in ten minutes."

Pierre rolled off the bed in a fug, pissed and sloshed his face in the bathroom, smoothed his crumpled clothes. He'd slept in his shoes. His socks felt like somebody else's. Someone with bigger feet. A cigarette. A wedge of Toblerone. A swig of Johnny Walker Black. Eyes closed for a few seconds. A vision of Zouzou in their cosy bed in Camden Town.

There was no convoy this time, just a speeding Land Rover with the three of them perched up front: A taciturn army driver, Ali sweating and red, and Pierre jammed between the two. They drove an hour or two down the coast road to Misrata, stopping for coffee and ablutions at an army post outside town, where the driver swapped jokes in an impenetrable dialect with his cronies. The heat outside the airconditioned car wilted Pierre's soul. And then inland through scrubby desert by way of a dump of a town named Tawergha. After three hours they rejoined the coast road, and by early afternoon entered Sirte.

"This is the Guide's birthplace," Ali said. Pierre tried to look reverential.

"Is the Guide here in Sirte?" It didn't look much of a town - a dull waterfront and unremarkable concrete houses. Ali didn't answer, but conferred with the driver in some language Pierre could not identify. Berber, perhaps?

They left the dull town behind and fetched up at an airport. The road signs said 'Ghardabiya'. Ali and the driver wore grim faces. They passed through a checkpoint and pulled up at a concrete blockhouse. A deafening clatter rocked the Land Rover. A helicopter landed fifty yards away. When the miasma of grit and dried donkey shit had settled, the helicopter door opened. An African woman with a Kalashnikov stepped down, followed by a blonde nurse in crisp white. Then the Guide emerged in a brown woolen robe and a black pill-box hat. He appeared younger than his press photos suggested. The eyes were sharp and wily, the face handsome but with a feral aspect. Pierre stared: The man was part wolf, part donkey, terrifying in his naive viciousness. The Guide's party went into a tent by the blockhouse. Pierre was led inside, placed on a rug next to Ali, and given a glass of sticky red soda pop. Gaddafi had settled on a pile of cushions six feet from Pierre. The black eyes drilled into his skull.

A man stood behind the Guide. It was the military officer with the aviator glasses and scrambled egg hat. The nurse and the African woman stood to each side, completing a bizarre tableau.

"If you don't mind, we will confirm your *bona fides*, Professor Cornelius," the officer said.

"Go ahead."

"Where were you born?" the officer asked.

"Casablanca, May 10, 1940."

"Who was your best friend at school?"

"Atom Aghabegian."

"Where were you between June 1962 and January 1963?"

"Living incognito in Beirut, but with a journey to Aden in November 1962."

"Who was your lover in Damascus in 1964?"

"Ingrid Hofmeyer."

"How did she die?"

"Strangulation."

"With what?"

"I did it with a tartan tie."

"What gift did Abu Ammar give to you in Tunis?" Fine company Cornelius Lamine moved in - receiving a gift from Yasser Arafat!

"Abu Ammar gave me a revolver."

"What was your role in the 6 September 1970 hijacking in Jordan?"

"Trick question," Pierre said, "I had no role."

The questioning stopped. The military man had a whispered conversation with Gaddafi. Pierre's bowels swirled.

Gaddafi straightened up in his cushions. He thrust a hand into his robes and pulled out a letter.

"Professor, what do you think this letter says?" Gaddafi's Arabic was impeccable. Classical Arabic. Not the words of a donkey.

"I have so little wisdom, your Highness. Perhaps you will enlighten an ignorant wretch, if God wills."

"This, by God, is a letter from Harold Wilson, the Prime Minister of Great Britain. I received it just an hour ago. And call me Brother Guide. There are no Highnesses in Libya."

"If I may be permitted, Brother Guide, what does the letter say?"

"The letter begs Libya - among other things - to desist from our fraternal relationship with the fellow revolutionaries of the Irish Republican Army, in exchange for a bribe of fourteen million pounds."

The Guide swept a look around the company. Silence.

The military man twitched and made a pained sound. It was possibly a snigger. Ali ventured a laugh, and the various hangers-on in the tent joined in. Gaddafi guffawed, brandished Harold Wilson's letter, slid it back into his robe, and settled into his cushions. He waved a hand at Pierre. Back to business.

"Professor Cornelius," the army officer said. "The Guide is satisfied by your *bona fides*."

He's easily satisfied, Pierre thought. Anyone could have learned those answers.

"But," the military man said. "There is a final definitive test." The opposite tent flap opened. A figure was led in by a guard and shoved onto a chair in front of Pierre. His head was covered with a cloth bag. The guard placed a complicated-looking tool on the knees of the captive. Pierre had seen one of these when the carpenters repaired the roof in Camden Town. It was a nail gun.

The cloth bag was removed.

The man in the chair was Zlotnik.

Pierre stared at his old friend, the Soviet diplomat he'd shared dinners and intellectual conversation with in Cairo. Zlotnik, the man who had entangled Pierre in his plot to sell Sadat's war plans to the West to secure his defection to Britain. Zlotnik, who'd been betrayed - as they all had - by Dimashqi.

The man looked gaunt. The limpid eyes stared vacantly at Pierre without acknowledgment. But was there a secret spark in that stare, a faint signal of recognition?

"What is wrong with him?" Pierre asked.

The wraith in the chair mumbled something in Russian. Pierre strained his ears; he and Zlotnik had exchanged lessons in Russian and Arabic. Did the Libyan officer speak Russian? Did Gaddafi? Only if they'd been pilots, and trained to fly MiGs in Russia; the Soviets had never translated the manuals into Arabic.

Pierre's instinct told him they didn't know Russian. Would Zlotnik pass him a secret message?

Why was the man here? Pierre knew exactly: What did Zlotnik want more than anything else in the world? To defect to Britain, to finally give MI6 something big enough for them to take him in. Whatever happened next, it would be part of Zlotnik's quest.

The officer with the half-pound of scrambled egg spoke to Zlotnik in halting English.

"Do you recognise zis man?"

"I do. We met once in Cairo at the Estoril restaurant." Zlotnik spoke English like an American, the result of spending his teenage years in Washington DC.

Pierre's heart pumped fit to burst his chest. Sweat poured down his back, cooling to ice under the blast of the air conditioner. The Estoril - they dined there once a month to exchange gossip - who was snooping, who was handing out cash, who was new in town on the diplomatic circuit.

He was sunk. Zlotnik was about to denounce him. He looked up at Gaddafi, whose eyes were on the nail gun.

"What is zis man's name?" the officer asked.

Zlotnik stared at Pierre for a full unblinking minute, and then winked, so faintly that Pierre hardly believed he had observed it.

"That man is Cornelius Lamine."

***

The weapons were stored in a warehouse inside the Tripoli dockyard. Part of Cornelius Lamine's job was to check the goods before they were loaded onto the Libyan patrol boat, which would rendezvous with the *Warda*. Pierre waited while soldiers prised open wooden crates to reveal shoulder-operated anti-tank missiles, grenades, assault rifles, wads of plastic explosive.

"Try to look like a professional," the men in London had said. But how on earth did a professional arms dealer behave?

Pierre had an idea.

"All very nice," he said to the senior officer - the one who had interrogated him. "But I've seen some tricks in my time."

"Tricks? By God, there are no tricks here."

"Convince me that that these aren't scrap weapons being palmed off on my clients. How about those?" Pierre pointed at the rocket launchers.

"What?"

"Do they work?"

"Of course they work," the officer said.

"Really? Show me."

"You want to see one working?" The officer was somewhere between incredulity and rage.

"Yes."

"Alright, but not the RPG. Perhaps just a rifle. This isn't a suitable place to fire that damned thing," the man said, sweat pouring off his brow.

"The rocket launcher."

The soldiers looked at each other and at the officer. Pierre waited, whistled a little tune. The officer cocked his head at one of the soldiers, who hefted an anti-tank missile launcher from a crate. A Russian RPG7 - just a tube that fired a rocket, basically - Pierre had seen the pictures in Stonehouse's file.

"And the projectile."

The soldier took a green pointed missile from another crate and began to slide it into the launcher. He was trembling. Pierre watched how the thing was loaded.

"Careful, Abdullah, by God," one of his comrades said, ducking to his knees. The rest crouched down, the officer too. If the thing went off in this corner of the dockyard, there'd be a massacre.

Pierre waited a full minute while the paralysed soldier stood grasping the loaded weapon.

"That's enough, comrades," he said. "Put it away. Let's finish the count and get this stuff repacked."

The Libyan patrol boat waited six hours before leaving to meet the *Warda*, which was completing the last leg of a circuit heading south-east. At two in the morning the engines rumbled and the moorings were let loose. Pierre watched the shore lights fade to distant twinkling. He was suddenly exhausted, the steady flood of adrenalin diminishing with the distance between himself and the coast of Libya. New possibilities opened before him: Possibilities that only pertained to a person who was actually alive, a person who had miraculously survived the bizarre circus that was Gaddafi's Libya.

Pierre allowed himself a moment to consider the future beyond the current complexities.

Somehow he would be reunited with Zouzou in Malta.

Someone would inform him that he had discharged his responsibilities to Great Britain.

Somebody in some office would give them passports with fresh US visas stamped within.

A lot of *somehows* and *someones*. A lot of *woulds*.

"Brother, half an hour till we rendezvous." It was the patrol boat captain, who had come down on deck. He offered Pierre a cigarette and they smoked in silence.

"How did you enjoy your stay in our *gamahiriyah*?" The captain had an Egyptian accent - saying 'g' for 'j'. It took Pierre back to the old worn streets of Cairo, his city, the city where he knew every alley, where he had an informer in every café, where he was owed favours by people in high places with secrets.

"Thanks be to God, you have honoured us, brother," Pierre said, using the customary polite formula.

"The honour is ours."

"You're Egyptian, yes?" Pierre asked.

"Yes, I married a Libyan woman and came here to work for the revolution. You sound like a Cairene, brother."

"Yes, I lived in Bab El-Louq," Pierre answered.

"By God, I'm from there too. Where did you live?"

"Huda Sha'rawi Street."

"What a coincidence! I lived in Muhammad Mahmoud Street, just around the corner. What's your family name?"

Pierre gulped. Fool! Smoke with a man and let your guard down! He made a grimace, forced a conspiratorial chuckle.

"Top-secret, brother. In my line of business, we keep a low profile. The revolution has too many enemies."

"A thousand apologies, brother. God be with you." The captain headed to the bridge, leaving Pierre to curse his carelessness. Cornelius Lamine, that's who he was for next day or two. Forget Pierre Farag.

The lights of the *Warda* twinkled up ahead. The patrol boat slowed and manoeuvred gingerly alongside. Curses, engines thrusting, black water boiling between the chafing hulls. Dark figures on the deck of the *Warda* winched the crates onboard. A rope ladder was slung down, and Pierre scrambled up. The Libyan patrol boat slipped away into the darkness.

Chapter Fifteen

On the third day after Cornelius Lamine departed the *Warda*, Ralph woke from a nap with tortured thoughts of Emma and Susan - Emma in the hands of that lout Mills, Susan probably in the same boat by now. What a bloody mess he'd made of their lives. He'd make things good somehow, anyhow. Then Ralph Stonehouse did something he'd never done in his life: He opened his mouth and screamed until his throat was raw.

The effect was extraordinary: His brain buzzed, his eyes cleared, the dull colours of the filthy cabin leapt into bright focus. Ralph was strong, Ralph Stonehouse was a man who could - well, could do any bloody thing he had to.

It dawned on him that the seasickness had left him and he was ravenous. He bashed the cabin door with a chair, imagining Waters' face disintegrating into red pulp. An alarmed crewman brought a bowl of greasy curry, which he wolfed down.

His thoughts now turned to duty. It was something in your blood as an Englishman, he told himself: Duty above everything. True, Ralph had been a little deficient in the duty department of late - well, for a few years now with this blackmail nonsense. But with a supercharged mind, he had the means to think things through: Something wasn't right with Operation Aqua.

Right-ho. Quick mental summary to refresh how Operation Aqua was supposed to work: 'Cornelius Lamine', a fictitious arms dealer, would approach the Libyans with a request from the IRA for a shipment of Soviet-made weapons. The enigmatic Lamine's fake credentials were to be unimpeachable; Lamine would never meet the Libyans directly during the negotiations, and the Libyans would never directly contact the 'IRA'.

Somebody hired to play the part of Lamine would travel by coastal freighter from Malta to moor off Tripoli, the main port city of Libya. Lamine would be transferred to a Libyan naval vessel and taken to onshore. There he would personally oversee the receipt of the arms and their transfer to the freighter. The freighter would then steam north to rendezvous off Malta with a yacht manned by British agents impersonating IRA personnel.

Meanwhile, Waters would receive a message appearing to be from his Soviet handler, telling him he was about to be exposed; he must travel immediately to Naples, where he was to join a yacht that would take him to Tripoli; from there, he would be flown to Moscow to join his girlfriend.

But the yacht would rendezvous with the coastal freighter off Malta, the arms would be were transferred to the yacht. Shortly after, a Royal Navy patrol boat would intercept it and arrest Waters and the fake IRA men.

Ralph Stonehouse gave himself a modest mental pat on the back.

But there were questions. He had neither pen nor paper, so he set out a mental list of issues that needed answers:

1. Why had Operation Aqua been modified so that he, Ralph Stonehouse, was now an active player?

2. Why was he being held captive with his daughter as hostage?

3. Who was the man playing the part of Cornelius Lamine, and could he be trusted?

4. Since the plan had one modification so far, could there be others?

Even though he had no conclusive answers to any of the questions, he thought it prudent to adopt the working hypothesis that Operation Aqua had somehow been compromised. If that was the case, his duty was to get it back on track.

Jolly good, then. He had the framework, next he needed an action plan. But as he pondered his options, an Indonesian crewman wrenched open the cabin door, yelling, "Mister, come. Kapten *sakit.*" Ralph ran after the man. It was mid-afternoon. The sun was hot, but a stiff breeze dried the sweat on his shirt.

"Kapten *sakit.*" Whatever *sakit* meant, it must be serious.

It was serious. Bloody serious all right. The master lay on his back. One side of his face was limp, the mouth drawn down. An Asian man in shorts stood at the wheel, staring at the waves and saying *The Lord's Prayer* in English. A heavy crucifix swung from his neck. He must be the Filipino mate. At least someone was driving the damn boat.

Ralph clicked back to the master. Stroke, got to be. Check his speech, movement. The old St. John's Ambulance training clicked in.

"What's your name, Sir?"

"Hrmmnph."

"Try to grasp my hands." The man's left hand floated up, wavered, dropped.

"Do you have any pain?"

"Hrmngg." A deep frown, the left hand pointed to his head. Definitely a stroke. But hang on, what was next? Ah yes - was the airway clear? He didn't fancy feeling inside the master's mouth, but was saved the ordeal when the man coughed up a clot of chewed meat. His mind ticked off the next step: Into recovery position. He rolled the master onto his side. Last thing - dial 999. On a boat, that would be Mayday, he supposed. But where the hell were they? And who was in charge?

Ralph had an idea. A bloody bonkers idea really, but why not? He addressed the dribbling man.

"Sir, you are incapacitated. As a senior civil servant of the British Crown, I assume command."

"Hrmnnphng." The master's good hand pointed shakily at Ralph. His cap had fallen off, and Ralph stuck it on his own head.

"D'you hear that?" he said to the Filipino at the wheel. "Me boss now." The man broke off his prayers to say, "OK, Boss."

Ralph hoped to hell the Filipino knew how to navigate this tub.

"Where are we going?"

"Stop two miles off Tripoli. Pick up cargo. Then go north to discharge cargo off Malta."

That was something. Everything to plan, and the mate speaks English. Hopefully, this Lamine fellow would have the goods.

"You know how to navigate?"

"Got my certificate, good navigator."

"What about the engines?" Ralph was moving rapidly out of his depth here. He knew that a ship had to have someone to get it from A to B, and to keep the engines going. Beyond that it was guesswork. He'd glossed over the details of the coastal freighter in Operation Aqua.

"Indonesian fellow, he's the engineer."

"OK. Radio?"

"My job. Got proper certificate."

"What's our course?" Ralph asked. It popped out like a line from a film.

"Due south, eight knots. We gonna bear south-west in ten minutes. Destination in one hour, Boss."

"What's your name?"

"Joseph."

"Very good. Carry on, Joseph."

The master was asleep, now snoring roughly. Ralph took a jacket from a peg and rolled it into a pillow for the man's head. He was damned if he was going to get Joseph to put out a Mayday call. The Libyans could take the sick man off at the rendezvous.

Ralph needed to get familiar with his surroundings quickly. He hurtled down a steel ladder into the crew's quarters - a short smelly gallery of bunkbeds garlanded with vests and caps and kitbags. A pile of greasy cinema magazines sat on a shelf under bars of soap and packets of dried noodles. Beyond the crew's gallery was a closed door - the master's cabin. Inside, it stank of tobacco and unwashed clothes. A photograph of a portly woman and two apple-cheeked boys was pinned to the wall. An open book on a tiny wooden desk showed log entries in Danish. The desk had a drawer. Ralph looked around for a tool of some kind: A tin opener with a rusted spike. The drawer gave way easily. There was a revolver inside. Ralph pocketed it. Ammunition? No time to check - he'd take his chance. Washhouse next - ugh, you'd come out dirtier than when you went in. Lastly, the stomach-heaving lavatory.

Next, he made his way to the engine room. An Indonesian crewman approached him, frowning.

"Boss *sakit*. Me boss now." Ralph pointed at his cap.

The frown changed to a grin. "OK, Boss."

The engine room was hot as a furnace. It stank of fuel. A filthy man in underpants sat gazing at his charge - a giant diesel engine throbbing on its mountings. He looked up and saluted Ralph. Must be the hat. We probably all look the same to these buggers.

That was about it: Bridge, cabins, engine room, and a hold somewhere below. Back to the deck.

The *Warda* was slowing; the mate must be closing in on the location where Lamine would return with the arms. Yes, there was a naval boat just fifty yards away in the gathering dusk. It was a similar size to the *Warda* but obviously built for speed. Ralph called to two crewmen smoking in the shadows.

"Hey, boat come. You help." The men saw the nearby boat, conversed rapidly in whatever they spoke in Indonesia, and beckoned Ralph to follow to a small crane near the stern. One of them scrambled up to the controls and switched the motor on. A stubby arm swung out over the side of the boat. They'd evidently been briefed to receive the cargo.

The naval boat was manoeuvring to come alongside. Joseph was holding the *Warda* steady. Suddenly the boat loomed very close. Ralph saw the bow bearing the number P514, a wicked-looking cannon, armed sailors. Men shouted, hooks swung, cable hummed on the drum of the crane, and four crates wobbled and swayed, one by one, until they lay in an untidy heap on the deck of the *Warda*. Transfer the master? Fat chance in the midst of this bloody bunfight. Last of all, the imposter flopped over the rail, rolled over and ended up at Ralph's feet staring into the barrel of the revolver.

"Cornelius Lamine, I presume?"

"You presume correctly, Sir," the man said.

"That's a most interesting presumption since I'm the one who invented Cornelius Lamine, so by all the laws of the universe you can't be him. What's your real name? And don't say James flipping Bond."

The patrol boat blasted into the dusk, and the *Warda*'s engines rumbled into action. The boat heeled to the right. Joseph had set course for Malta.

"Sir, my name is Pierre Farag, and you must be Mr Ralph Stonehouse."

"How do you know who I am? Give me one good reason why I shouldn't chuck you overboard?"

"The reason is," the imposter said, "your daughter Emma".

"What do you know of my daughter, you bastard?"

"I was with her a week ago in London. She gave me your file."

"Get up." Ralph waved the revolver at him. "Go on, head for the bridge. I'm right behind you." The imposter started up the steel staircase, but tripped. Ralph stumbled over him, the gun waving in every direction as he tried to regain his balance.

"Is the safety on, Mr Stonehouse? I'd rather get up those steps alive."

"Of course it's bloody on." Cheeky sod. He looked down at the gun. Where the hell was the safety anyway? "Just move yourself."

Inside the bridge, the master was slumbering on the floor. Joseph was apparently in full control of the boat.

"Sit down and talk. Now. What do you know about my daughter?

Farag looked around the cabin and back to Ralph.

"You know, Mr Ralph, that we are on the same side."

"Cut it out and start talking."

Chapter Sixteen

The three women waited silently in the main bedroom of the farmhouse until darkness came. Next door, Mr and Mrs Buttigieg bustled on their terrace, the husband supervising the roasting of fragrant meats, the wife chopping vegetables and chatting in Maltese.

"They'll be in bed by ten," Emma whispered. Zouzou dozed in the crook of her arm. Susan lay on the other side of the big bed, with the Egyptian woman curled between her and her daughter.

"Is she asleep?"

"Yes, she can sleep at will." Emma stroked Zouzou's hair. "She calls me *oukhti.*"

"What's that?"

"'Sister', it means 'sister'. Funny, really. I love her like a sister, but I hardly know her," Emma whispered.

"Poor lady. Tell me about her, Emma."

"That's what's even funnier. I just know what she told me in those hours on the ship. She was a film star in Egypt. Men found her very sexy, she said, and women hated her."

"You told me you met her husband."

"Pierre, yes, just for a few minutes. A little man, nothing special - you wouldn't notice him if he walked past you. But there's something intense about him when he speaks to you - something intense, God knows, I can't find the word. And together, him and Zouzou, it's as if they're in a weird bubble of their own ..."

"Emma, what's happened to you? You've changed, I'm seeing an Emma I don't know."

She leaned across Zouzou and kissed her mother's brow. "Changed, yes, Mum, something changed me."

Susan was right. The day of madness when she stole the file, the acid trip at Southwark Cathedral, the turquoise-trailing early morning after, the kindness of the old taxi driver in the checked hat. The moment with Solange in the restaurant when Emma had seen Susan Stonehouse in herself. She'd surely passed through a door, no a dozen doors in a few weeks.

She dozed for a while, replayed the scenes of her recent life, arranged them, shuffled them, wondered what next, didn't care much except for the warmth of Zouzou's body and her mother's perfume.

They must have all slept. Emma woke when Zouzou crawled over her to find the lavatory.

"It's two in the morning," Susan said.

"Are you all right?" Emma asked Zouzou when she came back.

"My body is healing, sister, but I cannot speak for my soul."

"I'm sure we're all feeling rather knocked about," Susan said. "But we've had a nice nap and it's time to buck up and make some decisions."

Emma smiled in the dark. Susan Stonehouse, at her finest in a crisis. She had delivered a baby between London and Cape Town in her BOAC days: "I told the lady to buck up and get on with what nature intended," she'd said.

"We must speak to the authorities," Susan said.

"No," Emma and Zouzou said in unison.

"Mum, there's nobody we can trust in Malta. We can't stay here. We need to hide somewhere and then try to contact someone in England. I don't know who."

"Daddy's boss. The Old Man they call him. Sir something Mountjoy, I think."

"Mum. Look at the facts. You told me how they set Daddy up as a nutcase, and now he's disappeared. Has anyone been in contact with you? No. And you've been too nervous to call the High Commission. And look at me and Zouzou - teeth knocked out, locked up on a stinking ship. We need to talk to someone at *The Guardian* or *Private Eye*, someone who'll kick up a fuss, find out what's going on."

Susan slumped on the bed in the darkness. "My poor husband. Where is he?"

"He's strong, Mum. He's resourceful. He'll turn up in a couple of days right as rain."

A wind rustled the grove of eucalyptus trees behind the house. A dog barked in the night, and a doggy friend barked back.

Zouzou spoke: "Mrs Susan, your husband is with my husband."

"What?"

"Yes, they are surely together."

"How do you know?" Emma hissed.

Zouzou lit a cigarette. "You English ladies have not the familiarity with wickedness and intrigue that I, a poor Egyptian woman who endured the sobriquet of 'the national bitch', has experienced," she intoned.

"Go on." Emma knew these stories could take some time.

"It is a question of deduction, a matter of weighing instinct against known facts."

"Zouzou, spit it out, where are they?" Susan's voice rose in irritation.

"Since you ask, Mrs Susan, they are on a ship sailing to Libya."

"The one we were on?" Emma asked.

"The one we were on as hostages, Emma, of course. We were there to secure the services of Pierre and your father."

"For God's sake, what do they want them for?" Susan asked.

"My husband Pierre is to play the part of Cornelius Lamine - the bogus arms dealer from the file. It is obvious to me now."

"And Dad, what part does he play?"

"He is ... *kabsh fida'* ... it means the boy sheep which is ransomed ..."

"Scapegoat?"

"Scapegoat, Emma, yes."

"The utter, unspeakable bastards," Susan said.

They sat in silence for a few minutes as the truth soaked in.

"But Zouzou, why didn't they track us down after we escaped from the Pig?"

"Because they are at sea now. We are no longer needed as security. We have played our parts."

"How do you know all this about hostages?" Susan asked.

"I played in *The Price of a Princess*. I was a rich and beautiful girl who had been paralysed in a skiing accident, and I was kidnapped by a criminal who needed a million dollars to pay for an operation for his granddaughter who had ..."

"Zouzou, we've got the message."

"Stephanie's house, that's where we should go," Emma said.

***

The first ferry of the day puffed out of Gozo as dawn came up. The three women lay quiet on sacks in the flat bed of Mr Buttigieg's cousin's lorry. A wall of vegetable crates lined the flat bed - capsicums, potatoes and tomatoes. A tarpaulin in the center covered the women, and a layer of dried seaweed was spread atop the canvas. Mountains of the stuff was washed up in storms on Gozo. It made terrific fertilizer after it had rotted. Emma eased her fingers under the tarpaulin to make a ventilation tunnel. The air under the tarpaulin stank.

Mr Buttigieg had been persuaded to help - even at 2.30am in vest and pyjama shorts.

"May I say," he announced on the doorstep, "that your appeal for neighbourly assistance does not come as a surprise. Put candidly, you are in the soup. My observations," - he produced a small notebook - "indicate that your residence has been under surveillance for the last thirty-six hours."

"My God, by whom? " Emma asked.

"Unsavoury fellows, no doubt. I spoke to my nephew at the police post just this morning, and there is now a watch on the ferry for troublemakers."

"And what does your nephew think?"

"He advances the hypothesis - or perhaps a mere suggestion - that they are foreign provocateurs of some kind. In the morning, he intends to raise a report for HQ in Valletta."

Zouzou spoke up. "Sir, they are Libyans, secret agents of the despicable Colonel Gaddafi. I will permit you into a confidence seeing that you are clearly a man of integrity and a patriot who deplores the incursion of the sword and crescent into this sacred Christian land."

Mr Buttigieg's chest swelled in his vest.

"Sir," Zouzou went on, "I am an Israeli counter-terrorism expert working with the British High Commission. Mr Ralph is on a secret mission to wrinkle out these villains ..."

"Winkle," Susan said.

"To winkle them out and to rid Malta of the scourge of the infidel. To cleanse these enchanted isles of ... "

Zouzou had a knack of cooking up this kind of high-octane nonsense. Mr Buttigieg was nodding sagely. Emma didn't know much about Maltese history, but she remembered her dad saying how touchy the Maltese were about the Arabs. Zouzou seemed to be hitting the spot. But she'd better shut up before it all blew up in her face.

"The lady is right. But can you help us, Mr Buttigieg? We have to get to Valletta to a, er ... safe house," Susan said.

Mr Buttigieg planted his sandals firmly on the flagstones and cast a searching look at the three women. Evidently convinced, he said, "Let me telephone my cousin. He has the ideal means of transportation."

"Isn't it a bit late?" Susan asked.

"Not at all. He will be loading his lorry as we speak."

***

At 2.45 am, Stephanie picked up the phone after the first ring. Led Zeppelin was up high in the background. "What a fucking blast, Emma! I'll leave the key under the mat. Hey, I'm gonna crash soon. Don't wake me up till lunchtime. Are you bringing the Egyptian goddess?"

"Yeah, and my mum too, so keep the you-know-what out of sight."

***

At Cirkewwa harbour on the main island, the vehicles in the lower deck started their engines. Emma choked on the fumes mixed with the rancid smell of rotten seaweed. She could make out her mother's face in the gloom under the tarpaulin; it was smudged with tears. Zouzou's foot nudged hers and she nudged back. The steel gates of the roll-on-roll-off ship ground open and they bumped onto the concrete ramp.

Mr Buttigieg's nephew pulled up at Stephanie's house within the hour. The three women scuttled up the side path. The key was under the mat and they let themselves into the spare room of the flat. Emma opened Stephanie's bedroom door a crack; her friend was fast asleep with a man wearing just his socks.

"Forget *The Guardian* and *Time Out*, Emma," Susan said when they'd rinsed out their reeking clothes. "The person we must telephone is Margaret Thatcher."

Chapter Seventeen

The man impersonating Cornelius Lamine talked. There was enough in his story for Ralph to piece together what Emma had done: Pierre Farag's search for a stolen briefcase, his wife Zouzou tracking down Emma and getting the file from her. His arrest at the café, Emma's escape from the police. It meant only one thing: The 'thin person' Mrs Littleproud had seen at the house was Emma. The 'why' could wait for later, but his bitter heart knew that he, Ralph Stonehouse, had been responsible in some way for whatever ghastly choices his beloved daughter had made.

Ralph stared at the little man's face. Perhaps they were on the same side. And how many damned sides were there? Two men on a rusty tub with four crates of deadly weapons. The only side they could be on was the one when they got onto dry land. He needed to know more of Farag's story. But first he had his duties as master of the *Warda*:

"Joseph," Ralph said to the Filipino at the helm. "How long till the next rendezvous?"

"Ten hours, Boss."

He turned to the imposter. "Now, you'd better explain how you got involved in this thing in the first place, and make it ruddy well convincing." He wiggled the gun around.

"Would you mind terribly if I made the revolver safe first?" Ralph hesitated. He was struck by something in Farag's expression: The man looked honest, somehow, or at least not dishonest. Ha - that would make a sodding change! He wasn't exactly threatening - a skinny little runt in a grubby linen suit. Well, why not? They both knew he wasn't going to shoot anybody. Ralph shrugged and handed the gun over. Pierre Farag took it, made some clicks, and handed it back with two loose bullets. Ralph shoved the gun in one pocket and the bullets in another.

As Farag related his story, the fog of confusion lifted - not to reveal a pretty vista, but an ugly truth - that Ealing had a sniff of Operation Aqua and had hired the man to find out more. The unremarkable Pierre Farag - you wouldn't give him a second look if he passed you in the street - told an extraordinary tale: His friendship with Zlotnik, the Russian who had slipped Ralph the evidence about Waters; his embroilment with Dimashqi, whose name had popped up when Ralph had tried to probe Waters' involvement in the cock-up in Egypt during the '73 war; and the deal Pierre had made with Waters to get himself and his girlfriend out of Egypt.

"Did you ever meet Mark Bellamy and Lucy Vickers?" These were the poor sods Waters had got packed off to Moscow from Cairo.

"I knew Mark Bellamy for a short time," Pierre said. "We became friends. He was an honest and brave man but he was out of his depth."

Ralph turned to the mate again. "Joseph. Time to rendezvous?"

"Nine and half hours, boss."

"What happened in Libya, Mr Farag?"

"I did my job, Mr Stonehouse." That was that, then.

Plenty of time to work out their next step. Yes, *their* next step; he was now sure that Pierre Farag was as much a dupe as he was, and that they had a common interest in getting out of this jam. But the story was still muddy. How much did Ealing know? Had they infiltrated the operation? Was Mills moonlighting for Ealing? Perhaps. If they'd subverted Aqua, what could that purpose be? To have it fail in order to discredit the Joint Intelligence Organisation, so that Marjorie Byers had a clear run in Middle East operations? No - ridiculous - she'd know from the file that Waters was a suspected Soviet agent. Start again. And who was the matinée idol Lieutenant Mills anyway? Ralph had never heard of the arrogant sod around the Cabinet Office. His head thumped. Trust? Duty? Bollocks!

Ralph addressed Pierre. "What is most important to you in the world, Mr Farag?"

"My wife of course, Mr Ralph." Ralph had heard this funny usage before among Arabs - given name after title. Made them sound like kids.

"Your wife. Not your country? Your duty?"

Pierre laughed. "My country? My duty? Unstiffen your British upper lip. My life has taught me that every man is his own master. The only country I have is the one on my bogus passport. My only duty is to survive for the sake of my wife and the child she is expecting."

Ralph said, "Where is your wife?"

"They have her in Malta, I presume. She was on this very boat when it was moored there. And Emma, your daughter? They have her too?"

"Yes, they have her. There's no doubt. She caught a ferry to Malta from Italy but she disappeared."

"Do you have a wife, Mr Ralph?"

"Yes, and they probably have her too. They are hostages."

"So what of duty, Mr Ralph?"

"Excuse my French, Mr Farag, but fuck duty."

"So, Mr Ralph, we are united in our purpose."

"Indeed. And how would you characterise our purpose?"

"It is, Mr Ralph, to fuck duty, to get off this fucking boat and to rescue our fucking womenfolk."

"Well yes, but easy on the f-word if you wouldn't mind, old chap."

"I apologise. I have never mastered the precise usage of that barbarous word."

***

Pierre's spell of national service had been an investment. Wasn't it a truism in life that even from adversity we learn? No experience was wasted, each nugget of knowledge was stored, each new idea tested and filed away. He'd been a radio operator during national service with the Egyptian Army: Two years of pointless, sweaty slog, long patrols into the desert regions, hours in the company of cow-faced village boys in scratchy uniforms. He was the lowly Corporal Pierre Farag, the man who went unnoticed, the man crouched over the radio, learning this and that, who was who, where they were next bound.

With his degree in English, he'd been sent for officer training but deliberately failed the exams by writing with his left hand. Officer? Lieutenant Farag? What did he want prancing about with a shiny belt, brass pips and responsibilities? Pierre Farag, the half-Armenian, half-Coptic master of many languages, hoarder of secrets, a man 'turned in on himself'?

But for now, he was faced with an alien maritime radio - a small grey set with a dial for the channels, a squelch button, and a handpiece with a SEND switch. Simple - nothing like the green Soviet-made monster he'd dragged on his back in his army days.

The plan he had devised with Mr Ralph was to find out who was at the other end of the line, to convince them that the *Warda* was *en route* to the rendezvous, and make a sudden break for Sicily. The Englishman claimed he knew Sicily like the back of his hand. They'd tell Joseph to pick up the Tunis ferry sea route off Marsala, slipping between the island of Favignana and Isola Grande till they reached Trapani. Somehow they'd get ashore at Trapani, where Mr Ralph would telephone the office of the Leader of the Opposition and alert them to what had happened. "Talk to someone with some bloody common sense," he'd said. "Margaret Thatcher'll put a firecracker under their backsides." Well, Pierre couldn't disagree with that; the magnificent Margaret was a lioness.

"Joseph, when do we make contact?"

"One hour before rendezvous, Mr Farag. Eight hours from now."

"Channel?"

"F for Freddy."

"Call sign?"

"We are *Warda*, they are *Evening Star*."

"Now, Mr Ralph. The gun and ammunition, if you please." Pierre had to be sure they could rely on the weapon in an emergency. He was sure that the Englishman knew next to nothing about firearms. Not that he, Pierre, was an expert. The last gun he had handled was an Israeli-made Beretta he'd received as part payment from a gangster client in Cairo. It lay hidden behind the skirting board in his aunt's boarding house.

This one was an old revolver, barely serviceable. He replaced the two bullets and tried to spin the chamber. From the brief weapons training he'd had in the army, he guessed the revolver was probably more dangerous to the person firing it than to the target.

"Perhaps I should look after it."

The Englishman nodded.

"Now, Mr Ralph, you say you might have to kill Donald Waters. Did they tell you how it was to be done?"

"No."

"Do you believe they ever really intended you to kill Waters?"

"Of course not. I wouldn't have a clue about killing a man."

"So what do they want, Mr Ralph?"

"This is my best guess, Mr Farag. You and I heading for a rendezvous with a British warship and twenty years in jail for gun running."

"But you are a senior Civil Servant. How could you be a gun runner and an assassin to boot?"

"Insurance, Mr Farag. There's a terrible stink about this story - a lost file, those poor buggers stuck in Moscow, a blackmailing double agent twenty minutes' drive from No.10. Do you know what my job really entailed? Plausible deniability - making sure that the Government didn't have to know about our dirty business in the Middle East. They don't just want Waters in jail. They want us locked up with him so we can't spill the beans."

"For myself - yes, I see that I am a mere pilchard in this sea of sharks," Pierre said. "But you, Mr Ralph, in your eminent position?"

"Ah, that's where you don't get it, Mr Farag. They don't trust me. I've let the team down. They'll say I'm a Soviet agent, I suppose. After all, I met with Zlotnik in a field in Berkshire. The Russians could have been cultivating me for years. This arms-running job would be my last hurrah before I defect to Moscow. It's madness, I know."

"I have seen worse madness, my friend. But your lamentable story could hold water. After all, you are in league with the mysterious arms dealer Cornelius Lamine, who has just been hob-nobbing with Libyans. And your daughter, if I may be so bold, is a young radical who you must have employed to get the file to Great Britain's enemies, thus diverting suspicion from yourself."

"Of course. And I arranged to have myself beaten up in my own house."

"A fine pair we are, Mr Ralph."

A bank of clouds obscured the moon and a brief splatter of rain sprayed the windows of the bridge.

"Joseph, how long?" Pierre called out. He wound his watch and set it, indicating to the Englishman to do the same.

"Seven hours, Mr Farag. Radio contact in six hours."

"Joseph, listen carefully."

"Listening good, Mr Farag."

"One hour before the rendezvous, we change course."

"What course, Mr Farag?"

"North-west for Sicily."

"Where we going in Sicily?"

"Trapani."

"OK, Mr Farag."

"You're sure you know how to get there, Joseph?"

"No problem. Nice harbour at Trapani. Eight metres deep."

"Do you know what our cargo is, Joseph?"

"I don't ask, Mr Farag. Maybe washing machines?"

"We need to get some sleep," the Englishman said. "We'll take the master's cabin. One sleeps for an hour, the other on watch outside." He turned to the mate. "Joseph, we'll be outside for a while. Watch over the master."

"OK, Boss."

They headed towards the sleeping quarters, but Pierre took them to the stack of contraband on the deck first. The crate containing the RPGs had split open during the unloading. Between them, they prised it off.

"Mr Ralph, we will borrow a rocket propelled grenade for protection." He hefted the launcher on his shoulder and handed one of the projectiles to the Englishman. Down in the sleeping quarters Pierre insisted the Englishman slept first. The man was dead on his feet, but adamant in his foolish British way that Pierre should take the first watch.

"If you insist, Mr Ralph, but take the revolver. Sit at the top of the steps there. One hour and you must wake me."

Pierre placed the RPG on the floor and flopped onto the bunk. He was instantly asleep.

***

A hand was shaking his shoulder. He turned back to Zouzou, who dissolved. His late mother was weeping as his father, terribly burnt, crawled along an alley towards him. The voice in his ear was frantic, English. Pierre reached out to touch his father, but his knuckles cracked on something hard - the bunkbed frame - and then Ralph Stonehouse was shouting in his face.

"We've been boarded, for God's sake."

Pierre leapt out of the bunk. It was three hours too early for the rendezvous. He grabbed the RPG launcher. The image of the soldier loading the projectile in Tripoli replayed itself- nothing wasted, every memory like money in the bank. He calmly loaded the projectile with its pineapple-shaped warhead on the end of the shaft. The deadly thing sat snug.

"Where are they, Mr Ralph?"

"At the top of the steps. I fired a shot and they stayed put."

Pierre edged around the cabin door, holding the RPG in front of him.

"Who are you?"

Silence. These were supposed to be the fake IRA men. Wouldn't they identify themselves? Something was wrong.

"I've got an RPG. Tell me who you are or this boat goes up in flames."

Silence.

And then a voice. "No need for that my friend. We all want to get out of this alive."

Irish! Pierre knew the accent. He'd had to learn the sounds fast when they first arrived in London. Half the city seemed to be Irish. All called Paddy.

"What do you want?"

"We want the feckin' prick who's calling himself Cornelius Lamine."

Pierre looked at Ralph Stonehouse, who shrugged.

"He's not feckin' here, Paddy." Pierre said.

"Are you trying to be funny, you cunt foreigner?"

"Mind your feckin' mouth, Paddy." Pierre was getting the hang of this Irish talk.

"Who the feck are you, anyway?"

"That's my business." Pierre said. "You don't muck around with me, Paddy. I'm coming up. Clear away from the doorway - and no weapons. I'll sink this feckin' ship otherwise. Yes, I'll sink the feckin' ship."

"We're getting off," he whispered to Ralph. "Stick close behind me."

Pierre counted for thirty seconds. He marvelled at the calm he felt. Certain death faced him. The last seconds of his life ticked away. A drenching sadness enveloped him. Zouzou singing under a spotlight in a black dress. A son or daughter he'd never see. Cairo, his home; Cairo, his father; Cairo, his mother. Cairo, *umm il-dunya* - mother of the world.

He was up the ladder in a flash, braced at the top with the RPG on his shoulder sweeping the scene before him: Six men in woolly caps and their hands up like paddles. One was Donald Waters. The sun wasn't up yet but Pierre had seen the faintest stain of orange on the horizon behind him. There was a chance to live!

"You." He pointed the RPG at a big white-faced fellow. "Get that lifeboat into the water." Pierre twitched the RPG towards an Indonesian crewman, who followed the big man to the gear that lowered the boat.

"Who's in charge here?"

A man with a ginger beard put his hand up.

"Your name, Sir?"

"Feck you, you cunt Arab."

"Mr Ralph, please shoot him now." Ralph raised the revolver.

"OK. Don't shoot. Me name's McTiernan. You and me's got a problem."

"What problem?"

"Whoever you are, you've feckin' short-changed me. That's a quarter of what we was promised." He pointed at the boxes of weapons.

"You can blame Donald Waters. He ordered the goods." Pierre said.

"He's lying," Waters said. "Shoot him."

"Shut yer feckin' gob. Do you want him to fire that thing and the whole boat blows up?"

"Paddy, it's true," Pierre said.

Time for some creative thinking. Just a minute more. One more minute.

"Gaddafi told me he didn't trust the IRA. Waters has got the rest of the consignment stashed away till ..."

Waters broke away from the ring of men.

"Come on Pierre, you know that's rubbish. Just leave the RPG and get into the lifeboat. You owe me anyway. Didn't I get you out of Cairo? It's your best chance."

"Like Mark Bellamy's best chance?" Ralph yelled, brandishing the wobbly revolver. McTiernean grabbed Waters. "What's this, yer feckin' English git? Are you and the Arab cunt running your own little game?"

The lifeboat splashed into the water on the opposite side of the boat. Ralph spun around at the sound, and the revolver struck a stanchion. It discharged with a crack, and Waters fell to the ground gripping his foot.

"You bastard, Stonehouse. How bloody dare you? How bloody dare you shoot me?" he screamed.

A sliver of orange light suddenly blinded the ring of men. The lip of a fiery sun had risen above the horizon behind Pierre. As the men shaded their faces, Pierre gripped Ralph's arm and scuttled to the rope ladder. He shoved the Englishman over the edge, all the while swivelling the RPG towards the ring of men.

"Get this ship moving or I sink it!"

McTiernan pushed one of the other men in the direction of the bridge. "Get it done!"

Pierre slid down the ladder and lay in the gunnels with the RPG aimed at the boat. Ralph grabbed an oar and shoved it against the rusty hull of the *Warda*. A gap opened up - ten feet, twenty feet. The Englishman began to row like a demon. A line of heads appeared over the rail of the *Warda*. McTiernan tossed something at the lifeboat just as the *Warda*'s propeller thrashed into life. The swell of the propeller tossed the lifeboat sideways, and whatever Tiernan had thrown splashed into the water a dozen feet away. A roar from below the water threw the lifeboat up and forward.

"Grenade!" yelled Pierre. Gunfire from the *Warda* splintered the gunnels of the lifeboat. Another grenade fell short and exploded under the water. Pierre braced himself and fired the RPG in the peach-coloured dawn light.

***

The fire must have sparked off the arms cache, judging from the erratic explosions that rocked the early morning calm. The boarding party leapt into the sea, clambered aboard their yacht, and motored off into the open water until they were no more than a smudge. The superstructure of the *Warda* burnt to the deck. Another lifeboat with a huddle of men bobbed a hundred yards off the smoking hulk.

Ralph Stonehouse lay in the belly of the boat suffering a single bullet wound. In through his shoulder and out through his side. God knew what organs it had ploughed through in its deadly track. There was little bleeding to see, nothing Pierre could do to stop the inexorable catastrophe in Ralph's chest and abdomen.

***

The sun was hot now. A strip of land approached and receded in the distance as the lifeboat drifted. Ten miles away? Twenty? Tunisia perhaps? Malta? Pierre tore his linen jacket along the back seam to fashion two sun hats. He cupped his eyes. Smoke in the distance. The *Warda*. They were drifting back towards the wreck.

A plane approached, flew lower, and circled. Pierre waved the shreds of his linen jacket. He saw RAF roundels on the fuselage. The plane flew away.

The Englishman was fading. He talked a lot, hoarsely, urgently. Sometimes his words rambled without meaning, sometimes he was coherent.

"Do you have a kid, Mr Farag?"

"I'm to be a father."

"He'd be a fine boy. What's his name?"

"I'll call him ..." Pierre stopped. This was something, he supposed, that expectant parents discussed together. "My wife and I have decided he will be Michael."

"And how old's Michael? Twenty, you said. My Emma's twenty."

"Emma's a fine young woman, Mr Ralph."

"She's an angel."

His eyes glazed, refocussed, glazed again. "Emma, thank you, darling. It's such a thoughtful present." He began to hum a tune that Pierre faintly recognised. Then Ralph flinched and coughed up some blood.

"Rest now, Mr Ralph."

The man waved his arm on the uninjured side. "Lovely party, Susan. Let me hug you both. Sort of going away bash, is it? Emma, you'll be careful in London."

The man wrenched his head around to stare at Pierre. "Will they ever forgive me, do you think?"

Forgiveness? What was it in Pierre that caused people - strangers, enemies like Dimashqi - to ask his forgiveness? How was it that people trusted him, even if they didn't know him from a dung beetle? It was, he supposed, a kind of gift, the only gift he could bestow on wretched Ralph Stonehouse.

"Mr Ralph, you believe in Jesus Christ, I think? He will forgive you."

"I spurned Christ, Mr Farag. But I know that he will wash away my sins."

"Of course he will, Mr Ralph. There, rest your head."

"Will you hear my confession, Mr Farag?"

"I am no priest, just a man among men."

"I cannot die a Christian until you do this for me."

How to achieve the poor man's wish? He remembered that in the Armenian Apostolic church, one confessed before taking Holy Communion. One adopted a contrite frame of mind and merely stated, "I have sinned against God". But then he'd seen dramatic confessions in the movies: The penitent behind a screen, the priest hearing some tale of murder ...

And after Mr Ralph had confessed, what next? Pierre had just the faintest glimmer of belief in God. How was he to absolve the wretched man's sins?

He'd do it the Armenian way. Just have him say, "I have sinned against God". Why should Stonehouse recount the shameful details of his misdeeds to a stranger? The dying man would surely agree to this.

But it was too late. Ralph Stonehouse slumped back and gasped his last breath.

Chapter Eighteen

Pierre was jogged awake by a bullhorn. Through crusted eyelids he saw that the sun had passed its zenith. A motor throbbed nearby. His hand brushed against a body. He shuddered at sticky blood on his hands from Ralph's abdomen.

"Easy goes, old chap." It was a sailor climbing from a large inflatable dinghy into the lifeboat. A Royal Navy patrol boat stood a hundred yards away. Another hundred yards beyond lay the mournful shape of the *Warda*, still smoking.

A couple of sailors gently wrapped the dead man in a tarpaulin and transferred him to the dinghy.

"You next, Sir." Pierre hauled himself across. One of the crewmen attached the lifeboat to the dinghy, gunned the outboard and headed for the patrol boat.

"Rough time, Sir?" a sailor asked.

Pierre said nothing. His mind was on Zouzou. Where was she? Would they be reunited soon? What trick would these English demons have in store next?

A man in crisp white cotton, ornate epaulettes and an aura of authority stood waiting on deck; surely the captain.

"Is this him?" he asked the officer holding Pierre's arm.

"Aye, aye, Sir. Mr Lamine or whatever he calls himself."

"Take him down to the medico for a quick check up and bring him to the bridge."

Down below, the Danish master of the *Warda* lay dozing on a narrow bunk in the sick bay. The boat's crewmen squatted on the floor, sooty-faced and patched up with bandages and ointment.

"Will he be all right? He's had a stroke," Pierre said.

"He'll live," the medical orderly said. "Looks more like epilepsy to me judging from the pills in his pocket. Now let's have a look at you."

Apart from sunburn and dehydration, Pierre was in reasonable shape.

On the bridge, the captain was seated next to the tall strapping fellow who had revealed to Pierre that he was to meet with Gaddafi. The man wore a thunderous expression.

"I've been anxious to speak to you, Mr Lamine," the captain said.

"Mr Farag, not Mr Lamine."

"Lamine, Farag, as you wish. Now, my orders were to intercept a yacht transferring arms from a coastal steamer, and to arrest yourself, a gentleman by the name of Donald Waters, and the deceased person who I assume is Mr Ralph Stonehouse. Instead, I've been diverted here to find the coastal steamer burnt to a crisp. I'd like some answers."

"So would I," Pierre said. "I would like to know what you people have done with my wife."

"What's your wife got to do with anything? I want to know why that damned vessel has been blown to bits and a senior civil servant shot dead."

"Ask your colleague. He was in charge. I'm saying nothing until I see my wife."

The captain turned to Mills. Pierre watched, captivated by the scene of the two warriors locked in a clash of wills: The captain, older than Mills, with his aura of authority and experience; Mills, tough and dangerous, a man hired to do perfidious Albion's dirty work. Why, oh why, was Pierre Farag, a man 'turned in on himself', a player in this ludicrous tableau? How many trials must he endure before those passports were his, and he and Zouzou could fade into a crowd?

"I'm waiting, Mills," the captain said.

"It's obvious. This man's a double agent. He was working for us, but he was running his own little game on the side. He whacked the master of the *Warda*, took Stonehouse prisoner, and ordered the boat to sail to some quiet harbour in Tunisia where he could stash the weapons and arrange to sell them."

"Then what?"

"The crew overpowered him, he took Stonehouse hostage in the lifeboat, and shot him when the poor beggar fought back."

"And how did the *Warda* get blown up?" the captain asked.

"The swine lobbed a missile at the *Warda* and it hit the contraband."

The captain stared at the *Warda*. Mills stared at his feet.

What was the expression the English used, Pierre thought? Yes, 'a load of bollocks'. It was one of his favourites: Mildly vulgar, satisfyingly euphonic, anchored somewhere between the comic and the ironic. A swear word that distilled half a millennium of the lives and manners of the English.

"You'd better try harder, Mills." The captain fixed him with a steely stare.

An officer peering through binoculars turned to the captain. "Sir, there's a small vessel approaching. With a mast, I think. One mile and closing."

The captain sprang to his feet and grabbed the binoculars. The radio operator called out, "It's the *Morning Star*, Sir. They're asking permission to come alongside."

***

As the *Morning Star* drew near, Pierre laughed out loud. Two yachts! What was the expression from *Hamlet*? 'Hoist with his own petard.' So apt, Shakespeare's image of a man lifted off the ground by a bomb he has set off. These English had been too clever, and the Irish not so far behind them.

But he didn't have the luxury of *Schadenfreude*. The more immediate problem was how this mayhem might affect his chances of getting his wife back and a couple of passports in his back pocket.

After the *Morning Star* had tied up alongside, four men wearing shorts and sullen faces filed onto the deck - the fake IRA men, Pierre assumed. A fifth man - in handcuffs - was helped aboard.

"Who's in charge of this vessel?" the captain bellowed.

One of the fake IRA stepped forward.

"Name?"

"Not authorised to say, Sir."

'Who is he, Mills?"

"Not authorised to say, Sir."

The captain pointed at the handcuffed man.

"I see. Mills, are you authorised to say who this is?"

"That is Donald Waters, Sir," Mills shot back.

The man in handcuffs laughed out loud. He was about forty, slightly built, sandy hair.

"What's the damned joke?" the captain asked.

"You lot, you're the joke," the man said. "My name's Alan Ebury, and I want the two hundred and fifty quid I'm supposed to get from someone called Mills. The bloke in Naples said I'd get the rest of my money when the Royal Navy turned up."

"What bloke in Naples?"

"Donald Waters, he said his name was."

"Do you often agree to impersonate complete strangers for money, Mr Ebury?" the captain asked.

"No comment."

Mills roared, "He's Waters, I'm telling you. He's a clever bastard."

"One more word, Mills, and you'll be put under arrest," the captain said.

"I command this operation and I protest your impertinence!" Mills rose from his seat and loomed over the captain. An armed sailor gripped his shoulder and sat him smartly down. Another sailor appeared from a doorway, saluted the captain smartly and handed him a piece of paper. The captain read the note and nodded.

"Mills, this is a radio message from Whitehall. You are relieved of your command. I have full responsibility for cleaning up this mess. Take him below."

Two sailors locked arms with Mills and began walking him away. He twisted around and yelled, jerked his head in Pierre's direction. "Ask him. He knows Waters. He'll tell you I'm right."

"Well?" the captain asked.

Pierre smiled. "I regret to say that this is a load of bollocks. The man is not Donald Waters. Mr Waters is on a yacht somewhere north of here with a bullet in his foot."

***

While uniformed men bustled about clearing up the chaos of the bungled operation, Pierre was left to sit on the steel cover of some piece of naval equipment. It was as if he were invisible, or perhaps an unlabelled object with no logical place to be stowed. He adopted the existential stare of a man 'turned in on himself' and was transported to other times: An evening on the beach at Agami, shyly smiling at the teenaged Aziza Faris; the early morning drive across Cairo just days before the outbreak of war, when he brought Zouzou to the villa on the Giza Road; the weeks when they travelled through France under false names *en route* to England; and the night she first sang at the Orient in Soho. If any sailor gave the man on the steel bench a second look they might have said, 'That funny little bloke - where did they say he was from?' The reply might have been, 'Don't ask me, mate'. He faintly noticed the *Warda* slipping below the waves, the clatter of a helicopter, the smartly executed commands of the officers as the patrol boat's engines powered up, the sun sinking towards the horizon to their left-hand side. Somebody took him by the arm and led him below, where he ate a pan of food, not knowing what it was. After, he pushed the pan away, laid his head on his hands, and slept with no dreams whatsoever.

Chapter Nineteen

Stephanie and the man in socks were gone when Emma woke the next morning. There was an envelope with a note scribbled on it: 'Gone to Sicily for a party with Silvio. Help yourselfs to anything'. Inside the envelope was a small wad of assorted foreign banknotes and some yellow pills. Emma made tea and toast.

"That smells good. Actually, it smells normal." It was Susan, looking surprisingly fresh.

"What do you mean by 'normal', Mum?"

"I don't know, like at home in Berkshire. There's something very English about the smell of toast." She went to open the blinds.

"No, keep them closed, Mum. And we'd better not talk too loudly. Is Zouzou awake?"

"Still snoring. That woman could kip for England." They had all slept in the same room in the downstairs flat, spread across two big foam mattresses.

"Is there a phone, Emma?"

"Try upstairs. Steph's dad must have one. Are you going to call Margaret Thatcher?"

"Of course not. I don't have her number. I'm going to try Bill Worthington. He'll track her down."

"Who's Bill Worthington?"

"Our Member of Parliament, silly. Don't you remember? Daddy and I handed out blue rosettes, well not Daddy really, being a civil servant, he helped on the tea trolley. And look what happened - we got that dreadful Harold Wilson."

"I voted for Screaming Lord Sutch."

"Yes, dear, that says everything about England nowadays."

Emma drank her tea while her mother went upstairs. Mum's sense of calm was extraordinary - her old BOAC training, perhaps. But it was more than that. It was the strength of a woman who'd held onto her beliefs and values despite the way her husband had treated her. Zouzou had it too, a woman who'd guarded her integrity in a world where brutal old men called the shots. Did Emma have the kind of strength Mum and Zouzou had? Yes, she bloody well did. She'd proved it that night on the boat. *The Night of the Coat Hanger.* That had a good ring to it, like the title of one of Zouzou's films. She'd shown she had guts, even if things had been a bit misguided before, well bloody stupid really for her to steal the file. Well, all that strength stuff was fine, but right now they were in deep shit, and her mum was upstairs ringing some crusty old fart Tory MP to get them out of it. As for Dad, he'd be back, she knew. Nobody who cooked up something like Operation Aqua would get himself into a jam he couldn't get out of. It'd all be sorted out.

Stephanie had left a carton of cigarettes. Lovely, long, duty-free Pall Malls. She thought back to when she filched poor Eric's last fag. It seemed like ten years ago.

There was a noise from upstairs that didn't sound right - scraping, scratching or something.

"Mum?" Silence.

The scraping sound again.

"Mum, are you OK?" Still silence.

Zouzou came into the kitchen, face puffy, charcoal eyes. "I will die without coffee."

Emma shushed her and pointed upstairs. Zouzou frowned, nodded and let herself out the side door. Where the hell was she going? For a walk?

She looked up just as the staircase exploded in violence. Two figures grappled at the top of the stairs. Her mother was scratching and kicking a sandy-haired man who was holding her in a bear hug. His foot was wrapped in dirty bandages and he was unsteady on the stair.

"You leave my mum alone, you bastard."

"Emma, he wants us for hostages. Leave me and run for help," Susan gasped.

"Put your hands on your head or I'll kill your mother right now," the man shouted. "You're going to walk slowly past me and phone a number. We're all going to stay calm."

"Get off my mum first."

"No way. You get up here to that phone. Where's the Egyptian bitch?"

"Asleep down here. Now let my mother go, you animal."

"Get up here or you'll end up like your bloody father," the man snarled.

"What do you know about my dad? Who are you?" Then it struck her like a hammer - he was Donald Waters.

She wasn't going to submit to this shit. She scrambled up the stairs, sobbing and flailing her arms. Grabbed the bandaged foot, twisted it, hands sticky with blood, the man howling, releasing his grip on Susan. A fist whacked

Emma's head. She tumbled back down the stairs but caught a glimpse of a figure behind Waters. Something shiny and hooked whipped in front of his face. Screaming, a lashing arm, Zouzou raising him up like a puppet by his nostril. Susan gripped Waters around the waist with both arms and hung her whole weight on him.

"Where's my dad? Tell me, you bastard," Emma shrieked.

"Get her off me." Another jerk of the hooked coat hanger. Waters let out a high-pitched yap of snot and blood and fury.

"Where is he?"

"He's dead, you stupid cow."

Susan made a long animal howl. She released one of her arms and grappled with the man's belt - no, with a band of silver duct tape around his waist with something round and grooved under it. "Got it!" was the last thing she said before she hugged Waters close and the room exploded in smoke and blood and flesh.

***

Emma tottered into the street, ears ringing, lungs rasping. She looked down and saw her clothes were a few tattered rags. Foul chemical stink. A passer-by veered onto the other side of the street. A figure staggered towards her covered in blood from the waist up. Barefoot. Dimpled legs under the shreds of a dress. Zouzou, mouthing words from a lopsided jaw. Emma mouthing back, hearing nothing but a metallic whine. Glass under foot. An ambulance. A small child offering an ice cream. Fragments of distorted sound. Embracing Zouzou, clinging, wailing, until a medico prised them apart and she fainted.

Chapter Twenty

The patrol boat landed Pierre in Malta. They put him in a military prison cell.

"No hard feelings," a chummy Lance-Corporal said. "Apparently they don't know what to do with you yet. Anyway, the grub's good."

On the fourth day, he was taken to an interrogation room, where Margaret Thatcher's double sat at a table. Marjorie Byers, yes, that was the name in the file. He remembered she was the head of Ealing.

"Where is my wife?"

"You will see her tomorrow."

"Why do I not believe you?"

"You have no choice. Now, I have questions for you."

It went on all day, a thousand questions about his journey into Libya, each question asked again from a different angle, every fact checked and rechecked. The Byers woman sat steady as a rock, apparently not possessing a bladder. Pierre squirmed and perspired. The sheets of paper filled with tiny purple writing. At last she opened the handbag, placed the writing materials inside, and took out a large envelope.

"Your travel documents."

Pierre opened the flap. Air Malta tickets from Luqa to Rome and another by BOAC a week hence to ... where? Melbourne? A joke surely? Wasn't Melbourne in Canada? No - New Zealand of course. He fished in the envelope for the passports. Mr Kevin O'Donnell. Mrs Rhonda O'Donnell. His photo on one, Zouzou's on the other. And what were these creatures on the coat of arms? A kangaroo face to face with an ostrich. They were going to Australia!

"I don't want to go to Australia."

"Hwot?"

"The old fellow in Whitehall. He promised me America. And your man Mills showed me different passports."

"The individuals you speak of are no longer in our employment."

"Am I discharged from the ten years that Donald Waters demanded of me?"

"I am afraid that name is not familiar to me, Mr O'Donnell," Marjorie Byers said, and left the room.

***

The next day, a man from the British High Commission arrived and announced that they were going to the hospital to see Zouzou. Hospital? How? But the official was otherwise mute.

She was here in Malta! Alive! He quelled his excitement. Was it a trick? Another ruse to engage him in a new ill-fated mission?

She was propped up reading a *Paris Match*. Her jaw bulged and she was missing some teeth. The skin on her brow was blistered and her hair was scorched. They embraced. She winced but gripped him hard.

"I knew from your message on the ship that you were close."

"Message?" she asked. "I left no message."

He looked closely at the injuries. She had suffered horribly.

"What devil did this to you, my heart? Tell me his name and I will ..."

"Hush, Pierre." She forced the words through the unbroken teeth on one side of her mouth. "It was the Waters man, and he is dead. His head flew off and broke my jaw."

"Flew off? How does a man's head fly off?"

"With a grenade, of course. But I am alive, thanks be to God."

"*Al-hamdulillah.*" Pierre repeated the ancient invocation. "And how is the baby?"

Zouzou flicked the *Paris Match* open. "Ouf, the things they get up to in Monaco."

"Our baby, Zouzou."

"Baby?"

"Our child. *Habibti*, I have ached to talk to you, to hold you close, to listen to the sleeping child in your belly, to choose a name for him - or her."

Zouzou looked out of the window. "I know nothing of a baby, *habibi*."

Pierre slumped on the bed. Why had he let the old man fool him? How could they devise such cruelty? Worse than devils. Who could imagine the mind of a person who might invent such a story to entrap him? He had been violated. Zouzou had been violated.

But what about the Wimpy burger she had demanded, her tenderness, her fatigue? Could it be that her denial sufficed for the truth? Had a baby been lost somehow? But pregnancy was a sea where he possessed no chart. "I'm sorry, my heart. I must have misunderstood a remark someone made."

"Pierre, there will be a baby - in America, three babies, four, however many you want. Be patient." She kissed his brow. "And now we will tell one another our stories."

Zouzou began, working backwards. Pierre listened carefully, slotting the events into place. Yes, now he saw it: The IRA men must have dumped Waters at some remote beach in Malta, perhaps shoved him off in a dinghy. Considering the arms cache had been destroyed, it was a wonder they hadn't tossed him in the sea. Waters must have filched the grenade from the cache to protect himself before the *Warda* blew up. But how had he known where the women were hiding? Did he have a *shabkah*, a network of informers, someone with transport? Anything was possible in this world of - what did the English call it? - 'smoke and mirrors'. He tried it in Arabic - *ad-dukhaan wa-l-maraya*. No, better in English.

Zouzou's account of the coat hanger in Waters' nostril turned his stomach, but by the time she had worked back to the escape from the Pig, he was seeing a violent streak in his wife he was not quite comfortable with.

"You see, Pierre, I knew that the Pig would take pity on a sick woman. When he knocked on the cabin door, we put our clothes on - it was so hot in there - and I lay on the bed groaning while little Emma shouted, 'She has a bursted appendix, she will perish shortly'. And sure enough, *il-khanzeer* came in and bent over me and I raised my knee to crush his manhood, then rushed behind him with the coat hanger ..."

She conked out in mid-sentence, switched from high animation to deep sleep.

"Rest now, *habibti*, finish your story tomorrow," Pierre whispered to the sleeping woman.

He hadn't mentioned Australia. Tomorrow perhaps, or when he'd had time to prepare her.

Chapter Twenty-One

'I'm an orphan,' Emma thought for the first time. Stupid idea. How can you be an orphan at twenty? She swigged back her fourth sherry.

The double doors of the sitting room in *Ghawdex* had been opened so that the mourners could flow into the conservatory. The fierce summer heat had broken; now, ragged English clouds drifted in a sky of milky blues and limpid greys through the glass-paned roof. Gently clinking glasses and muted chatter provided a soundscape to the unreal - no surreal - scene of Mrs Littleproud offering canapés and fish-paste sandwiches to the guests. A pale teenager - apparently Mrs Littleproud's niece - circulated with a tray of pound cake and sherry.

It had just happened, the Littleproud takeover of the funeral. Grudging and grim-faced, that was the neighbour's style of generosity: "It's the least I can do for your poor parents."

If only they'd let her bury Mum and Dad in Malta, but the High Commission people had found endless reasons why she couldn't. Truth was, they couldn't get the Stonehouses out of the country quick enough.

Another sherry - ugh, so sweet and sticky - and the alcohol in Emma's brain hit the spot where caution verged on rashness. A drunk orphan. Something between a sob and a smirk bubbled out of her nostrils. A bloody rich orphan actually. Did she actually think that, or was it an evil alien whispering from a dark corner of her mind? But she knew the gang of Emmas behind that whisper: The Emma in a bitter sink of resentment against the father who had never reconciled with her; the Emma who prayed to whatever god would listen, that she would be forgiven for destroying him; the Emma who cried for herself and the bloody awful world that had set everything up so that it would all go to shit; the Emma who drifted into a reverie where a grenade hadn't blown her mother to smithereens, where she and Mum mourned Ralph Stonehouse together until another voice hissed, 'She's dead, you little fool'.

"Lovely service, Emma, dear." Auntie Florence with her face creased in the deepest sadness. Hug, moist kiss on cheek, fish-paste on the breath. "Thank you, Auntie." Behave, keep your head from wobbling. Here's Pound Cake girl. Grab another amontillado.

Somehow, she'd written a eulogy for Mum and Dad, amazed the mourners by delivering it cold as ice in the church, but just as she was to finish, a great welling of grief filled her eyes and nose and face, and sobs shook her shoulders. A pair of uncles helped her to a pew, and the rest of the service trickled on in a blur, and then blurred into the sherry-soaked bash at the house: 'Brave, Emma's been so brave ... they were a beautiful couple ... best parents in the world ... great future ahead of him ... cut off in his prime ... supremely loyal, a wife in a million ... bedrock of his life.' One fucking cliché after another. How she yearned to shout, 'He was a selfish shit who treated my mother like rubbish', or 'She was a bloody slave to her stupid meaningless middle-class morals'.

"Steady on, Emma. Let me get you a coffee." It was cousin Neville, a dopey prick from some dopey town with a dopey weak-chinned wife.

"I don't want any shitting coffee." Was that her voice squawking above the restrained chatter? Sideways glances, Neville backing away. 'She's under tremendous strain ... It's amazing she's held up so far ... anybody would crack in her circumstances.'

Emma muddled her way to the upstairs bathroom, sat on the toilet laughing and weeping all at once. A writhing snake invaded her mind, hissing 'Rich orphan, rich orphan,' over the drone of a sitar. She closed her eyes and the snake's head morphed into the sweet face of her mother. 'That'll do Emma. Go down now. Daddy and I want you to go downstairs. Behave, please, just for us,' the turquoise face said.

She descended to the sitting room in a cloud of calm, with the knowledge that she was in shaky control of herself. The family and friends absorbed her into their midst with smiles and kindness. Her thoughts turned to the night in the squat when Kit's friends shared joints and chocolate and sausages. She floated on all the kindness in the world.

As it got dark, Emma stood at the door shaking hands with the procession of mourners being shooed to their cars by Mrs Littleproud. The pale niece stacked the plates in the dishwasher, and rinsed the glasses in the big kitchen sink.

"I can't thank you enough, Mrs Littleproud."

The neighbour stared ceramically. "As I said, it was the least I can do for your late parents."

"Mrs Littleproud, I'm sorry."

"For what?"

"I don't know. I don't know anything."

"Will you manage tonight, Emma?"

"I'll be fine. I'm a rich orphan."

"I beg your pardon?"

"Nothing, Mrs Littleproud. Thank you."

***

Emma woke to a noise. She looked around the dark sitting room. She'd fallen asleep on the sofa. Her watch said ten o'clock.

"Who's there?" Shuffling. Something clacked on a tiled floor.

"Bollocks!"

"Who's that? I've got a golf club. Show yourself." Her heart bounced against her ribs.

"It's me." A familiar voice.

"Who's me?"

"Eric, of course." Bloody Eric, the CND boy. He'd been with a bunch of her old school friends at the funeral. They'd talked their way past Mrs Littleproud.

"What are you doing here, Eric?"

"I fell asleep in the scullery. Too much of that bloody sherry."

She rummaged in the freezer and found enough bits and pieces to make them toasted sandwiches. They ate them on the sofa with cold beer.

"What happened, Emma? There was nothing in the papers."

"Must have been a D-notice."

"What's that?"

"Christ, Eric, typical engineering student. Don't you know anything about politics?"

"My mum and dad were communists, remember. I kind of grew a carapace."

"Twit! A D-notice is when the government tells the papers they can't mention a certain subject."

"So you can't say anything?" Eric asked.

Emma took Eric's hand and wrapped his arm over her shoulder. "Nope. You wouldn't believe it anyway."

The fact was that the woman who'd debriefed her at that old mansion in deepest Hertfordshire had scared the wits out of her. Two days she'd sat telling her story over and over again while the posh old bat wrote it all down in purple ink. When Emma got to the bit about Zouzou pawing her on the ship, the woman blushed slightly and asked for much more detail than seemed necessary. "Is that a qualification for your job, a dirty mind?" Emma had asked her, but the woman just opened her enormous handbag, took out another notebook, wrote in it in green ink, and put it back. At the end, she made Emma sign a document, and reminded her for the tenth time about how many years in prison she could get for breaking the Official Secrets Act.

"What about the posthumous medal they gave your dad?" Eric asked.

"Oh, that was just some Civil Service thing for sticking it out for so long."

She grasped his free hand and caressed her cheek with it.

"Got a fag, Eric?"

When they had finished smoking, she asked, "Eric, can we go to bed?" She couldn't bear the night alone. He'd grown up, swotty Eric. The arm around her shoulder held her firmly. He had a nice profile, kind eyes.

"You mean to ..."

"If you want to." She didn't mind either way. Eric's eyes shone.

"Wait, I'll put on some music." She found a cassette. It was *The Girl from Ipanema.*

"That's nice, Emma. My mum used to play it."

"My mum too."

They stripped off and grappled on her old bed, with Abba and Pink Floyd looking down from their curling posters.

He fumbled in his wallet for a condom.

"Let me help you," Emma said.

"Nah. It's all right."

"You've got it inside-out."

"Oh fuck."

"OK, Eric. You can put it in now."

"Is that the right place?"

"No, let me help you."

He gasped and it was all over. "Oh shit, sorry, Emma."

"Honestly, it doesn't matter."

"I feel such a prat."

"You're not a prat. You're a good guy. It happens all the time."

"Does it?" She felt the tension in his shoulders relax. He was just a boy. She was a hundred years older. She stroked his head and he went to sleep. Her arm went numb and she eased him away, picked up the wrinkled condom that had slipped off him, and dropped it on the floor. He murmured, "I love you, Emma," and snored like a tractor. She spooned into him, gazing around her teenage girl room in the full moon shining through the net curtains. My past. Gone. I'm not that Emma anymore. But who the heck am I? What next? What does a rich orphan do now?

The family solicitor had rambled on about shares and unit trusts. She'd signed endless documents that apparently gave her control over a serious pile of cash, substantial investments, as well as the houses in Berkshire and Malta.

She had no idea what was next, and strangely, she didn't give a damn.

***

The man at the desk at the Polytechnic tutted and shook his head.

"You didn't submit your forms. You can't just turn up without your forms."

"Can I fill them in now?"

"Miss, a lot of applicants would give their right arms for a place here. Do you have any idea of how many people are turned down?"

"What's that got to do with me?"

"It's the regulations. And what about your grant?"

"I don't need a grant."

"Well, you're very lucky. But I can't make exceptions."

"So I can't take my second year?"

"It's the regulations, Miss. You'll have to apply for next year."

Fuck them. She'd only gone up to London to enquire at the Poly for lack of any other ideas: Do another year, see how it works out. But the rupture in her life was so devastating that nothing she'd done before her act of insurrection had any meaning now.

And she was alone, lonely. No Mum, no Dad, nowhere to go all day, camping downstairs in the Berkshire house. Her teenage bedroom filled her with sorrow. She couldn't bear to go into the other bedrooms where her parents' clothes and possessions remained undisturbed: A book on siege engines by her father's bedside, her mother's night cream on the dressing table.

She hauled a mattress into the sitting room and closed all the curtains, watching TV and smoking all day. When the phone rang, it rang. When the food in the fridge and pantry ran out, she stopped eating, just riding a bike to the off-licence for wine, cigarettes and bags of crisps. When she got really hungry, she took the Range Rover to the Indian take-away in town.

September drifted into October, the days were greyer, the nights colder. The heap of mail on the hall mat grew deeper. She spotted a letter with FINAL DEMAND on the envelope, and sent off a cheque for the electricity bill a day or two before she was to be cut off. She knew the sitting room stank of stale food and unwashed sheets; she felt the greasy knots in her hair; she saw in the bathroom mirror the pimples on her face; she smelt the comfy animal pong of the T-shirt and underwear she hadn't changed in weeks. Who cared? What difference did it make to anyone if she spent the winter holed up in here?

Mrs Littleproud knocked from time to time. Emma, wrapped in a blanket, would open the door a crack and say she was unwell. One day, Auntie Kay turned up complaining that Emma hadn't answered her calls.

"I've been studying. I won't ask you in, Auntie. I've got my you-know-whats and I've been lying down. The place is a bit untidy."

A boy came around, the one who fed the dogs when Mum and Dad were away.

"I've still got your dad's dogs. Can I bring them back?"

"He's dead. Keep them. Fuck off." The boy's jaw dropped.

"I'm sorry, that was a nasty thing to say. Thanks for looking after them, but there's nobody here who wants dogs anymore."

On a dead, cold day when the morning sky was slate-grey and crows bickered in the leafless trees, Emma carried the sitting room rubbish into the back garden. She threw the filthy bedsheets and blankets onto the pile, peeled off the T-shirt, and hobbled to Dad's shed in her grubby bra and panties. A splash of paraffin, and the whole pile blazed up. She went inside, upstairs to the bedrooms, snatched clothes from cupboards, cushions, books, handbags, shoes, framed photographs, and flung it all from the windows into the garden. She toiled for half an hour until a plume of dirty smoke hung over the garden in the still air. Bare feet torn and muddy, fingernails broken and bleeding, sooty smuts, snotface, howling like a toddler. Fuck them, fuck all of them.

"Quiet now, dear." A policewoman was suddenly behind her, a blanket was draped around her shoulders. A police car in the driveway, a worried policeman talking into a radio. And then a boy wearing a CND jacket jumping off a bike. Eric. What's Eric doing here? Worried faces. Christ, I'm so cold. What do you want, Eric? Questions, questions, back inside the house, nice cup of tea, sobbing on the sofa. The cops writing in their notebooks.

***

"I'm home from university for the weekend. I was riding past and I saw you dancing around half-naked in front of the fire, and the police about to arrest you."

"You're a pal, Eric. How did you get rid of them?"

"Said you were my girlfriend and you'd asked me over for a bonfire and a drink. You were a bit upset 'cos your dog had died, I said."

"Genius, Eric!"

"Engineering student, see. Problem solving, that's what they teach us."

Thank Christ he'd come along. From the look on the cops' faces, she was a hair's breadth from being carted off to the looney bin. She looked around the sitting room over the rim of a mug of sweet tea Eric had made.

"Sorry, Eric. This place looks like the council tip."

"What's that brown stain?"

"Vindaloo, I hope."

"Want some more tea?"

"No thanks, Eric. You're sweet, you know."

"A lot of girls say that to me, Emma, but I'm still a prat."

"Have you got a girlfriend?"

He blushed and looked away.

"Sorry, Eric. It really didn't matter, what happened after the funeral."

"Just forget it, Emma. Anyway, what are you going to do with yourself?"

"Dunno. Become a hare krishna, study French, take up sword-fighting, join a band, write poetry, start a commune. I haven't got a bloody clue. What about you?"

"I'm going to get a job in Africa as soon as I get my degree."

"Wow, why Africa?"

"It's my plan."

"Plan?" Emma asked.

"Plan, you know, a plan for my life. Hey, look, I'd better get going."

Eric helped her rake the half-burned bits of clothing and picture frames into the centre of the bonfire, where it flamed up merrily and settled into a bed of crimson and grey ashes. It was exhilarating to be outside. The air had an autumny tang. She noticed layers of sound all around her: The *waak-waak* of the crows in the bare oaks, the twitter of sparrows and finches, the sough of a gentle wind in the trees. She watched her friend wobble off on his bike, a goodbye hand raised, past Mrs Littleproud's, and he was gone.

This would be the last time she'd see the house. No going back. She'd sell it. Could she do that? Well, she was a rich orphan, so she could do what she liked. She packed a rucksack with some clothes, her passport and cheque book, slammed the door and set off on foot to the railway station two miles away. No actual plan, but maybe it was time she made one.

***

Linda had rented out her old room, so Emma booked into a hotel in Russell Square. It was expensive, full of foreigners - Arabs and Persians, they seemed to be, always huddled in meetings in the lobby. She wandered around Bloomsbury for a couple of days - the British Museum, the galleries, the pubs. The constant pestering by men started to irritate her, and by lunchtime on the third day she hadn't spoken to anybody except shop assistants and bar tenders. That afternoon she took a bus over the river to visit Kit's squat, but when she tapped on the corrugated iron flap a filthy-looking guy with needle tracks on his arms tried to drag her inside.

She went down to the pub at Southwark and hung around for a couple of hours in case Kit and his friends might turn up. Perhaps they'd moved and still came to their local? Nobody. Around seven she finished her drink and put her Levi jacket on, but a voice behind her said, "Could I have a word, Miss?" He was an ordinary-looking fellow, wearing a cardigan over a shirt and tie.

An old-fashioned, affable git, like somebody from a fifties comedy film. If he thought he could get off with her, he needed his head tested.

"Who are you?"

"Oh, nobody really. I work for the lady you met at your debriefing."

"Have you been following me?"

He made a snuffly chuckle. "Nothing that dramatic. It's just that we like to keep an eye on our people."

"Your people? What are you on about?"

"Well, you're not technically one of our people yet, but ..."

"So piss off and leave me alone."

The man swung his face into Emma's. The affable smile switched to a snarl.

"Now listen, Missy, I'll say it just once. Shut up and listen."

"Leave me alone." His hand crushed her elbow. It hurt like hell. This bastard was serious.

"OK, say what you've got to say."

"That's better." Mr Affable was back. "Emma, you know a lot of things you're not supposed to know. Upset a lot of people. On the other hand, you've proven yourself to have guts and initiative. We like the cut of your jib. You're going back to college next week, and you're going to work for us when we need you. You know - like a holiday job."

"I can't go back to college till next year."

"That's been sorted out."

"What if I don't want to work for you?"

"Ah, now that's where you don't get a choice." He opened his wallet, humming a little *doo-dee-doo* tune. "Here's my card. We'll be in touch."

J. Cardew, Pensions Review Section, it said, with an address in Ealing.

THE END

I love to get feedback on my novels. Readers' comments motivate me to keep writing, and help me to spread the word about my work. If you enjoyed *Bury me in Valletta*, scan the QR code below to tell me what you liked. You can write an essay or just a few words! Thank you very much – Stuart.

You can find out about Books One and Three of the trilogy *Cairo Mon Amour* and *The Sunset Assassin* at my website.

www.stuartcampbellauthor.com

Notes on sources and historical events

I have taken some artistic liberties with the representation of Gaddafi's Libya. As far as I can determine, Gaddafi did not start using the title 'Guide' until about two years after the action in the book. Similarly, his African bodyguards do not seem to be mentioned in accounts from 1975.

My fictional descriptions of the Bab El-Aziziya barracks and Gaddafi's tent were inspired by works like Lindsey Hilsum's biography of Marie Colvin *In Extremis*, Annick Cojean's *Gaddafi's Harem*, and *Blair Inc* by Francis Beckett, David Hencke and Nick Kochan.

The letter from Harold Wilson brandished by Gaddafi was reported by the Daily Mail here: https://www.dailymail.co.uk/news/article-1218205/Documents-1970s-reveal-Britain-offered-Libya-14million-stop-supporting-IRA.html

I have used the (more or less) conventional spelling 'Gaddafi' for the late gentleman's name in the narrative, but 'Gathafi' when I reference the *Green Book*. This is the spelling that appears in the Ithaca Press edition.

The importation of Libyan arms by the Provisional IRA is detailed in this Wikipedia article: https://en.wikipedia.org/wiki/Provisional_Irish_Republican_Army_arms_importation

The 'Arab mafia' is discussed here: https://www.jta.org/1977/06/02/archive/behind-the-headlines-pro-arab-bias-in-british-foreign-office .

The *Times of Malta* archives was an invaluable source of information about the Mintoff years.

Although Emma caught a ferry from Catania to Malta, I have been unable to confirm (even from authoritative sources in Malta) whether such a route was in operation in 1975.

Emma says she voted for Screaming Lord Sutch, but in fact Sutch stood as a candidate in the 1974 general election in the constituency of Stafford and Stone, far away from Berkshire.

About the author

Stuart Campbell was a university Pro-Vice Chancellor and a Professor of Linguistics before he took up writing fiction in 2011. His other books include the novels *An Englishman's Guide to Infidelity*, *Bury me in Valletta*, *The Sunset Assassin* and *The True History of Jude*, as well as the novella *Ash on the Tongue*. He is also the author of numerous academic works on Arabic-English translation, and on the Arabic component in Malay and Indonesian. Stuart lives at Manly Beach in Australia.